WHEN I FIND YOU

GEORGIA E BROWN

ISBN: 978-1-3999-7045-7

Cover and interior design by Socciones Literary Consultancy
www.socciones.co.uk

Other books by Georgia E Brown

The Stalker's Song

ACKNOWLEDGEMENTS

My gratitude to the following people for their help in producing this novel: For proof-reading, editing and her sound advice and support, not to mention her suggestion for the book title, my thanks to Steph Boulton. Thanks to Kathy Bacovitch for her scrutiny of the first draft and detailed feedback with pertinent suggestions for improvements. For her constructive feedback and helpful advice, Angela Coils.

The team at Socciones (voted 'Best Self-Publishing and Editing Company 2023 — England & Wales' at the SME Enterprise awards) for their invaluable guidance, professional cover design and publication of this book. For their patience and constructive help with my author website and social media marketing, my granddaughters Georgia Glennon and Holly Bolton.

For valued help with police procedural matters, thanks to Simon Atkinson and Michael Robson.

Finally, thanks to my husband and family for their unstinting encouragement, patience and support throughout the whole process.

CHAPTER ONE

December 2022

Where did this bloody snow come from? It wasn't forecast yet it was now falling thick and fast, covering the ground quickly, building into a deep layer. Driving would become difficult if he stayed on this hilltop much longer. *Shit* he thought, *this car wasn't built for this*. What had seemed the ideal solution was going horribly wrong. The right spot was proving elusive, and with this damned snow it was getting more difficult by the minute.

Parked up at the end of Hillside Road in Rothbury, where he had driven in the hope of finding a suitably secluded place, he was becoming extremely frustrated and dismayed to find the area crawling with hikers. *Fucking nuisance.* Even the snow and approaching darkness wasn't putting them off. In the end, after sitting around for as long as he dared, he decided it was too risky, and was left with no option but to turn the car around and head back the way he'd come. The last thing he wanted was to be stranded up here. He'd have to find somewhere else to dispose of his burden.

He drove slowly and carefully in the freshly fallen snow, but the unfamiliar car was an automatic, and as it crested a rise in the road it seemed to change up a gear and increase its speed. If he'd been driving his own car in these conditions, with its manual gearbox, he'd have changed right down into first gear at that point, remembering that the road ahead sloped steeply downwards on the approach to a hairpin bend. The car surged forward, seemingly taking on a life of its own and he quickly realised it was out of control. Trying to slow it down, he grabbed the manual override lever but, not being used to an automatic, didn't know what to do with it and his feeble efforts to find a gear came to nothing. Desperately he tugged on the handbrake. All to no avail; inexorably the car ploughed on, continuing to gain speed. Frantically, he tried to steer into a hedge at the side of the road. Nothing worked. The car was stuck in a skid, speeding straight ahead into the driving snow.

As it gathered speed, hurtling towards the flimsy wooden fence atop the snow-covered bank ahead, he tried one last time to steer out of the skid. But the car was fixed firmly in its trajectory. When he realised there was nothing more he could do, he finally accepted whatever fate awaited him. A thrill of fear coursed through his veins. Whatever happened next was in the lap of the gods.

Strange saying that, "thrill of fear" he thought as he realised that's exactly what he was experiencing. An immense surge of extreme excitement passed through his body. He felt alive in every fibre of his being as he faced what he believed was probably going to be his death. He wasn't sure how steep the descent was on the other side of the bank, but he knew that he was on the highest point of the hill, and from there, there was only one way to go. As he headed towards his destiny, fat snowflakes continued to hurl themselves at the windscreen, the wipers working overtime in a futile attempt to keep the screen clear.

A solid white wall raced towards him, and with a violent thud the car hit the bank, throwing him forward against the steering wheel. Then it was flying upwards at a steep angle, and his body was jerked backwards. He felt the back of his head bang hard against the headrest and fleetingly thought that if the headrest hadn't been there, his neck would have snapped. The car seemed to become momentarily airborne before it crashed through the wooden fence with an ear-splitting crack. For a few heartbeats time stood still, before he became aware the car had come to a halt. Incongruously, the wipers continued to swish, thudding back and forth in the sudden silence. Peering into the impenetrable blackness ahead he couldn't see anything but big white flakes filling the air. The car creaked ominously.

Slowly, hardly daring to move, he unclipped his seatbelt and gingerly opened the door, just a crack. Snowflakes swirled in, as he looked down. *Shit.* Below him was nothing but a black hole. He eased the door closed, then as gently as he could, squirmed over the central console into the passenger seat. As he did so, there was another, louder creak and the car tilted forward, then stopped again. His heart missed a beat. He tried the passenger door, pushing tentatively against it, then again, harder. It wouldn't budge. *Don't panic, don't panic* he told himself. *Think.*

As carefully as he could, trying to still the mounting panic in his throat, he squeezed himself, with some difficulty, between the front seats, and crawled into the back. Holding his breath, he tried the nearside door. To his immense relief it opened and he could see snow below. He quickly slipped out falling to his knees in the soft snow, praying there was terra firma beneath, before scrambling to safety on all fours. As he did so, with an audible groan the front of the car slipped even further, dipping forward, its back rising up to expose the undercarriage, its rear wheels high in the air. Still the car held on the edge of the drop, and he could see that its chassis seemed to be caught in the barbed wire strands that formed part of the fence.

"**The Driver of this car will never be so lucky again**" was the caption to the photograph on the front page of the Rothbury Gazette the following day. The image was of the car, teetering on the edge, prior to going over. When he saw it, he surmised that one of the nearby residents must have taken the photo and immediately forwarded it to the paper. Several people had braved the blizzard and come out of their houses on hearing the car crashing through the fence. They had all stood and watched in fascinated horror as the car finally tilted over the edge and went crashing headlong down the steep slope, accompanied by muffled bangs as it hit obstacles on its descent.

'My God, it's a bloody good job you managed to get out of that,' said one resident, his clipped tone reminiscent of an army officer. 'Are you hurt at all?' he asked, peering at the driver. The driver shook his head, keeping his head down.

'Look, our house is just here. Why don't you come in whilst we get things sorted out?' He and his wife led him, into their home, pressing him to sit down, asking again if he was sure that he wasn't hurt. He put his head in his hands, breathing evenly in an effort to quell the violent beating of his heart. 'Here you go, old chap,' the man said, handing him a small glass. 'Brandy,' he stated. 'You've had a hell of a shock. Get that down you, it'll do you good. Now you just sit quiet, and I'll make a few phone calls. I take it you'll want to stay in the hotel in the village? Not much else you can do tonight, with no transport.'

In what seemed no time at all, a large, red-faced man arrived, bringing with him swirling snowflakes and a blast of cold air. His bulk filled the doorway and his booming voice the room. 'Won't come any further. Boots are caked with snow. Name's Bill Dawson,' he announced. 'By God, you've had a lucky escape. You ok?' he asked, peering at the driver, who kept his head down, but nodded. 'My farm's just down the road. I can take you into the village now in the four by four. Then, tomorrow I'll recover the car with the tractor. You ok to come now?'

The driver knocked back the remaining brandy, before mumbling his thanks to his host and following the farmer out into the night. Everything felt surreal and he couldn't wait to be on his own to work out how get his head around the situation.

Once alone in the hastily arranged hotel room, he paced the floor, running one hand through his hair, trying to think what to do next. What a situation to find himself in, bloody sod's law. Eventually, he lay down on the bed, but sleep was out of the question. Going to the window, he pulled aside the chintzy curtains, and gazed out over the snow-covered hills for a long time. Feeling agitated and jumpy, he tried to order his thoughts, form a plan. He had to get out of the village as soon as possible. He needed to be far far away by the time that farmer went to collect the wreck of his car.

For the next hour, he tried in vain to get a taxi. There were very few taxi businesses in the area, and no-one was willing to risk the roads in the dark in blizzard conditions. One said he would attempt to get him to Newcastle at first light but advised it would be safer to wait until the gritters had been out. With a fatalistic groan he accepted he was stuck in the hotel for the night. Tomorrow, they would look in the boot of the car and the shit really would hit the fan. *Fuck.*

He was awoken by the insistent buzz of his phone. Groping around on the unfamiliar bedside table, he located the phone and was surprised to see that it was eight forty-five. He had a vague recollection of crawling under the duvet at some unearthly hour. He must have fallen into a deep sleep.

'Hello?' he answered tentatively, trying to orientate himself.

'Morning,' said the familiar booming voice. 'Bill Dawson, I gave you a lift to the hotel last night?'

'Oh... yes, hi... Sorry, I've just woken up...'

'Just wanted to let you know we've recovered your car this morning. Wasn't as hard as I thought it would be to get to it. It had bounced right to the bottom of the hill, so we just had to go over the bottom field to reach it and tow it off. Covered in snow, it was, we didn't see it at first. Anyway, we've taken it to the garage in the village, just along the road from the Turks Head. It's in a bit of a state. Complete write-off. Bloody lucky you managed to get out in time.'

'God...' he muttered, waiting with bated breath for what would be said next.

'You'll need to let your insurance company know right away. They'll settle up with me.'

'Yes... yes, I'll do that. Thanks for recovering the car for me... I'll get on to them straight away.' *They mustn't have looked in the boot yet.*

The booming voice continued. 'If you need anything out of the car, you'll need to go to the garage, but be prepared for a shock when you see it. There's not much of it left; all the windows are shattered, one of the back doors torn off, boot ripped open.'

Boot ripped open. 'Oh... I see... bloody hell. I'll ring the insurance people right away. Tell them where the car is.'

'Ok,' he said, then added with a laugh. 'You take care now. That's one of your nine lives gone.'

His hand was shaking slightly as he ended the call, hardly able to believe his good luck. He'd certainly had a lucky escape, in more ways than one by the sound of things. He took a few deep breaths. Feeling calmer, less panicked, he picked up the phone again and began to key in the number for his taxi.

CHAPTER TWO

January 2023

Nearing the end of his daily afternoon walk with Jess, Joe was ready for his pint at the Queen's Head. Today he quite fancied one of their steak and ale pies. Usually, he was content with just a sandwich but today the cold air must have built up his appetite and he was almost drooling at the thought of biting into the succulent pie, which from past experience he knew to be delicious. Since losing his Nancy two years ago, he couldn't be bothered to cook much for himself anymore, and he found the Queen's a godsend. The manager and several of the regulars had become his friends, assuring him of a warm welcome and good conversation. Most importantly, Jess was welcome too.

Jess's bark brought him from his culinary reverie, and he looked around to see what she was up to. With darkness falling fast, he could just make her out, on the far side of the snow-covered field alongside the road. She seemed to be pawing at something on the ground.

'Jess,' he called. 'Here, girl.' Usually obedient, the dog ignored his command and went on pawing at the ground, occasionally pausing to look in his direction and bark excitedly. Joe recognised the urgency in her tone. 'What have you found now, girl?' he sighed, muttering to himself as he began to trudge through the deep, virgin snow towards her. The last time she'd been agitated like this, she'd presented him with a decaying pheasant.

As he got nearer, he could see something poking up out of the snow where she'd been scrabbling at the ground. What was it? 'Leave it Jess,' he commanded, and she sat back on her haunches, obediently waiting for him to reach her. 'What on earth have you got there lass?' The object of her attention was greyish, with frozen snow clinging to it. Crouching down to examine it, he dusted off some of the snow to reveal what looked like a knobbly stick. On closer examination, it became clear that the 'stick' was a big toe, attached to a large, stiff foot, clearly that of human being.

'Good girl, Jess,' he said, rubbing her head. 'We'd better ring this in, hadn't we?' Taking his mobile from his pocket, he tapped at the keys. 'Police please,' he said in response to the call handler's question. 'Former Detective Inspector Joe Barnes here,' he said once he was put through. 'I'm reporting a body buried in the snow in Rothbury. Male, if I'm not mistaken.' He went on to give the exact location. 'I'll stay here until you get a team over.' *Bugger,* he thought, *there goes my pie. They'll have run out by the time I get there.*

When DCI Gayle Jones took the call from the duty officer, just as she was preparing to leave the station in Wallsend, her first reaction was *shit.* After making a note of the details, she barked 'Right. On my way.' Shrugging on her parka, feeling in the pockets for her keys, she yelled, 'Georgia, we need to get up to Rothbury. Body found on Hillside.' She heard a barely suppressed groan from her sidekick, Georgia Green, a twenty-eight-year-old DI whose wild partying lifestyle was well-known around the station. 'Sod's law, I'm afraid, looks like your weekend's up the spout... here, catch.' She threw the keys to Georgia. 'You're driving.'

In the car, Gayle took the opportunity to put in a call to her mother, to let her know it could be very late before she was off duty, explaining that an urgent case had come up. 'I know, mum, I know,' Georgia heard her say. 'I'm sorry... but I'll come round first thing in the morning and do you some breakfast. Ok...? Alright, see you then.' She terminated the call with a heavy sigh and began massaging the back of her neck.

'Everything alright boss?' asked Georgia glancing at Gayle's troubled face.

'My mother,' said Gayle. 'She's getting worse. You know she's been ill for quite a while? Well, she needs more help than I can give her now. But she's so bloody stubborn. Doesn't want strangers in her house. But something's got to give...' She took a deep breath. 'Anyway, let's focus on the job in hand. The only info I've got so far is the body of a male has been found by a dog walker. He's a former DI as it happens, the dog walker, not the John Doe,' she clarified with a grin. 'I used to work with him, back in the day. The body's in a field just down from Hillside Road.' She shivered. 'God, it's bloody freezing in here. Can't you turn the heating up a bit?' Teeth chattering, she rubbed at her arms dramatically.

Georgia fiddled with the dashboard controls, muttering that the car hadn't had time to heat up yet. Within a few minutes, much to their mutual relief, warm air began to flood the interior, taking away the intense chill. Turning on to the A1, they headed north, the car's headlights bouncing off the piles of snow banked up at the sides of the road. The gritters had done their work, evidenced by the constant ping of tiny pebbles worrying the underside of the car. The North East was in the grip of one of the worst winter months in living memory, but a temporary thaw had now thankfully begun to set in, although of course the temperatures still dropped to below zero once the sun set.

Before too long, Georgia slowed down as they reached the turn off for Rothbury. Indicating left, she took the slip road on to the narrower, unlit, B road leading to their destination.

'Thank God the snow ploughs have been out here too,' said Gayle, grateful to see that the road ahead was snow-free. Flanked by trees, their network of branches silhouetted against the moonlit sky, Gayle thought how menacing they looked in the dark, in contrast to how picturesque she knew them to be in daylight. The twists and bends in the narrow road slowed their progress considerably, and Gayle could feel her impatience growing.

'Fuck,' muttered Georgia, leaning forward to peer through the windscreen, her unruly curls falling over her face. 'I wish people would dim their bloody headlights.' She flashed her own headlights, yelling 'Wanker' as the lights of an on-coming vehicle momentarily blinded her.

'Charming. You've got a foul mouth for someone who looks as though butter wouldn't melt,' laughed Gayle. 'Must be the red hair.'

It wasn't too long before they reached Rothbury and made their way slowly through the semi-deserted village. Along the main street, a few shops and a couple of pubs were still open, their lights reflecting on to the snowy verges. Frost-rimmed halos surrounded the streetlamps, lending an eerie air to the place. Not far ahead, an intense beam of light sliced downwards through the dark sky, accompanied by the faint whir of rotor blades.

'Got the chopper up, I see,' observed Georgia.

'Yep. Take a right just along here,' instructed Gayle. 'Follow the road... basically head for the light.'

Georgia obeyed, climbing a sharp bank for a few hundred metres, before turning left to drop down onto an unlit snow-covered road skirting a field at the base of a steep hill. On the far side of the field, they could see blue flashing lights, reflecting intermittently on the white snow.

'Let's see what we've got here,' said Gayle, as Georgia brought the car to a halt. 'We'll need the wellies,' she instructed, opening the passenger door so she could more easily remove her ankle boots.

'I'll just wade through the snow to get them then, shall I?' grumbled Georgia, getting out of the car and immediately finding herself almost knee-deep in crisp snow. Once she'd retrieved them and slammed the boot closed, she sat back in the car and struggled into the wellies in her by now wet socks and trousers. 'Bloody snow, I hate it,' she muttered under her breath.

On the far side of the field, bathed in the bright searchlight from the helicopter, they could clearly see the forensics tent and make out several small white clad figures moving around. The noise of the helicopter now hovering overhead was loud in the still air. Gayle took in the whole tableau thrown into stark relief in the glare from its powerful beam, thinking the scene looked almost biblical.

As they trudged across the field, snow spilling over the top of their boots from time to time, Gayle felt the adrenalin begin to kick in. It was always the same at the start of an investigation, and she loved the rush, the feeling of excitement building up inside. The anticipation of a juicy case. *With my luck*, she thought, *it'll just be natural causes*, then chided herself for hoping it would be a violent death.

'What a way to spend a Friday night. And to think I should be getting ready to hit the town,' complained Georgia, pouting as they made their way over the field, swearing as she tripped and almost fell into the snow. 'I was supposed to be meeting some mates...'

'Well, that would make a change. Not,' Gayle interrupted. 'Come on, keep your mind on the job.' Georgia was a good officer, but she could be irritating at times. *God, I must be getting old* Gayle thought as she realised how grumpy she was sounding these days. *I must try and lighten up.* 'Was it for anything special?' she asked.

'No, just the usual,' said Georgia. 'I don't mind missing it really. I'll save some money and a hangover, no doubt. Anyway, this could be interesting,' she said, nodding at the scene ahead. They reached the cordoned-off area, where they were greeted by a young PC, stamping his feet, and rubbing his arms.

'Everything's secured, ma'am,' he told them, his breath forming a white cloud. He handed them protective shoe covers, and waited while they put them on, Gayle nearly losing her balance in the process, before leading them to the tent. It had been erected underneath a large oak tree; its branches laden with snow. The SOCO team was busy, flashlights going off as details of the scene were recorded.

'The Divisional Surgeon's inside.' The PC pointed to the tent opening.

Just then, David Dawkins emerged, his greying beard glistening in the arc lights. 'Good evening, Gayle,' he said, grinning like a Cheshire cat, 'we'll have to stop meeting like this.'

'It's getting to be a habit, that's for sure,' she responded, laughing. She and David often crossed paths at crime scenes. 'What have we got this time?' she asked.

'Male, white. About forty. I'd say he's been here for some time, buried under the snow. The body was found by a dog walker. One of yours. Said he knows you. He's still around somewhere if you need to talk to him. Not sure yet about cause of death. There's an obvious head injury. A deep gash to the back of the head. But also, a stab wound to the upper body and multiple lacerations to the face. Lot of blood on his clothes. I need to get him back to the mortuary to take a proper look. Too cold to work here.'

'So foul play, then,' stated Gayle, with a frisson of excitement. 'Do you think the body could have been here since before the snow fell?'

'Well, there appears to be a small amount of snow underneath the body,' explained David. 'But we'll check that when we move him. My first impressions indicate that he could possibly have been here since just after the snow started to fall. That would be about three weeks ago, you remember that blizzard that started it all? Of course, it's possible he could have been buried here later than that, but the lack of any disturbance of the snow around the body makes that unlikely.'

'Hmm... Any ID on him at all?'

'Not that we've found so far,' David replied. 'He's not dressed for walking. Trainers. Clothing too flimsy for being out and about this time of year, so I don't think he was a hiker.' He hesitated, and Gayle wondered what was coming next. 'There's something else, Gayle...'

'What?'

'The body's been mutilated; not a pretty sight... the genitals have been almost severed.'

'Bloody hell. That's nice. Before or after death?' asked Gayle.

'Probably after, but I need to take a proper look. Lividity suggests he died elsewhere, and the body moved here, post-mortem. I'll be able to confirm or otherwise once I can do a proper examination. We need X-rays. The sooner we get him back, the sooner I can give you accurate information.'

'I'll just take a quick look,' said Gayle, turning towards the opening. 'And there's no sign of a wallet or anything that would give us a clue as to who he is?' she asked, over her shoulder.

'No, nothing at all,' said David. 'If we find anything when we move the body... I'll let you know.'

Gayle ducked her head and entered the tent. The body was still lying where it had been found, on its back, the head turned to one side. A wound was just visible on the back of the head, the skull showing through a deep gash. She moved around the body to get a better look at the face.

'What a bloody mess.' Despite having seen a fair number of corpses during her career, including some in various stages of decomposition, she was momentarily taken aback at the sight before her. The entire face was pulp, criss-crossed with deep slashes, some down to the bone. Whoever he was, she was sure no-one would be able to recognise him right now. She let her eyes travel down the body, noting the pulled up grey sweatshirt, exposing a pale abdomen, skin puckered around a dark gash. Denim jeans had been pulled down to his knees, exposing the grotesque sight of the mangled blood-covered scrotum, on top of which lay a greyish, flaccid penis. For some reason, the sight of the pathetic member invoked an unexpected surge of pity in Gayle, and she turned away to get control of her thoughts.

'Someone didn't like him very much,' murmured Georgia, in a hoarse whisper.

'You can say that again,' said Gayle, taking another look at the mess. Turning to David, she asked 'Is this how he was found, with the jeans pulled down?'

'Yes, the body was wrapped in a sheet,' he indicated an evidence bag through which a heavily bloodstained off-white sheet could be seen.

'How soon can you do the PM? I'd like to establish cause of death as soon as possible and try to figure out a timescale and just what's happened here.'

'Just for you, Gayle, I'll do it in the morning. I can make a start before noon. Say eleven forty-five, if that's soon enough for you?' Gayle nodded and he asked, 'You attending?'

'Thanks, David. Yes, I'll need to be there. Can you give me a call if there's any change in the time?' asked Gayle, before adding with a grimace, 'Another weekend down the pan.'

'It was ever thus, kid. See you tomorrow.' As Gayle turned away, he called after her, 'Sweet dreams.'

Gayle laughed. 'You too. See you in the morning.'

'Ma'am? Thought you'd want to speak to the person who found the body?' It was the officer who'd shown them to the tent. 'He's over there in the van. The dog's in the back.'

As they approached the blue van, Gayle could hear excited barking. She remembered Joe used to have a very lively collie and wondered if it was the same dog. It had been a while since she'd last seen him, around two years if her memory served her right.

'Well, hello Gayle. You've got this one, have you?' asked Joe coming around the van and extending his hand. 'Long time no see. How are you?' They went to shake hands, but Joe suddenly stepped closer and put his arms around her, muttering 'Sod handshakes, c'mere sunshine,' before planting a kiss on her cheek. 'It's good to see you. How are you?'

'I'm good, Joe. Nice to see you. I hear you've been sniffing out bodies for us?' she grinned.

'Well, not me. Jess is the culprit,' Joe said, indicating the back of the van with his thumb. Jess, perhaps sensing an old friend was nearby, increased her barking to an unbelievable crescendo. 'Quiet girl,' Joe shouted and miraculously the barking ceased.

'I believe you've already given a statement, Joe,' said Gayle. 'You say Jess found the body?'

'Yeah, she was off the leash and ran over the field. When she started barking and pawing at the ground, I wandered over to see what the fuss was about. By the time I got there, she'd uncovered a foot. I put her on the lead and got in touch straight away. Guarded the site 'til forensics arrived.' He scratched his chin, and then added 'Apart from Jess's paw prints, I couldn't see any other disturbance in the snow.'

'Good,' replied Gayle. 'Thanks for that Joe. We'll see what Dave Dawkins finds.'

'Yeah, I gather it's a murder case?' queried Joe.

'Between you and me, it certainly looks like it,' nodded Gayle.

'Well, when you've solved this one, DCI Jones, you and I will have to get together for a drink and a catch up.' He enveloped her in another bear hug before wishing her good luck and returning to Jess.

CHAPTER THREE

It was midnight by the time Gayle got home to her flat. Still feeling wired, she poured herself a strong vodka and tonic, taking it over to the panoramic windows to watch the lights dancing on the River Tyne as she got her thoughts in order.

She loved the flat. She'd moved in a few years ago, after living with her mum and saving long and hard until she had enough money for the deposit. She really appreciated what she now had. On the third floor of a relatively new, prestigious block right on the quayside, it boasted a spectacular view of the Tyne and four of its many bridges. Looking directly opposite, on the south bank she had a view of the shiny, steel caterpillar-shaped building that was the internationally renowned culture and live music venue, the Gateshead Sage, where she'd once seen Andrea Bocelli perform. Her favourite tenor. To her left, further east on the same bank, she could see the Baltic Centre for Contemporary Arts rising starkly from the river. Gayle remembered what an eyesore it used to be when it was an old, disused flour mill. Now, with a new lease of life it looked funky and current. She'd been to see a fabulous collection of Beryl Reed paintings there recently and afterwards had gone up to the top floor for a spectacular bird's eye view of Gateshead and Newcastle. She remembered that had been in the early days with Frazer when he'd been fun. Before becoming a pain in the arse.

Just in front of the Baltic, spanning the Tyne, was the pedestrian Gateshead Millennium Bridge. A beautiful arched structure, known as 'The Eye' because of its similarity to an eye blinking when raised to allow shipping to pass underneath. From her vantage point, she could also see, to the west, the iconic Tyne Bridge, and beyond that the High-Level Bridge where she could just make out a train on its way to Edinburgh via Newcastle Central Station. In the distance, a glimpse of the Swing Bridge completed the panoramic view.

Gayle would often stand at her floor to ceiling windows drinking in the view, just as she was now. She thought it positively beautiful, especially at night, when the bridges were illuminated in various colours, the lights reflecting in the river below like a sea of moving jewels.

Tonight, before her evening was so rudely interrupted, she had planned to spend a bit of time with her mother, make her supper, chat with her for a while. It hurt Gayle's heart to know that there was no cure for her mum. After being diagnosed with inoperable cancer of the womb seven years ago, her mother had undergone an intense course of radiotherapy, which had eradicated the existing tumour but not before, unbeknown to them, the cancer had managed to send out its insidious spores to other organs, ensuring its certain return in the future. Her mother experienced three and a half years of relatively good health, leading a normal life, and Gayle had begun to believe she was truly cured. It was at that time that she bought her flat and moved out of her mother's house.

Then, gradually, the health issues began and slowly her mum had deteriorated to the point where she was now almost bedridden, and Gayle knew it was only a matter of time. Feeling constantly guilty, trying to juggle her demanding career with caring for her mum, she spent as much time as she could with her. But she never felt it was enough, although her mother never complained and was always pleased to see her.

She had also planned to end things with Frazer tonight. To dump him, she supposed, although that was a term she didn't like or use. It sounded like putting someone into a bin or onto a scrap heap, and that was not what she wanted to do. She simply didn't want to see him any longer. Things had run their course since she'd first bumped into him seven months earlier. Not really his fault, she acknowledged, admitting to herself that as a workaholic with a sick mum to attend to, there was little room in her life for a partner right now. She was honest enough to admit to herself that she would miss the sex, which was great, but lately he'd been putting pressure on her to set up home together and that had focused her mind. She had realised that commitment was the last thing she needed, and besides she wasn't sure she'd ever feel for anyone what she'd felt for her cheating ex, so why bother?

Now, thanks to Mister John Doe's body surfacing, she knew that all her focus would need to be on the case, making it more urgent that she free herself up. Wanting to get it over and done with, she decided to do it by phone, there and then. With a deep sigh, she threw the last of her vodka down her throat and reached for her mobile.

CHAPTER FOUR

2007

Curling her legs beneath her as she settled down to watch the film, Charlotte tucked a tartan throw around her knees as she basked in the warmth emanating from the wood-burning stove in the hearth. She wriggled into a more comfortable position, sighing with contentment as she listened to noisy hailstones drumming in waves against the patio doors with each gust of wind. What better place to be tonight than here at home?

'Ah, cosy nights in are just lush,' she said, picking up the remote. 'Especially when the weather's like this. Don't you think, Ricky?' She looked over at her partner of five years sprawled on the other end of the settee, long, skinny legs stretched out, bare feet propped up on a dark grey footstool. 'This is supposed to be a really good movie. Sandra Bullock is in it, so it should be good,' she informed him.

'Not sure Premonition is gonna be my cup of tea, but whatever makes you happy, my little plum duff.' Ricky grinned over at her, showing slightly crooked teeth beneath a narrow moustache. He suddenly reached out and picked up a nearby cushion, playfully throwing it at her. 'The sacrifices I make for you,' he teased. 'The footie's on ITV.'

She laughed and batted the cushion away, then groaned as the sound of the theme tune to the Muppet Show filled the room. 'Oh please, not tonight,' she muttered reaching for her mobile on the floor, its screen lit up with the incoming call. Glancing at it, she recognised the number, and her fears were confirmed. 'Shit!' she exclaimed under her breath before quickly answering, 'Charlotte Clarkson.'

'We've got an emergency, love. Social worker needed urgently at Longstaff Road,' the disembodied voice advised her through noisy static. 'Violent domestic in progress. Young child at risk. A toddler, about three years old.'

'I'll be there right away,' snapped Charlotte, quickly scribbling the address on the back of her hand with the pen Ricky had grabbed and held out to her. Pushing the throw to one side, she jumped up from the sofa, all thoughts of cosy nights and Sandra Bullock banished.

'Oh shit,' said Ricky. 'Just when you were looking forward to a nice night in... Do you want me to drive you? I can just stay in the car, out of the way.' Swinging his legs to the floor, he made to get to his feet.

'No, no need, darling,' said Charlotte, firmly pushing him back down. 'I'm not sure what I'm going to find there. And no need to spoil both our nights. You can watch your beloved team now.'

'Such a shame sweetheart... but if you insist,' he pulled a face, trying hard not to look too pleased at the prospect of football instead of a girl's film. As she went into the hall, he stretched over to reach the remote.

Going through to the bedroom, Charlotte donned her black parka and pulled on black Ugg boots over her leggings. She grabbed her keys from the console table in the hall, after draping a thick woollen scarf around her neck. 'Bye, sweetheart,' she called out.

'I'll do some supper for when you get back, Hun,' offered Ricky, coming into the hallway. 'Any idea how long you'll be?'

'No idea,' she said. 'How long's a piece of string?' Then, looking at the disappointment on his face, she added, 'Why not do something that we can heat up in the microwave later if I'm not back in time? That would be good. I'll try not to be too long.'

'Ok. Give us a hug then,' he said, putting his arms around her and nuzzling into her dark curls for a moment. 'Take care, sweetheart.'

She hugged him back, kissing his cheek, before turning and hurrying out into the cold night air. Heading towards her old blue Mazda parked at the roadside, she pulled up her fur-lined hood, tugging it forward to shield her face from the driving sleet. She started the engine, leaving it running while she retrieved a child car seat from the boot and fixed it securely into the back seat.

The adrenalin was pumping as she drove the fifteen minutes or so to her destination. What would she have to confront when she got there? She recalled the last time she'd had to remove a child from a dangerous situation, a boy of eleven. Trying to prevent his father from continuing to beat his mother, he had inserted himself between them. The poor little bugger had been punched in the stomach for his efforts, and by the time Charlotte arrived, he was being loaded into an ambulance, and his mother was unconscious on the floor. She'd arranged temporary foster care for him on discharge, but before too long she was dismayed to learn that he'd been allowed to go back home to his dysfunctional parents, albeit closely monitored by child protection services.

Wary of black ice, she drove as fast as she dared, wipers working overtime, anxious to get to the premises as soon as possible. As she got nearer to her destination, she noticed that the neighbourhood looked fairly decent. Although she knew Twickenham well - she had grown up there after all - she'd never been in this part before. Under the light of the frost-rimmed streetlamps, the row of semi-detached houses looked well kept, with tidy front gardens and neatly trimmed hedges. She easily located the house she was looking for; hard to miss it with three police cars and an ambulance outside, blue lights flashing. A few of the neighbours had come out and were standing in small groups in their gardens, huddled under their hoods, watching the proceedings, their faces intermittently lit up blue.

The house looked just like its neighbours, only the screaming and shouting emanating from within differentiated it from the others. She got out of the car, grabbing a thick blanket from the back seat before hurrying up the front path towards the noise, thinking *here we go.*

It was all kicking off when she walked into the crowded living room. Police and paramedics seemed to be everywhere. Two paramedics were standing to one side, watching a struggle between two of the police officers and a well-built man. They were attempting to drag him away from a woman who was lying on the floor, curled in a foetal position in a desperate attempt to protect herself from his vicious kicks. Even with his arms behind his back, he continued to scream obscenities and kick out at her, trying to reach her where she lay. His eyes looked wild, unfocused, and Charlotte thought he was clearly on something, and probably drunk into the bargain. As he was roughly manhandled out of the house, still shouting at the woman, she could hear one of the officers cautioning him.

Charlotte turned her attention to the woman, who was now being attended to by the paramedics. She looked young, not much more than a teenager. Her unfocused eyes suggested that she too was high as a kite. Her face was swollen, lips split and bleeding, torn skirt riding up around her thighs, revealing red marks on her legs which no doubt would soon turn to deep bruises.

Charlotte looked around the room, searching for the little girl. The place was a shambles, upended furniture, and broken glass everywhere. She spotted a couple of needles on the floor, near an overturned, half-empty bottle of vodka. 'Where's the little girl?' she asked the nearest paramedic, an urgent note to her voice.

'Over there,' he nodded to the far side of the room, where a staircase led to the upper floor. Under the stairs, an officer was crouched, his back to her, apparently trying to coax the girl out of the corner. Over his shoulder, she could just make out a pair of big fear-filled eyes staring out from a white, pinched face.

'Let me talk to her,' Charlotte said quietly, taking his place and squatting in front of the girl. 'Hello sweetheart,' she murmured. 'I'm Charlotte. Can you tell me your name?' Charlotte's voice was soft as she smiled encouragingly at the child.

The little girl studied her, sucking vigorously on her thumb. After a few seconds, she removed her thumb and whispered, 'Chloe.'

'Well, Chloe, everything's going to be alright now. I'm going to take care of you. Will you come with me?' The girl hesitated, backing further into the corner, her dark eyes round with fright.

'It's alright, Chloe, there's no need to be scared,' said Charlotte, smiling and putting her arms out. 'You'll be safe with me.'

The child put her thumb back into her mouth and studied Charlotte. Wearing a red top with red-patterned leggings, Charlotte thought she looked well enough dressed, but undernourished and thin, her little face white and pinched, dark circles beneath her eyes. After a few moments, the girl seemed to make up her mind, and took a tentative step forward, before putting her arms out. Charlotte quickly scooped her up and got to her feet.

Despite her injuries, the mother was quick to react when she realised her daughter was to be taken. Pushing the paramedics out of the way and jumping to her feet, she grabbed Charlotte's arm, digging her nails in and screaming in her face, trying to wrestle the girl from her. Charlotte knew that once the drugs wore off, the woman would feel the effects from the severe beating she'd just taken, but right now she was like a wildcat. Holding on tightly to the girl, Charlotte turned away as the paramedic attempted to restrain the mother.

'Fuck you,' the woman yelled, tightening her grip on Charlotte's arm, pulling her round, away from the door. 'You're not taking my baby.' She spat in Charlotte's face. 'You're not fucking taking her...'

The two officers jumped to Charlotte's aid and quickly restrained the mother, holding her arms tightly to allow Charlotte to escape with the little girl.

'Come on, love,' the female officer said to the mother. 'Let her do her job. The girl must go, she's not safe here. And you need to go to hospital.'

'She's not fucking going anywhere,' she screamed, trying to wrest herself free, her eyes wild. 'I'll fucking kill her,' she threatened. 'I'll fucking kill her if she takes her.' Her eyes were glassy, pupils unnaturally enlarged.

Seizing her opportunity, Charlotte hitched the little girl further up on to her shoulder and hurried from the house, the screams of the woman following her.

'I fucking know who you are, bitch. I know where you live. I'll fucking get you.'

As she carried the child down the path, Charlotte wrapped the warm blanket around her thin little body, trying to protect her from the worst of the elements. As she did so, she felt the child's arms slide around her neck as the girl snuggled into her. A little plaintive voice came from the folds of the blanket.

'It's alright, I'm safe now.'

Years of tough social work, had to a certain extent hardened Charlotte, yet Chloe's words pierced her heart. *Poor little mite* she thought. As she lowered the child into the back of the car, and tucked the blanket tightly around her, she could still hear the woman shouting obscenities and screaming out Chloe's name.

'Come on, little one. I'm going to take you to a nice lady, who will take good care of you.' As she was being strapped in, the little girl looked up at Charlotte with big, brown eyes, and smiled.

It was a further two hours before Charlotte was finally able to get home, after ensuring the little girl was in the safe hands of emergency foster carers. Drawing up outside her house, she took a few moments to get control of her feelings. She sighed deeply, emotionally and physically drained. Once inside and picking at the lasagne Ricky had heated up for her, she vowed to herself that she would keep an eye on Chloe's progress, so moved had she been by this particular child. She fervently hoped the authorities wouldn't allow Chloe to be returned to those two junkies. She deserved so much better.

'It's not like you to get emotionally involved, Charlotte,' said Ricky, looking at her in consternation as she wiped tears from her eyes and pushed away her plate.

'I know,' she said. 'Not very professional either, but... I don't know; the kid just got to me. Bless her; she just wanted to be safe.'

Over the coming months, Charlotte followed Chloe's case and was pleased to learn that she was to be adopted by her maternal grandparents, with access denied to her mother and father. The history of violence in the family apparently preceded Chloe's birth, and they'd been on the radar of the police and social services for some time.

A year later, she learned, tragedy struck. Both grandparents were killed outright in a road traffic accident. Chloe was left alone and vulnerable once again. Charlotte was gutted; the poor little kid had done nothing to deserve the shit that life was throwing at her.

CHAPTER FIVE

2011

Sandra Howard sank gratefully down onto the shabby blue sofa, with an audible sigh of relief. Fishing a pack of cigarettes and a lighter from her coat pocket, she lit up with shaking hands, and took a deep drag, the tip glowing brightly in the dim room, highlighting the deep hollows of her cheeks. Resting her head against the back of the sofa, she slowly exhaled a long stream of blue smoke, beginning to feel the calming effect of the nicotine on her frayed nerves. She knew she shouldn't be smoking in here, and told herself it would be just this once, to settle herself down.

She'd done it. Thank God. Unbelievably, she'd managed to get clean, thanks to the tough love at the clinic. It had been a hard road; one she knew she was never going to go back down again. Ever. Not to the drugs. And not to him. From her first desperate approach to that policewoman, she had begun to dare to hope that things could change for the better. And they were, slowly. She took another deep drag, sucking her cheeks in and savouring the hit.

She should have left him long ago. Why had she put up with his violence and intimidation for so long? In the early days, when she was young and naive, he'd seemed charming and charismatic. All an act of course, as she soon found out. Not long after she moved into his house, the facade began to wear off, revealing the controlling bully underneath. Subtly at first, putting her down, constantly criticising and undermining her. Then, gradually alienating her family and forbidding her go out with friends or have them to the house. Inexorably, bit by bit he eroded her self-esteem, until there was nothing left of the confident, vibrant young girl she used to be. Then the physical abuse began, escalating until she was thoroughly cowed and intimidated. She knew about coercive control, how on earth had she let it happen to her? Where was her courage? Why did she let it go on for so long?

Early on in their relationship he introduced her to drugs. At first, she only smoked a bit of pot he brought home, finding it helped her to get through the day. But soon he bullied her into trying stronger and stronger stuff and soon she was using regularly. By then, she was totally under his control, completely dependent on him and the supply of drugs he drip-fed her. Her life spiralled down to the deepest depths. A good metaphor, she thought, as she recalled the feeling of being under water most of the time, floating aimlessly through the murk that defined her life. He began bringing men home, charging them to have sex with her. He always introduced them as a 'mate' and she was expected to comply with whatever they wanted. To refuse was to invite his wrath. She sighed again, closing her eyes, thinking back to the day she finally broke free.

It had been a bad night. He'd brought yet another 'mate' home and she'd told him she couldn't sleep with him as she had her period. He'd flown into a rage, punched and kicked her and told her he would throw her out of the bedroom window if she didn't do as she was told. In the end, she'd had no choice but to perform a sex act on the man, whilst her partner watched, pleasuring himself and shouting encouragement to the man.

It was the straw that broke the camel's back. The next morning, when he left to give his mate a lift home, she had simply walked out of the house. In a daze and with no idea where she was going, she got on the first bus that came along, eventually finding herself on Ealing

Broadway. After wandering aimlessly for ages, attracting odd looks, she finally asked for help from a police officer patrolling the shopping centre. She must have looked a sorry sight, with a black eye and split lip enhancing her battered face. At the station, after the police surgeon had examined her and attended to her wounds, the police tried to persuade her to press charges against her partner. Terrified she'd have to see him again, she refused. After that they put her in touch with a local Women's Refuge.

At the lowest point in her life, wretched and ashamed, dependent on drugs to get through each day, the people from the Refuge had reached out to her and literally save her life. The practical help, support, and tough love they'd given her was nothing short of miraculous. In response to the call from the police, they immediately sent someone to collect her. She was in a bad way, upset and shaking, terrified he would somehow be able to find her. And by then, she was also beginning to crave a fix.

Looking back, everything seemed to happen fast, and the precise sequence of events evaded her memory now. She remembered her relief to find that nobody judged her. They simply offered practical help with a down-to-earth, no-nonsense approach. Sandra found herself agreeing to go into a rehabilitation clinic near Leeds, where she went on to face the biggest battle of her life. The agony she experienced as the drugs were purged from her system was something she never thought she would get through. Several times, she got to the point where she didn't think she could take any more and decided to quit. But with the dedication of the staff and the tough love from the Refuge people, she had somehow stayed with it. And she had done it. She had actually done it. And now she was here. This morning, Hayley, one of the Refuge team, collected her from Leeds in her battered old Range Rover, and brought her here to Sanctuary, a

Women's Refuge in Morpeth, Northumberland. It was comforting to be hundreds of miles from her old life, and *him*. She often wondered what his reaction had been when he'd come home to find her gone. He would have been apoplectic with rage, probably smashed the place up in his temper, unable to believe she had left him. She could hardly believe it herself. Even now, she still wondered where she'd found the courage after all those years of oppression. But thank God she had, and it was the best thing she had ever done.

'Sandra, you there?' The voice was loud, interrupting her reverie.

Startled, she jumped up and quickly ground out her cigarette in a nearby plant pot, waving her arms around in an attempt to dispel the smoke, before opening the door and looking at the cheerful countenance of the small, plump, blonde-haired lady standing there.

'Oh, it's you, Linda.'

'Hi, how are you doing?' asked Linda in her soft, Glaswegian accent 'I've just come to check that you're ok? Did Hayley get you settled in alright?' As she spoke, she followed Sandra into the small room. Linda sniffed the air as she looked around, but to Sandra's relief didn't mention the smell of smoke, although she couldn't have failed to detect it.

'Well... yes. Everything's happening so quickly all of a sudden... hard to believe I'm here...' she gestured with her hands, looking around the room.

'It'll feel strange at first, Sandra. But you'll soon settle down. You know that you're safe here, well away from harm. Has Hayley fixed you up with everything you need?'

'Yeah. I didn't need much... just some shower gel and shampoo. I'd run out of those.'

'Good. Now, do you fancy a cuppa? We can get one in the kitchen, and you'll be able to meet some of the other residents if anyone's around.'

Before being brought here, Sandra hadn't known what to expect. Would the Refuge be a big, impersonal place? She'd pictured dormitories and queues for the loo but was pleasantly surprised to find it was just a normal house, quite large, but a far cry from the institution she'd dreaded. Just five rooms, a communal kitchen/eating area, and a bathroom.

As she followed Linda along the narrow hall, she took several deep breaths, trying to control her anxiety. To Sandra's relief, the kitchen was unoccupied, and Linda quickly made them a cup of coffee which they sipped sitting at a small wooden table in the centre of the room.

'Did Hayley explain how this place works?' Linda asked, taking a tentative sip of the hot coffee.

'Yeah... and she went through the rules and all that stuff. Told me about the rent and having to do my own cooking and that.'

'Good. So how did you find rehab, Sandra? You were there for about ten weeks, I think. I know you nearly gave up a few times. Was it very bad?'

Sandra took a deep breath before giving her response. 'It... it was hard. Very hard. Especially at first. And I know I'm not out of the woods yet... but I'm determined to make a new life. I won't go back to it.'

'It's not an easy journey. Rehab can be vicious, especially in the withdrawal stages.' Linda placed a hand on Sandra's arm. 'But we're here for you. We'll help you to stay clean and to start rebuilding your life. You know that your mentor, Jill, will continue to work with you for as long as you need her. And we have counsellors on hand to support you too,' said Linda, patting her arm.

The kindness was getting to Sandra. She couldn't remember the last time anyone had been nice to her. Suddenly, before she realised it was going to happen, big, noisy sobs erupted from her as the floodgates opened. Linda didn't say a word but Sandra felt her continuing to gently pat her arm as she dropped her head into her hands and howled, her body wracked with convulsions.

Eventually, the storm of emotion eased, and Sandra raised her head, trying to wipe away the tears with the heels of her hands. 'I'm sorry... sorry...' she sniffed loudly.

'It's alright, Sandra,' said Linda, pressing a man-size tissue into her hand, retrieved from her pocket. She watched as Sandra wiped her eyes before blowing noisily into the handkerchief. 'No apologies needed. This is perfectly normal. You've been on a huge emotional journey, you know. Everyone feels like this when they first come here. Better out than in, girl... now finish your coffee and we'll go back to your room.'

As they sipped their drinks, Linda took the opportunity to tell Sandra a little about the other women currently staying at the Refuge. 'We have three women here at the moment, Sandra. Like you, they're all fleeing violent and abusive men. One of them has her two small children with her.'

'Children?' whispered Sandra, an ache beginning in her chest. 'How old are they?'

'Four and five. Just little tots. They've seen far too much in their young lives.'

As they walked back to her room, Sandra felt her optimism beginning to drain, the heavy weight of guilt on her shoulders threatening to overpower her. Once inside, she slumped abruptly onto the settee, putting her head in her hands.

'What is it?' asked Linda. 'Your face drained of colour when I mentioned the children. Is that what it is, Sandra?' She crouched in front of Sandra, trying to see her face. 'Tell me.'

'I... I had a little girl,' she whispered, raising her head to face Linda. 'They took her... it was my fault... all my fault.' She gulped and took a deep breath. 'Oh God, sometimes I wish I was dead... I can't stand the guilt...'

'Where is she now?' asked Linda, gently.

Sandra wiped her eyes and took another deep breath. 'She was only three... they gave her to my parents... on condition I didn't go near. The social workers said I was an unfit mother... and they were right...'

'Don't be so hard on yourself, Sandra. You were young and in the clutches of that awful man.' Linda grasped her hands. 'Anyway, now that you're clean, there might be a chance that you'll be able to see her again. We'll help you...'

'No... You don't understand. My parents were both killed a year after she went to them... a car accident. She was adopted after that... I don't know where she is now.'

'That's really tough...' Linda squeezed her hands. 'I'm not going to give you platitudes, Sandra. Some things you just have to learn to live with, but you have to stop taking all the blame. It's very hard, losing a child like that, but at least you know that she'll be in good hands, well looked after and having a good life. When was she adopted?'

'Three years ago... She'll be seven now.'

'Right now,' said Linda in a firm voice, 'we need to concentrate on getting you well. Look at you; you're all skin and bone. You can't weigh more than seven stone. I want to see you eating regular meals. You'll be surprised how much better things will look once you've built up your strength.'

Over the next couple of weeks, as Sandra got to know the other residents, she realised that her story was not so different from that of many women who had suffered at the hands of violent men. Some had endured far more than she had. One of them had been brought to the refuge directly from hospital where she had nearly died after a severe beating from her partner. She'd been repeatedly kicked in the stomach and the resulting miscarriage and internal damage had almost proved fatal. In every case, just like her, the women blamed themselves for the predicament they were in.

Katie, the lady with the two children, left the Refuge a few days after Sandra arrived, but not before she and Sandra had established a rapport and promised to keep in touch.

'Try to get housed near me, Sandra,' Katie begged. 'At least we'll have one friend each.' She was being moved to a safe place on the outskirts of Newcastle, far away from her abusive former partner. The Refuge staff had arranged everything. Found her the house, liaised with social services, arranged benefit payments and located schools for the children. They also continued to support her emotionally every step of the way.

'When you're ready to leave, Sandra,' Linda explained to her when she asked about being near Katie, 'you'll be able to start a new life. With a new name. You'll have a chance to rebuild your life. We'll try to find you somewhere near Katie, but I can't promise anything at this stage. The main thing is that you'll be safe. Even if your former partner decides to try to find you, he won't be able to. You'll be safe,' she reiterated.

'Safe?' whispered Sandra. 'That would be so good... But... the thought of being on my own scares me... How will I manage? Please let it be somewhere near Katie. Otherwise, what will I do? I won't know anyone... what will I do for money...'

'One step at a time,' said Linda. 'Let's take one day at a time for now. The main thing is that you're safe and can make a new life for yourself, free of his clutches. You need never see him again.' Words that would return to haunt her.

CHAPTER SIX

2012

I had the nightmare again last night. The same disturbing dream that has been haunting me for as long as I can remember. At first I can only see dark shadows, and then suddenly I hear a woman screaming. A piercing, long, drawn-out, blood-curdling, "Noo…" that hammers into my brain and wakes me up.

Thankfully the nightmare doesn't come as often as it used to. It's been months since the last one and I was beginning to think it had stopped altogether. But it was bad last night. Really bad. When it comes, it's so scary. It sounds as though she's in my room, screaming right into my ear. Last night, when I jolted awake, shaking with fear, and crying, I yelled out for my mum, and she came rushing in. She sat on my bed, stroked my head, told me it was just a bad dream. When I couldn't stop sobbing, she slipped into bed beside me and eventually I must have fallen asleep in her arms.

Today, when I came home from school, the strangest thing happened. My mother said she wanted to have a talk with me and told me to come into the kitchen and sit down. It all seemed very serious, and I thought, uh-huh what have I done now? I was racking my brains to think when I'd last been naughty.

'Eva, there's something important I need to tell you,' she began. 'You're eight now, and I think you're old enough to understand.' She stared at me across the table. 'I haven't told you before because I didn't think you would be able to fully understand. But, after last night, I'm hoping that what I'm about to tell you might help you to know why you have the nightmares, and hopefully stop them from coming back.'

Puzzled, I didn't say anything. Perhaps I wasn't in trouble after all? I waited, swinging my legs under the table, noticing the anxious look on mum's face, wondering what she was talking about and hoping it wouldn't take long. Blue Peter was coming on the television in five minutes.

'You see, sweetheart, there's a reason why you have the bad dreams.' She reached across the table and got hold of my hands. Crikey, this must be serious.

'I need to tell you about something that happened when you were very young, too young to remember.' I noticed her take a deep breath, and she waited for a while before she started speaking again. 'When you were very small, you used to live with your grandma and granddad,' she told me. 'Not the nanna and grandpa you have now. You were with a different family then. This is a photograph of them, see?' She handed me a small, silver frame, and pointed to a pretty lady with a round face and dark curly hair, looking into the eyes of a man in uniform. 'That was taken when they were quite young when your granddad was in the army. He was an officer,' she said, pointing to his peaked khaki cap. 'That's an officer's hat, you see.'

She wasn't making any sense to me. 'How can they be my grandparents? I've got my own nanna and grandpa. Your mum and dad.' I pulled my hands free, using one to begin picking at a loose thread on the cuff of my blouse, aware that as she talked Blue Peter was starting.

'Eva, do you know what adopted means?' mum asked, and the penny began to drop.

'I think so... is that when you go to a new family?' I asked, thinking about Lucy Jefferson at school who had told everyone she was adopted.

'Yes, that's right, darling. It means you were specially chosen by dad and me. It's a sad story, Eva, but one with a happy ending because you came to us, and we love you so very much.' She again took hold of my hands, saving my cuff in the process. 'You used to live with these other grandparents until one day they were in a very bad car accident on the motorway. Your grandma and granddad were badly injured and taken to hospital, but unfortunately, they both passed away soon after.'

'Does that mean they died?' I asked, puzzled by "passed away".

'Yes, sweetheart. They both died from their injuries. It was very sad. You were so little, just nearly four years old. You were in the car with them, strapped in your car seat in the back.' She squeezed my hands and studied my face. 'We think your dream of the lady screaming might come from the accident. You were brought out of the

wreckage unharmed. Everyone said it was a miracle.' She leant over the table and took my head in her hands, planting a kiss on my forehead, before continuing. 'Now you're our miracle. You came to us to be looked after soon after the accident and then, later, we were able to adopt you.' She smiled her bright smile, the one she uses when she wants you to agree with what she's saying.

'I was in a car accident?' I asked, fascinated, the television temporarily forgotten. 'And that's why I hear the scream?'

'Yes, that's right. The doctors believe that's where it stems from. You began to have the dreams soon after you came to us. At first, you would wake up screaming nearly every night, but gradually, as you settled down here with us and your new brother, they became less frequent. But, as you know, they haven't gone away entirely yet.'

'Why can't I remember this other grandma and granddad?' I asked. 'I can only remember always being here with you and dad.' I was trying to understand this new information.

'You were too young to remember, darling. Just a baby, really.'

'So, I'm adopted,' I said slowly, and I suddenly had a thought. 'But what about Sam? Is he adopted? Does this mean he's not really my brother?' The thought that my big brother who I hero-worshipped was not my real brother made me feel sick.

'Of course, he's still your brother. Nothing has changed,' mum said quickly. 'We adopted Sam, too. He came to us when he was a baby, many years before you came along.'

'Oh, is that why his skin colour is different from mine?' I'd often wondered why Sam was so dark and me so fair-skinned. He's my hero. Although he's nearly ten years older than me, we are very close and the best of friends. He always looks out for me. I remember once, when I was about six, getting upset when a boy in our street had been mean to me, taunting me in the school yard, telling me I was skinny and ugly. Sam had 'had a word' with him. I don't know what was said or done, but the boy didn't bother me again after that and kept out of my way whenever our paths crossed.

Tonight, I told Sam about what mum had told me, and asked him if that meant that he wasn't really my brother. He became very angry. Took hold of my shoulders, put his face close to mine.

'Don't you ever say that,' he hissed at me. 'I am your big brother and I'll always be your big brother. Right?' Then he put his arm playfully around my neck, pretending to choke me. 'And you'll always be my little sis, right? Even when I go away to Uni. Never forget your big bro is always there for you'. He gave me a great big hug and I felt much better.

'I'm going to miss you when you go away,' I told him. 'Oxford sounds so far away. Mum says you're 'gifted'. Is that true?'

'No, I'm just an exceptionally clever language student,' he replied with his usual modesty. 'The working-class boy from Wallsend done good.' He grabbed me again, got me in a headlock, and began tickling my ribs until I begged him to stop.

At eight years old, you tend to take things in your stride. You just accept things. In the days that followed the revelation of my adoption I didn't feel any different, but it did make me realise that I have always had a very vague sense, just wispy feelings really, of not always being with mum and dad. Now I understand why, and although I was surprised at what mum told me, at the same time it feels good to have been specially chosen. As for the accident, because I've got no real memory of it, or of my grandparents, I'm not thinking too much about that. Even though I realise how sad it is that my grandparents died like that, I couldn't wait to tell the story to my friends at school. Giving my classmates the gory details has given me a kind of mini-celebrity status which, to my shame, I'm happily basking in. It seems that learning about the accident might have helped put my mind at rest about the scream, because up to now I haven't heard it again.

I don't know why, but it didn't occur to me to ask who my real mother and father were, or where they are now.

CHAPTER SEVEN

2015

'Ah, there you are Gayle. Come on in.' Detective Superintendent Charles Duncan looked tired, a grey pallor beneath his salt and pepper beard. Due to retire in just six months, Gayle thought he looked more than ready for it. 'Just got a report in,' he said, holding out a thin file. 'Young girl of eleven reported missing by her parents. Lives in The Crescent, Wallsend. According to the parents, she went to see a friend in Woodbine Avenue and hasn't come home. It's been nearly four hours now since she left the friend's house. Said she was going straight home. The Crescent is, what, ten/fifteen minutes' walk, from Woodbine? I want you to be Senior Investigating Officer on this – you'll need to start with the parents. Get the details. I'll get Frank to draft in some uniforms and put a team together, ready to go if needed. When you give the word.'

She took the file, quickly scanned it. Looking up, she shrugged. 'Hmm... she hasn't been missing for long, Gov. She could have just gone to see another friend, something like that.'

'Could be,' he said, taking off his glasses and polishing them with a handkerchief fished from his pocket, 'but the parents are convinced something's happened to her. Completely out of character, apparently.' Gayle noticed his face looked even more tired and washed out without his specs.

'Let's hope they're wrong,' said Gayle. 'Anyway, I'm on it. I'll take Dave with me.' She turned to leave.

'By the way, Gayle,' he added, 'how are things with your mother now? You coping alright?'

She turned back. 'Oh, not too bad at the moment, sir, thanks for asking,' she responded. 'She's stable for now, thankfully. We know it's inoperable, but they think with radio therapy they can keep her going, hopefully for quite a few years yet.'

'That's good to hear,' he smiled. 'Now go and find that girl.'

As she left the Super's office she found DI David Chapman by the coffee machine, just about to put a coin in the slot. 'Better bring that with you, Dave,' she said, slapping him on his arm as she strode past. 'We've got a missing girl. I need you to come with me.' Over her shoulder she added 'You can drive.'

She liked working with Dave. Valued his diligence and good humour. In his late twenties, he was mature for his age, with a keen intelligence. Gayle thought it likely he was destined for great things. He'd only been with the department for a year but was already making a name for himself.

As he drove the unmarked car along the Coast Road, heading west, Gayle brought him up to date with the little information she had so far. 'Her name is Eva Simpson. A good kid, according to the parents Rachel and Tommy. Never given any cause for concern before. She's been missing for nearly four hours, and the parents are certain something's happened to her.'

'Four hours isn't long. It's a nice day. She could have just decided to take off somewhere, don't you think?' he asked, glancing sideways at her as he drove, the early evening sun bouncing off the lenses of his Oakley's.

'My thoughts exactly. Anyway, we'll see what the parents have to say. With a bit of luck, she might even have turned up by the time we get there. This is the exit coming up,' she said indicating the slip road ahead.

'Yes, boss. I do know where The Crescent is,' Dave grinned. 'I've only lived in Wallsend all my life.'

'Sorry. Teaching my granny to suck eggs am I?' she laughed with him.

He took the slip road leading to Wallsend Town Centre, turned left at the junction and before long was swinging into The Crescent. They located the house halfway around the crescent-shaped street. Dave drew up outside a neat semi and cut the engine. 'This is it,' he announced, checking the number as he unclipped his seatbelt.

'Here goes,' said Gayle. Getting out of the car, she straightened her jacket as she crossed the pavement and pushed open the wrought-iron gate. A smooth concrete path led to a blue-painted front door. Neat borders of brightly coloured flowers surrounded the immaculately clipped lawns on either side. The stone birdbath in the centre of one of the lawns, cast a long shadow in the early evening sun. Breathing in the heady aroma of the flowers, Gayle, whose horticultural knowledge was sadly lacking, wondered fleetingly which of the many flowers smelled so strongly? Could be night-scented stock she supposed, thinking of one of the few flowers she could put a name to.

She pressed the bell and could hear it ringing somewhere in the house. The door was soon opened by a small, slim woman with dark shoulder-length hair. Gayle estimated her to be around forty. Anxiety was etched into her face as she looked at them.

'Mrs Simpson? I'm DCI Gayle Jones. This is DI David Chapman. Ok if we come in?'

'Yes... of course,' she said, opening the door wider to admit them. 'Is there any news? Have you found her?' she blurted, searching their faces.

'Not yet, I'm afraid. We've only just received the report that your daughter is missing,' explained Gayle.

'Oh... I see,' she said sounding dejected. 'Come on in.' She turned and led the way along a short, grey-carpeted passage into a light-filled living room, the rays of the evening sun streaming through the big picture windows. 'It's the police, Tommy,' she said to a stocky man standing with his back to them, staring out of the window.

'About bloody time,' he barked, turning to face them. 'I hope your lot are out looking for her?' he demanded.

'Mr Simpson, we came here just as soon as we received the report that Eva is missing. We have a team ready to start searching for her. But first, we need a few details, to focus the search in the right areas. Ok?' Gayle spoke firmly and kept her steady gaze on him.

'But it's getting late now,' he muttered, scowling, waving his arm towards the window. 'I just want her found.'

'That's what we all want, Tommy,' she said. 'Is it alright if I call you Tommy? Why don't we sit down?' Gayle indicated the grey leather sofa behind him, and he somewhat reluctantly took a seat. Rachel sat beside him, and Gayle took one of the armchairs. 'Please call me Gayle.'

'And I'm Dave,' said the DI, standing behind Gayle's chair.

Gayle looked around the room, noticing how neat and tidy it was. Dark wood flooring, pale grey leather three-piece suite, light oak sideboard with matching coffee table. There were a few family photos on the wall in the fireplace alcove, mostly she assumed of Eva when she was younger, together with one of Rachel and Tommy on their wedding day.

'Now, can you tell me exactly what's happened? When did you first realise Eva could be missing?' she asked, looking at Rachel.

Softly spoken, with a hesitant manner, Rachel began to explain. 'She left here at about two o'clock this afternoon...' she said, wringing her hands.

'More like quarter past,' her husband cut in, taking over. 'She asked if she could go to Sophie's for an hour or so – they're always in each other's houses. We said yes, of course. When she hadn't come back by half past four, we wondered what was keeping her. Eventually, at about quarter to five, Rachel rang and spoke to Sophie's mother.'

'What did she say?' asked Gayle, turning to Rachel.

'She told me Eva had left shortly after half past three. They only live in Woodbine Avenue so it's just a ten, fifteen-minute walk from there. She should have been back by quarter to four at the latest,' said Rachel.

'We gave her a bit longer. Thought she must have bumped into a friend. Got talking. Forgot the time or something,' said Tommy. 'But when it got to five o'clock and she still hadn't come back, Rachel started ringing around her friends and I went out to look for her.' His foot involuntarily tapping on the wooden floor, he continued. 'There was no sign of her anywhere, so I came back to see if Rachel had had any luck. It was gone six then and that's when we rang the police.'

'Where did you look, Tommy?' asked Dave.

'I walked down Kings Road, past the park and on to Woodbine. Then I looked in the back lanes around there, and some of the back yards, those where the door wasn't locked. On the way back, I checked the park. Just the bits nearest the road, on both sides of the street. It's a big park.'

'I've spoken to all of her friends that I can think of, but none of them has seen her,' Rachel said, her voice breaking. 'It's after seven now. Where is she? Why are we just talking? Something's happened to her. We should all be out there, looking.' She jumped to her feet and went to the window, shoulders hunched, staring out.

'Just a few more questions,' Gayle said gently, going to her and touching her shoulder. 'I know this is hard for you. But we need to get as much information as possible, to help us to find Eva. Come back and sit down.' She led Rachel back to the settee. 'Has Eva done anything like this before? Come home late or gone missing?'

'No, never, she's a good girl. And sensible...' answered Tommy.

'Can you think of any reason why Eva might have deliberately not come home? Have there been any rows or upsets?' Gayle asked, looking from one to the other. 'Could she have run away?'

'No, definitely not. She's a happy girl. A ray of sunshine. She'd never run away.' Tommy was adamant.

'What about boyfriends?' Dave asked, notebook in hand.

'Boyfriends? For God's sake, she's only eleven,' retorted Tommy, going red in the face and glaring at Dave.

'It happens,' said Dave evenly.

'Not in this house it doesn't,' spluttered Tommy. 'Eleven years old with a boyfriend? Never.'

'We have to ask these questions, Tommy,' said Gayle. 'Now, does Eva ever go into the park? It's been a lovely, sunny day. She might have fancied a walk?'

'She sometimes goes, with her friends,' said Rachel. 'But I don't think she'd go there on her own. She knows she's not allowed. And she told her friend, Sophie, that she was coming straight back here.'

'Maybe she bumped into some other friend or friends on the way back and went for a walk with them?' suggested Gayle.

'She wouldn't do that,' said Tommy. 'She knows we worry if she's not back on time. She would never stay out this late without letting us know where she is.'

'Does she have a mobile phone?' asked Dave.

'No, we think she's too young... It's caused a few rows, but we've told her she can have one when she's twelve,' said Rachel. 'All her friends have them, or so Eva tells us, so it's been a bit of a bone of contention. But her father's adamant she must wait.'

'I see. So has that caused any resentment?' asked Gayle, thinking *poor kid.*

'Oh, nothing serious,' said Rachel, quickly. 'Just typical kids' angst. There's never been any falling out over it.'

'What about social media?' asked Gayle. 'Does she have a computer?'

'She has a computer for schoolwork, but I won't allow her to go on the internet for anything else,' Tommy explained, before pompously adding, 'I've got strict parental controls in place to restrict what she can use it for.' Then for good measure, he added, 'And I have remote access, so I can check what she's up to at any time.'

'Hmm... you seem to have it all sewn up,' said Gayle, thinking to herself *What a control freak.* She was finding Tommy Simpson bumptious and overbearing, frequently interrupting his wife, and contradicting her. It was obvious who played the dominant role in their relationship and Gayle wondered what life was like for Rachel behind closed doors.

'Rachel, do you have a recent photograph of Eva that we can circulate?' Gayle asked. 'And we need to know what she was wearing when she left the house?'

Rachel jumped up, going quickly to the sideboard where she picked up a silver-framed photograph. 'This is the latest school photo,' she said, her voice wavering. 'It was taken at the end of term,' She held it out to Gayle, her hand shaking. 'When she left the house, she was wearing her black leggings and a pink crop top...' Rachel was making a visible effort not to cry, her bottom lip trembling. 'Oh, and she had her hair up in a ponytail... with a pink band. She loves pink... her favourite colour,' she whispered.

'That's good, Rachel.' Gayle tried to sound encouraging. 'What about her shoes?'

'Trainers, white. Converse. She had her pink rucksack...' Rachel lost her battle for control then and broke down, putting her head into her hands. Crying, she sat down again, her shoulders heaving as she sobbed. Gayle noticed that her husband made no move to comfort her.

'Thank you,' said Gayle studying the photograph. She saw a pretty, blue-eyed young girl. Pale complexion, long, light brown hair, a sprinkling of freckles. Wearing a green checked school dress. She passed the photograph to the DI. 'Dave, get this circulated with a description of what Eva was wearing. And update the team with everything we've got so far,' Gayle instructed, getting to her feet. 'And I'd like you to take charge of co-ordinating the search.'

'Yes, boss,' he said, taking the proffered photograph as he headed for the door. Through the window, Gayle could see him outside on his phone, gesticulating animatedly with his free hand, as he talked and transmitted the picture to the team.

Addressing the distraught couple, Gayle explained, 'The search team is ready to go. They'll be covering the route Eva will have taken. They'll go house to house, speaking to the residents, searching in back lanes and yards, garages, sheds, and outhouses. At the same time, a team will begin covering the park. You know, Richardson-Dees Park has an excellent reputation as a safe place for children, so try not to worry about the possibility of Eva going in there. It's a very busy place, full of families enjoying a day out. The team will be checking whether anyone has seen Eva.' Gayle wanted to reassure them their daughter would soon be found. 'We'll circulate Eva's photo on social media, too. I can assure you we'll do everything in our power to find her quickly.'

'I need to be out looking for her myself.' Tommy was on his feet, pacing around, getting more agitated. 'It'll be dark soon. And I can't just stay here doing nothing. I'm going to call a few mates, get them to help me.'

'Speak to Dave. Let him know where you'll be, Tommy. Make sure he's got your mobile number and keep your phone with you.' Looking at Rachel, she added, 'We need one of you to stay here, just in case Eva returns.'

'I'll stay,' said Rachel.

'I'd like to take a look at Eva's bedroom now, if that's ok?' Gayle asked, directing her question to Rachel.

Rachel nodded. 'I'll take you up,' she said, turning to the door. Gayle followed as Rachel led the way up the thickly carpeted stairs, her shoulders slumped in dejection.

'We'll need to take Eva's computer away, just to check it out for ourselves,' said Gayle as Rachel pushed open the door. As she entered Gayle was immediately struck by the neatness of the room, the lack of any of the clutter usually associated with the bedrooms of young girls. No posters or pictures on the plain, white walls. It was immaculate. Not a thing out of place. She thought it the tidiest teenager's room she'd ever seen, like a bedroom you might find in a show home on a newly built housing development.

'My goodness,' she exclaimed to Rachel, 'Is her room always this tidy? I've never yet met a youngster who knows the meaning of tidy, let alone pristine.'

'Tommy likes everything just so,' replied Rachel, looking slightly embarrassed. 'He's instilled his love of neatness into Eva...'

I bet he has thought Gayle. *Control freak extraordinaire.* Noticing Rachel gazing mournfully at her daughter's bed, Gayle gently touched her arm. 'Rachel, I'm assigning a Family Liaison Officer to you. She's on her way here now. Her name is Georgia Green and she'll stay with you to give you and the rest of the family help and support.' When Rachel did not respond beyond a quick nod, she continued. 'I'll just take an initial look around, if you don't mind?

'I'll leave you to it then...' whispered Rachel, tearing her eyes from the bed and turning to leave.

Gayle looked around. It was a pretty room, themed in lilac, purple and white. The bed, with its white cover, was neatly made, cushions, in various shades of purple and lilac piled up neatly at its head. In the corner, a white melamine desk, on top of which was jotter with a Lenovo laptop. Otherwise, there wasn't as much as a stray pen cluttering its surface. She opened the drawer at the front, to find that too was clutter-free, only housing some post-it notes, a ream of copier paper, a few pens, and a box of paperclips.

The first double doors of the floor to ceiling wardrobes stretching along the wall opposite the bed revealed Eva's clothes neatly hanging, all colour-co-ordinated, shoes tidily placed on shelves. Behind the next door, Gayle found sweaters and tee-shirts precisely folded and stacked. She was hoping to find a diary but despite checking everywhere, including under the pillows, and beneath the bed, she was disappointed not to come across one. After trying unsuccessfully to get into Eva's computer, she decided to leave it for forensics to remove and examine.

Returning to the living room, she let Rachel know that a forensics team would take a look at the bedroom and reiterated they would take away the computer for analysis to check for anything that might help in the search for Eva. Rachel, by then slumped on the settee, staring into space, simply nodded. She seemed to be almost in a trance and Gayle wondered if she needed to see a doctor. The doorbell jangled just then, and Rachel came to life, suddenly jumping up, hope suffusing her face.

'That'll be the Family Liaison Officer,' Gayle said, quickly, taking Rachel's arm to prevent her rushing to the door. 'You wait here, I'll get it.' After a few moments, she returned with a petite, young woman who was patting at her unruly curls. 'This is Georgia, the family liaison officer I mentioned. DC Georgia Green. She'll stay with you, to support you and the family. She'll also keep you up to date on what's happening with the search,' Gayle explained. 'And I'm told she makes a great cuppa.'

Georgia smiled. 'My reputation goes before me.'

Once the introductions were complete, Gayle told Rachel she'd leave her in Georgia's capable hands. 'Try not to worry, we'll find her. Usually in cases like this, the missing person is quite quickly found. Rest assured; we'll do everything in our power to find Eva.' The bleak look on Rachel's face, as she left, was one that Gayle had seen before with other missing children cases and she fervently hoped that Eva was found soon, safe and well.

In the hall, on her way out, Gayle had a quiet word with Georgia. She suggested Georgia should contact the family doctor, get someone to check on Rachel. She knew Georgia would delve deeply into the family background, find out details of Eva's life, her relations at school and with her brother, her hobbies, best friends, boyfriends, etcetera and report back any significant findings, all of which would be shared with the team back at the station.

CHAPTER EIGHT

He spotted her as she came skipping out of a back lane, long hair flying behind her in the summer breeze as she crossed over the road. Watching as he slowly drove down Kings Road, he saw two bigger girls stop her by the entrance to the park, then in his rear-view mirror he glimpsed the three of them turn and walk into the park.

Go home he told himself. *Just get the hell out of here.* He was still telling himself that as he parked his car a few streets further on, and when he was making his way on foot, back towards the gates. The urge was always stronger than his willpower. *I'll just have a walk around the park,* he thought, trying to convince himself, *no harm in that, is there?*

On such a warm, sunny day the park was teeming with people. He'd never been there before and, looking around, was mildly surprised to find such an oasis in the middle of Wallsend. A mixture of walking paths, small lakes, streams running through clumps of trees, shaded nature walks, children's play areas, a cricket pitch and more, all very well kept. The place was teeming; mothers pushing prams and pushchairs, dog-walkers, cyclists, groups of kids, some on roller skates or on bikes.

Casually strolling along the winding route, shirt sleeves rolled up, he hoped he looked like what he was, a businessman taking a break from the office, soaking up a bit of sun and fresh air. It was half-term and everywhere he looked, there were children. He deliberately did not linger around the children's play areas, nor loiter near the outdoor gym. It would never do to look like a voyeur.

The warm air was filled with shouts and laughter, and even music coming from a nearby bandstand where a trio was playing a catchy jazz tune. Further on, near a large open area, he stopped at a small cafe, ordered a prawn sandwich and a cup of coffee, and carried them outside onto the terrace. He was lucky enough to find a small, vacant table overlooking the park. Just a normal bloke, getting some relaxation in his busy day. To support that impression, he took out his mobile phone and took the opportunity to answer a few emails and texts. Anything, other than watch the children he'd just spotted playing nearby.

Lunch over, he found himself walking past a large pond dotted with noisy ducks of every variety and a few moorhens, when he suddenly saw the girl he'd noticed earlier. She was standing just at the edge of a wooded area, talking to the two older girls she'd entered the park with. They seemed to be arguing and she looked distressed. As he watched, one of the girls pushed her roughly before laughing and turning away to link arms with her friend and walk off, leaving the younger girl standing on her own. The lone girl turned to walk back the way she had come, and as she turned towards him, he could see that she was crying.

'Are you alright?' he asked, approaching her, walking alongside. 'You look upset. I couldn't help but notice those girls being nasty to you.' She briefly glanced up at him, as she walked on, muttering that she was alright. She was a pretty little thing, he noticed, with a retroussé nose, her long brown hair glinting in the bright sunshine.

'Are they supposed to be friends of yours?' he asked her. 'Because that's not how you treat a friend. I've got a daughter about your age, and I'd hate to think she had friends like that,' he said, keeping abreast of her. 'What were they saying to you? I saw one of them shove you away quite hard.'

'They told me I was useless. Just because I couldn't smoke their horrible cigarettes... they tried to force me to smoke weed...' the girl muttered, head lowered as she walked, 'but I can't smoke. It made me cough and I felt sick.'

'What? In the park? Couldn't people see?' he asked, looking round, indicating all the people with a sweep of his arm. 'Someone could have helped you.'

'They made me go up there...' she pointed to a wooded hill, just ahead of them now, at the top of which were dense bushes and trees. 'One of them held my wrists and the other one forced a cigarette into my mouth... she told me I had to smoke it to prove I wasn't a baby... I choked and was a bit sick. Then they stopped ...'

'And you still walked on with them?' he asked.

'They pretended to still be my friends. Then they started being mean again. They told me I had proved that I was a baby... to run back to my "mammy and daddy"...' she stammered, beginning to cry again.

'Hey. Don't be upset. Look, I've got an idea,' he said, holding her arm, preventing her from continuing to walk. He turned to her. 'I think these girls need to be taught a lesson, don't you? I think we should look for some evidence, and then you can get your parents to make an official complaint to the school. I'm a school governor myself, and I would like to think that if this happened at my school, we could identify and punish the perpetrators. Don't you agree?'

The girl nodded, biting her lip. He continued, 'Come on. Take me up there and show me where they made you smoke. I bet they've left some stubs. You'll be able to prove they tried to force you to smoke a joint.'

'But... well... I'm not sure...' she began, hesitating, her voice wavering.

'Listen, your father's not going to be happy about what's happened to you, is he?' He made his voice sound encouraging. 'If you can take him a discarded stub, to support what you're saying, it'll give him a chance to do something about it. I'm sure he'd want you to do that. Hmm? Come on, let's look.' Putting his hand in the small of her back he guided her up the steep slope, heading for the area she'd indicated.

CHAPTER NINE

The light was beginning to fade as the police search got fully underway. Eva's friends, classmates, teachers and neighbours were being located and interviewed. A team was going door to door, speaking to the occupants of every house on and around the route Eva would have taken on her journey home, searching gardens, back yards, outhouses, and garages. Another was searching for her in back lanes, parking areas, looking in wheelie bins and skips. Anywhere a person could be hidden. CCTV footage from cameras in the vicinity and surrounding areas was being sought and examined, and a social media appeal prepared. To some, it seemed an incongruous thing to be doing on a pleasant summer evening.

The largest contingent was deployed in Richardson-Dees Park, which lay to the north of Wallsend Town Centre and covered sixteen acres. DI Chapman was co-ordinating the search and had drafted in fifty uniforms to assist detectives, together with sniffer dogs. He'd also requested a helicopter to be deployed, hoping to take advantage of the remaining light, but the pilot was reporting his view of the vast park was severely restricted by its dense canopy of trees.

With the Wallsend Burn running through its centre, linking the River Tyne to the heart of the Borough of North Tyneside, the park had been further improved over recent years thanks to substantial Lottery funding. It now boasted four tennis courts, several state-of-the-art children's play areas with sandpits and water features, bowling greens, an outdoor gym, a lake, and woodland paths through densely wooded areas. It was very popular with locals and visitors from further afield. *Plenty of places to hide a child* thought DS Chapman.

By the time the police search started, most people were making their way out of the park or had already left. Mothers with pushchairs, some trailing tired, crying children, young teenagers hurrying home for their tea, some to get ready to go out on the town later. Those still in the area were questioned and shown a picture of Eva. Up to now, no-one could remember seeing a girl matching Eva's description.

It was becoming evident to the DI that something sinister must have happened to Eva. Nearly six hours had passed since she'd left her friend's house to take a ten-minute walk home. Sophie's mother told them she'd let her out of the backyard door herself and waved her off as she skipped down the lane towards Kings Road South. Where had she gone? What had happened to her?

In the park, progress was slow. There were so many areas to search. In mid-summer, the trees and shrubs were dense with foliage. Dave fervently hoped it wouldn't prove necessary to search the lake, but he was making contingency plans to do so if she hadn't been found by dawn. The light was fading now as rainclouds gathered overhead, hastening the onset of darkness. Soon, the search would continue by torch and searchlight. There was no question of halting the hunt overnight. Not with an eleven-year-old child missing.

Back at the office, Gayle was receiving regular updates from the various teams. She knew that if Eva wasn't found soon, the search would become much more difficult overnight. The thought of the girl out there in the dark somewhere, perhaps hurt, and terrified, if indeed she was still alive, filled Gayle with a determination to leave no stone unturned in the search for her. She knew rage was futile and a cool head was required to resolve this case, and God knows she'd seen enough of the dark side of human nature not to be surprised at anything, but when kids were involved, it really got to her.

CCTV footage from every camera found in the vicinity and surrounding areas was being examined. A camera sited in a window of a first-floor flat on the corner of Woodbine Avenue, had picked up Eva emerging from the back lane just after three thirty and crossing the road. A slight figure, skipping happily, heading for home.

The night wore on. Eva seemed to have simply vanished. There had been no sightings of her at all, after she left the back lane at Woodbine Avenue. The helicopter was using heat-seeking equipment to try to locate warm spots in the park. So far, it had pinpointed a number of animals moving around, as well as a few people who had turned out to be lovers, drug users, rough sleepers and the like, all of whom had been checked out and moved on. Of Eva there was no sign at all.

There was no question of Gayle going home, and she was heartened at the numbers of her team who volunteered to stay, wanting to help in any way they could. The shrill ring of the phone on the desk interrupted her thoughts.

It was Dave. 'No sign yet,' he said. 'This place is dense. We're doing a fingertip search. Got the dogs out and the chopper's looking for hot spots. They've found a few, but they've turned out to be false alarms. The park's closed now, but a few couples have managed to get in. We're screening them and clearing them out as we find them.'

'Nothing from the door-to-door team?' she asked, knowing he would already have told her if there was anything to report.

'No, they've covered all the immediate area around Woodbine. Using the list Eva's mother supplied, we've spoken to her friends and their mothers. Also, to her teachers. There's no suggestion that Eva was upset or acting differently lately. The picture that's emerging is of a normal, happy, kid. No-one can think of any reason she might have left home voluntarily or have any idea where she could be. It's not looking good, boss.'

'Ok Dave, keep up the good work. I'm doing a TV appeal soon, should be on the ten o'clock news. We'll see what that brings in. Thanks for your update. Keep me informed.'

With a sinking heart, Gayle ended the call. Just as she put the phone down, her mobile rang. She could see it was Georgia. 'Hi, how's it going?'

'I got the names of Eva's friends and classmates from Rachel, those that she knows, and passed the details to DI Chapman, boss. Rachel's in a state. The doctor's just left. He's given her a sedative, but it doesn't seem to be having any effect yet. Her only close relative is a sister who lives nearby, but she's away on holiday until tomorrow. Her mother's dead. A couple of the neighbours are close friends and they're coming over soon. She's frantic for news. Is there anything I can tell her?'

'Nothing yet. Dave's just been on. Tell her everything that can be done is being done, and we'll let her know just as soon as there are any developments,' said Gayle. 'Tell her we're going to get some coverage on the ten o'clock news on BBC and ITV. I'm just about to go into a press conference. We've managed to arrange one at short notice. We'll be appealing for anyone who might have seen Eva to come forward. Hopefully, someone will have seen something.'

'I'll let her know, boss.'

The night wore on. CCTV coverage taken from every camera located in the area was being painstakingly examined, team members bent over their screens, anxious not to miss anything important. Others were still out searching throughout the town, some still knocking on doors. Gayle, getting regular updates from the team, was beginning to feel like they were looking for a needle in a haystack. Press conference over, Eva's photograph and a description of her clothing was all over social media, with an appeal for anyone who may have seen her to contact the police.

Around midnight Dave rang again to let her know that following the appeal dozens of local people had come forward, volunteering to help in the search. He had arranged for them to be deployed combing the streets, back lanes, car parks, fields, and wastelands in and around Wallsend. Of Eva, there was still no sign. Surely, somebody must have seen her. She couldn't have disappeared into thin air.

The weight of responsibility on Gayle's shoulders felt heavier with every minute that passed. Dropping her head into her hands, she fought a wave of despair. Was she missing something? What else could she do?

Forensics reported they'd completed their examination of the computer taken from Eva's bedroom. As her father had said, it had only been used for schoolwork and some communications with her friends. There was no internet chat room stuff or any sinister activity that might give a lead as to what had happened to her. Gayle revised her opinion on the parental control thing, acknowledging that if all parents were as diligent, then a lot more children would be kept safe from on-line predators. Sod's law then, that such a well-behaved and well-protected kid was now at risk.

With a deep sigh, Gayle went to check on her team. Most of them had volunteered to stay and she was grateful for their diligence and loyalty. All heads were down in the office, some taking calls from the public, following the article on the ten o'clock news. Others were poring over CCTV footage from every camera located in the vicinity of the park and the wider surrounding area.

'Anything of interest?' she asked a young PC who'd been drafted in to bolster the team. He had just hung up and was completing his report of the conversation.

'Don't think so, boss. Not this one. I'll pass it on to be checked out, but it just sounds like someone under the influence and trying to blame their ex. Pissed out of her head or on something,' he grimaced. 'Another timewaster no doubt.'

The hours passed, with no real progress. Reports were coming in regularly from the field, but the result so far was zilch, nada, nothing. Gayle was considering asking Eva's parents to do a press conference in the morning and was wondering if Rachel would be strong enough. At around six o'clock she was brought abruptly out of her musings when, after a perfunctory tap on her office door, DC Felton entered with an air of urgency.

'Boss, I thought I should bring this straight to you. We've had a call from a woman who says she's got a photo of a girl on her phone that she thinks could be Eva. It was taken in Richardson-Dees Park, yesterday afternoon. The girl's walking along with a man.'

Gayle was suddenly on high alert. 'What makes her think it could be Eva?'

'She matches the description, wearing black leggings and a pink top. And she's carrying a pink rucksack... I asked her to forward the photo to us, but she says she doesn't know how to do that.'

'Where is this woman?' asked Gayle, jumping up and reaching for her jacket. He gave an address in Heaton. 'Just up the road then? Come with me, Doug. Let's go see this photo.' They hurried to the car park where she handed the keys to DC Felton. 'Won't take us long to get there. This could be interesting.'

Within fifteen minutes they were in Heaton, knocking at the door of Jackie Townsend. A tiny woman of about sixty, she looked nervous, frowning, and wringing her hands as she invited them in. 'Sorry I haven't contacted you earlier... we've only just realised this morning that it could be a photo of the little girl you're looking for... You can't see their faces... Oh, I do hope I'm not wasting your time...' Her words all ran into each other as they traversed a narrow, dingy hall into a large, high-ceilinged living room.

'I nearly deleted the photograph,' she explained. 'It's not a very good one of Bella, you see. That's my granddaughter... I was in the park with her, and she didn't want to leave, so she was sulking... now where's my phone...'

Gayle waited, trying to be patient, as the woman rummaged through her capacious handbag at length, searching for her phone. Eventually, after much muttering and with a pile of discarded items on the kitchen table, including several crumpled tissues, a half-empty packet of wine gums, a pair of sunglasses, a worn brown leather purse and a pink hair slide, she exclaimed, 'Got it.' Fishing it out of the bag, she held it aloft in triumph. 'Now, I'll just find the photo for you.'

It took an age, and Gayle almost snatched the phone from her outstretched hand when she finally offered it. Examining the photograph, Gayle could see it was of a decidedly sulky-faced young girl of about four. But, in the background was a man, holding the hand of a girl. The girl had to be Eva. Her clothes and hair matched the description Rachel had given, and she looked to be around the right height and age. To clinch it, as DC Felton had told her, she was carrying a pink rucksack, looped over one shoulder. Unfortunately, they were walking away from the camera, so their faces couldn't be seen. Still, it provided valuable information. It confirmed Eva had been with a man, in the park at four thirty pm the previous day and gave them a lot to go on in terms of details of the man.

He looked to be about six feet tall, medium-build, dark, wavy, shoulder-length hair, wearing a white shirt with the sleeves rolled up, dark grey trousers and what looked to be black shoes. After studying the photograph, Gayle asked, 'Can you remember which part of the park you were in when you took this picture?'

The woman frowned in concentration, deepening still further the furrow between her brows. 'Well, it was just as we were leaving. That's why Bella was in such a bad mood, you see...' she began. 'She didn't want to go home... So, it must have been just near the exit.'

'Which exit would that be?' asked Gayle, knowing there were several entrances/exits to the park.

'The one that comes out on to Kings Road.'

'Ok. And do you recall seeing the man and the little girl yourself when you were in the park?' she asked.

'No, no, I didn't notice them at all. I was too busy trying to sort Bella out. She was being a right little madam. It wasn't even me who spotted them in the photo, it was my daughter. I showed her the photos when I took Bella home, and she forwarded them to herself. When she saw the police appeal on social media this morning, she took another look through them. She couldn't believe it when she spotted the man and girl,' the woman explained. 'She got straight on the phone to me as soon as she realised. I'm just glad I didn't delete that picture. I nearly did because it's a horrible one of Bella.'

'She certainly doesn't look very happy in it,' agreed Gayle. 'Could I just check if this is the only picture the man and girl are in?'

'Yes, I've double-checked, but please have a look yourself, I only took five or six. Do you think that girl could be that little Eva then?' the woman asked as Gayle scrolled through the other images.

'We'll have to check it out,' said Gayle, satisfied there was only one relevant photograph. 'I'm forwarding the photo to my phone now,' she said, pressing "send". 'If we confirm that it is Eva, it'll be widely circulated in the press and social media. Now, just to reassure you, we'll blur Bella's face so she can't be recognised and of course no-one will know where we obtained the photo.'

'Do you think anyone will recognise him?' the woman asked eagerly. 'I know you can't see his face, but someone might be able to identify him by his clothes?'

'Let's hope so,' said Gayle. 'You've been very helpful, Mrs Townsend. Thank you again for coming forward, I really appreciate it.'

On the way back to the station, Gayle couldn't help but wish the man had been facing the camera, but still, there was a lot to work on. As Doug drove, prior to sending the photograph to the team, Gayle forwarded it to Georgia, before ringing to ask her to show it to Rachel. She could hear Rachel's screams of distress as she confirmed it was definitely her daughter. Gayle could only imagine how distressing it must be for Rachel to look at her daughter holding hands with a strange man. On the phone to the station she instructed the team to circulate it widely throughout the force, and to all media outlets. They had something solid now to get their teeth into.

Getting Dave on her mobile, she confirmed to him that Eva had definitely been in the park, and a man had been with her. She forwarded the photograph to him. 'I want you to draft in more people, Dave. We know she was in there, and the possibility that she's still in there somewhere is quite high. The photo was taken near the Kings Road exit. Have you made arrangements to search the water?' A shiver ran down her spine. *Please don't let her be in the water.*

'It's in hand,' he told her. 'The teams are on their way.'

CHAPTER TEN

Standing in the car park puffing on her cigarette, Sandra Howard told herself for the hundredth time that she should give up. Looking around at the drab, metal-clad factories that formed her view, she thought *How sad am I? Standing in a bloody car park, in the drizzling rain. Just so I can draw toxic fumes into my lungs. Probably killing myself in the process. I must be bloody mad.*

Ruminating, she felt life hadn't turned out too badly since her escape from her tormentor. After all this time, the events of what she now thought of as her old life seemed like a dream. Or rather a nightmare, albeit a distant one now. She would never be able to forgive herself for her actions, but she'd learned to live with the underlying guilt and remorse and get on with her life.

She felt enormous gratitude to the Refuge people, especially to Linda, who had helped her so much, and even now was always there to provide a crutch should she need it. Everything she now had, she owed to Linda. The neat little flat she'd found for her in Walker, that she now called home. Linda had even managed to find a place only a short walk from Katie's, and the two of them had become firm friends. It was thanks to Linda, too, that she had this job as a machinist, which paid well and enabled her to pay her rent and live a decent life. After such a turbulent past, all she wanted from life now was to live a normal, quiet existence.

And she had met a man. A decent, hard-working man. A Polish immigrant, Marek. A bit fierce looking, with wild unruly hair, he was a very gentle person underneath, with a generosity of spirit she had never experienced before. He was kind to her, and she couldn't remember a man ever showing her kindness. But then she supposed, she'd never been with a man who didn't put her down, and it took some getting used to. She kept finding herself apologising to him for every little thing, a habit he was helping her to break. She was content with her lot, and it was a good feeling, one she hadn't experienced since she was a child... Oh well, time to get back to work, she couldn't stay out here any longer. Dropping the cigarette to the pavement, she ground it out with her foot, picked up the stub and dropped it into the bin of sand as she turned to go back into the factory.

'That was a long fag break,' Anne said, looking up from her machine. 'They should dock the time from your wages.'

'You're just jealous,' said Sandra, laughing. She knew there was some resentment from the non-smokers about the time spent on cigarette breaks, but it was generally light-hearted. At least she hoped it was.

'Jealous that I haven't got black lungs?' retorted Anne. 'I don't think so.' She bent over her machine, putting the final touches to a seam on the duvet cover she was stitching. 'Anyway, it's nearly break time. You going to the canteen?'

During their morning break, over a cuppa, Anne usually brought Sandra up to date with the latest gossip. Swallowing a mouthful of millionaire shortbread, she wiped crumbs from the corner of her mouth with one finger before starting. 'Have you heard the news? About that girl in Wallsend that's gone missing. Hasn't been seen since yesterday afternoon.'

'Oh, yes, I heard. Terrible, isn't it? It was on the local news this morning,' Sandra answered. 'I hope she turns up soon. Can't think of anything worse for the parents.'

'She's only eleven, poor little bugger. We live near the park, and they've had a helicopter out all night. We could hear it and see the beam scanning backwards and forwards. And the park was crawling with police. And the streets too. Search parties all over the place.' Anne took another bite, catching the escaping crumbs in one hand. 'It's all over social media,' she continued, once she'd swallowed. 'You don't expect things like this to happen on your own doorstep, do you?'

'Oh, I hope she's just run away or something like that. Can't bear to think of anything nasty happening to a child.'

'Well, the police must think something's happened.' Anne put the last piece of shortbread into her mouth. 'Or there wouldn't be all this activity,' she mumbled.

The missing girl was the talk of the factory. Anne, who always had her mobile phone with her despite the rule that they were to be left in lockers, kept them up to date when new information was posted as the morning progressed. There were on-line appeals from the police, asking for anyone who was in or near the park, on the day of the attack to come forward. Even if they had seen nothing untoward, the police wanted to speak with them. They were also appealing for anyone who had taken photographs in and around the park the previous afternoon to come forward with their pictures.

Sandra was bent over her machine, concentrating hard on keeping a seam straight, when she became aware that Anne was talking to her.

'...and they've found one. I'll just have a look.'

'Found one what?' asked Sandra, looking up to see Anne peering at her mobile. 'Sorry, I was miles away.'

'A photograph. Someone's come forward with a photo of a man with a girl matching her description. In the park,' she said, excitedly. 'I'm just downloading it.' Head bent over her phone, she frowned in concentration, the tip of her tongue poking out between her teeth. 'Here it is' she exclaimed, examining the picture. 'Oh, you can't see his face. They've got their backs to the camera. But it's definitely her, from the description the police gave about her clothing and her pink backpack and everything.' Holding her phone aloft, she yelled 'Anyone want to see if they recognise him?'

The other machinists quickly gathered around Anne, expectantly. Unable to get near enough to see the phone, Sandra concentrated on finishing the piece of work she was busy with, listening to exclamations of shock and disgust from her workmates. Eventually, as the others drifted back to their machines, shaking their heads, and voicing strong opinions about what they would like to do the bloody pervert if only they could get their hands on him, Anne handed the phone to Sandra. There was just the one image, a rear view of a man holding the hand of a little girl. Her heart went out to the kid, and she felt a wave of revulsion at the thought of her being led away. At first glance, the photo of the man didn't evoke recognition in Sandra. Then she took a closer look. *No*, she thought. *No, it can't be. It can't possibly be.* Keeping her expression neutral, she handed the phone back to Anne, telling her 'Hmm... it's not very clear. Especially as it's just a view of his back. But I hope it helps them to find him.'

Unable to bear the tension, and needing to study the photo in detail, she decided to take a half-day. Trying to hide her concerns from Anne all afternoon did not appeal to her, so pleading a headache, she told the supervisor she needed to go home before it developed into a migraine. Part of her couldn't wait to take another look at the photograph, yet at the same time, she really didn't want her fears to be confirmed. As soon as the buzzer sounded for lunch break, she made her escape. She hurried to the bus stop, groaning when she saw that the bus was crowded. Managing to get the last free seat, next to an extremely overweight middle-aged man taking up one and a half seats, she wasn't able look at her phone with any degree of privacy. Although she was dying to take another look at the photo, she decided to wait until she was home. Alighting from the bus, she walked briskly along the two streets to her flat, stopping at the corner shop on the way to buy a copy of the Evening Chronicle displayed in the stand outside. Almost running up her street, she found her hand shaking as she inserted her key into the lock. Once inside the door, she ran up the stairs, dropped her handbag on the floor and laid the paper out on the kitchen table. The missing girl was front page news, but the paper must have gone to press before the photo had been released. Retrieving her phone from her pocket, she quickly located the photo, her tummy doing somersaults as she studied it closely. Although it was of his back, there was something familiar about the stance, the way he was holding himself... she wasn't sure... Without warning, she was overcome with nausea and had to rush to the bathroom.

For goodness' sake, she told herself, *pull yourself together girl.* She made a cup of coffee, lit a cigarette, cracked open the window and stood by it, blowing smoke through the gap. She tried to think what to do. She wished Marek was with her tonight, but unfortunately his job as a delivery driver meant he regularly had to be away overnight, and he wouldn't be back until late tomorrow. She wanted to talk this over with him, get his view on whether she was just being silly. After all, as far as she knew, Ian Cooper lived in the south. What would he be doing in this area? She didn't want to contact the police and waste their time on what after all was mainly just a feeling. Neither did she want to ring Marek and cause him any needless worry. After mulling it over, she picked up her mobile.

'Katie, I need to talk to you. Is this a good time to call round?' Sandra had found a kindred spirit in Katie, and they had become the best of friends since they'd first met in the Refuge. Katie displayed an empathy with Sandra, borne out of a shared experience of suffering and degradation at the hands of an abusive man. Katie understood Sandra and the understanding was mutual. Their friendship had begun at the Refuge but had grown in strength over the intervening years.

Walking the few streets to her friend's, Sandra went over in her mind the details in the on-line article. The police were asking for anyone who had any information or who thought they recognised the man in the photograph to come forward. Even if they were mistaken, it stated, it would at least allow the police to eliminate the person from the enquiry.

As soon as Katie opened the front door in response to her friend's impatient knocking, Sandra held up her phone, 'There's something I need to show you...'

'Well, come in first,' laughed Katie, opening the door wider before walking through to the kitchen. 'Kids, go and watch TV in the front room, please,' she said, shooing her two boys out of the kitchen. A few grumbles and protests ensued. They decided to comply only after extracting a promise they could have something from the sweet tin later.

'Thought they'd be at school,' said Sandra, nodding to their backs as they scampered from the room.

'Half-term. Keep up,' laughed Katie. 'Now, what brings you round here in the middle of a workday?'

Holding her mobile in one shaking hand, Sandra pointed at the image on the screen. 'You heard about that girl going missing in Wallsend? They're looking for this guy,' she indicated the photos, holding out the phone towards Katie.

'Yes, I saw that earlier. It's all over the news. Why...?' asked Katie, frowning as she looked at the photo, before handing the phone back.

'Katie, I think it's him,' Sandra interrupted, almost whispering. 'I think it's my ex...'

Katie snatched the phone back and took a closer look at the photo. 'Your ex?' she exclaimed. 'But you can't even see his face, Sandra. What makes you think it's him?'

'I know it sounds stupid when all I can see is the back of him, but there's just something about his stance, his build, the way he's holding his head...' Sandra s voice trailed off.

'But... well... you can't possibly be sure, from that? The stance? You haven't even seen him for years... But...' she said slowly, 'I suppose if you think it's a possibility, then you really should tell the police. After all, if you're wrong, there's no harm done. Have you rung them?'

'Not yet... I mean... I'm not certain it's him.... I don't want to waste their time.' Sandra was nervously wringing her hands, suddenly longing for a cigarette.

'If you've got any suspicion at all, you really should tell them, Sandra,' Katie decided. 'It's up to them to find out whether you're right. They won't consider it a waste of time. Look,' she said, pointing to the article, 'they give a number here to ring.'

'You're right, I know,' said Sandra. 'It's just... I'm scared... if he's interviewed, I don't want him to know it's me who pointed the police in his direction. I never want to have to see him again.' She was becoming agitated, tugging at her hair, a habit she'd developed when she was in rehab.

'I know you're still scared of him, Sandra. But you've got to do this.' Katie's voice was firm. 'If it is him, and he goes on to take another child, you'll never forgive yourself. And if it's not him, there's no harm done. And the police would never reveal your identity to him, especially not when you tell them your history.'

'I know... I know... I'll ring them now. Just as soon as I've had a fix,' she said, fishing a crumpled pack of cigarettes from her jacket pocket and heading for the back door.

'I'll join you,' said Katie, 'I could do with one myself right now. Then we'll call them.'

CHAPTER ELEVEN

Back at the Murder Investigation Room, Gayle brought them up to date on the visit to Mrs Townsend and showed them the photograph, which by then had been widely circulated. 'The search is still progressing in the park. More personnel are being drafted in and arrangements are in hand to search the water.

'Let's hope the photograph strikes a chord with someone. Expect an influx of calls on that. Pity they've got their backs to the camera, but it gives us something to work on. We now know that Eva was in the park, and she was with a man. I want all the CCTV coverage in the vicinity of the park re-examined, looking specifically for this man in the photograph. With or without Eva – you may have already seen him in some footage without realising the significance. Examine everyone on the tapes getting in and out of all vehicles. Did he leave a vehicle near the park? Did he abduct her and take her elsewhere? Or did he leave her in the park? We need to scour every street, lane, car park; literally anywhere he could have left a car. The sooner we find him, the sooner we find Eva.

'I'm grateful to you all for volunteering to stay. It's past nine o'clock now,' she said, glancing at her watch. 'And you all need a break... Wendy, could you organise a rota to let everyone have a few hours off to recharge their batteries? And that includes yourself.' There was a chorus of protests from the team, none of whom wanted to rest whilst Eva was still missing. 'I appreciate your dedication, but you need to rest. We don't want things missed because of tiredness. Most of you have been here all night. Take a few hours and come back refreshed. Ok? I've asked Doug to draft in a few more uniforms to help out.'

A few grudgingly agreed and one DC called out 'What about you, boss? When will you get a rest?'

'Don't you worry about me, DC Jensen, just take a break and do a good job when you get back. That's an order.'

The search continued, with not a sign of Eva. As the morning wore on, with each negative report from the teams, Gayle began to feel they were looking for a needle in a haystack. Dozens of calls were coming in from people claiming to recognise the man in the photograph. Each call was being meticulously followed up, but so far none was proving credible. Exhausted, Gayle wouldn't let herself take a break. She hadn't slept for over thirty-six hours and felt she was operating on autopilot, but she was so wired that sleep was out of the question.

'Come in,' she called on hearing a knock at her office door.

'Boss, I took a call from a woman who thinks she recognises the guy in the photograph. Thinks it could be an ex-partner,' said DC Doug Felton, coming into her office. 'She seems quite credible. I thought you might be interested in this one.'

'Oh?' Gayle was wearying of the false hope raised by the dozens of calls coming in from members of the public purporting to know who the assailant was. It was always this way in an investigation. Every call had to be followed up. You just never knew, and they couldn't afford to miss the right lead. 'Why? What's different about this one?'

'Well, she's lives in Walker, in one of those flats the Womens' Refuge provided...'

'You mean one of Carol's places?' interrupted Gayle.

'Yes. I knew that address was on the Refuge register, so I checked her out with the Refuge. Spoke to the manager, Linda. She says this woman, Sandra Howard, is a decent sort. Had a bad start in life and they took her in when she fled an abusive relationship. Said she's no fantasist, and to tell you we should definitely take her concerns seriously. She thought you should speak to the woman yourself.'

'Hmm, did she now? Ok... Walker's only a ten-minute drive. Tell you what,' she said rising and pushing her chair back, 'you and me will go to see her now.' She usually let the team handle these calls, but as she respected Linda's judgement, she decided to make an exception in this case. Also, she thought to herself, *I could do with a break from the office.*

'I got to know Linda on a case I was involved in a few years ago, when I was just a DC,' said Gayle to Doug on the drive over, by way of explanation. 'Quite a harrowing case, involving a stalker. The victim was a young widow, Carol Barrington. She'd been seriously assaulted in Barbados, and I was Family Liaison Officer on her return to the UK. Linda was with Victim Support at the time, assigned to support Carol. After it was all over, and Carol had recovered from her ordeal, well as much as anyone could recover after such a horrendous experience, she went on to set up the Women's Refuge in Newcastle. She recruited Linda to manage it. Now she's got a network of them right across the country. The three of us were closely involved at the time and we went on to become good friends. So, if Linda thinks this Sandra is sound, there may be something in it. I'll give her a call.'

'Hello Gayle.' Linda's chirpy Scottish tones filled the car. 'I was expecting you to call. I can certainly vouch for Sandra Howard's credibility. Like everyone who comes here, she has a lot of history, but she's sound as a pound. Used to live near Ealing. We moved her north, as far away from her abuser as possible and arranged rehabilitation. She's twenty-eight, clean now for at least three years. She's in steady employment and lives quietly with a new partner. If she thinks she recognises your perp, I would take her seriously. Your DC said he thought it could be her former partner? Tread carefully. She will be terrified at any thought of having to come face to face with her ex. She had a torrid time with him.'

'Thanks Linda, we'll bear that in mind. Appreciate your input. We're on our way over to speak to her now,' said Gayle. 'By the way, we must have another girls' night soon. Will you check on Carol's availability and we'll set something up? I fancy that new place on the quayside... I forget its name just now, but it'll come to me. Let me know some dates so we can get booked up. Be good to have a catch up.'

'Will do. It's been too long since the three amigos got together,' quipped Linda. 'Good luck with Sandra. Let's hope she's able to help you. Speak soon.'

'This is the place,' said Doug, turning into a street of old terraced houses where the front doors opened directly on to the pavement. 'It's not a bad little street. Nowhere near as rough as some of them round here.' Slowing down, he squinted as he searched for the right number. 'She lives in a first-floor flat, number thirty-nine.'

Number thirty-nine was located near the end of the street. Its freshly painted bright red door, made it stand out from the neighbouring properties, most of which were quite drab. The woman who answered their knock was wearing a brown paisley-patterned tunic with black jeans and pink furry slippers. Gayle thought her thin, careworn face made her look much older than her twenty-eight years. Deep frown lines and noticeable creases around her mouth put years on her.

'You must be the police?' she said as soon as she saw them. 'Come on up. I hope I'm not wasting your time.' They followed her up the narrow stairs, to a small square landing before turning right into a surprisingly large room with a high, corniced ceiling. Light flooded in through the large sash windows, showing a neat and tidy living room with dark wooden furniture polished to a high sheen and a large sofa upholstered in bright floral chintz. Through the windows, Gayle glimpsed the back yards and fire escapes of the properties opposite.

Gayle introduced herself and Doug. 'Thanks for contacting us, Sandra,' she said. 'I understand you told DC Felton you think you recognise the man in the photograph we published. I have a copy here.' She held out a print of the photograph.

'Yes...' Sandra took the photo with shaking hands. 'Well, I'm not a hundred percent sure,' she said biting her lip while she studied it. 'Obviously I can't see his face, but there's something about the way he's walking. His stance. If that makes sense?'

'His stance?' repeated Gayle. 'So, who do you think it could be? DC Felton said something about a former partner?' This woman didn't seem very certain at all and Gayle's spirits sank. Sandra looked anxious, her hands shaking as she studied the image.

'I... I need to know that he won't know I told you... and that I won't have to see him or anything...' Sandra stammered taking a deep breath. 'I think it could be my ex... But you mustn't let him know that I've pointed you in his direction. I never want to see him again. I... I ran away from him... and ...'

Her voice trailed off and Gayle, understanding how scared she was and noting the panic in her eyes, quickly sought to reassure her. 'Don't worry about that, Sandra, I understand. We never reveal our sources. I promise you won't be identified or implicated.'

Sandra seemed to relax then and explained it had been nearly four years since she had last seen Ian Cooper. She gave them the address of where he used to live. 'Course, he could have moved on since then,' she said. 'I don't know what he would be doing in this area...' Looking crestfallen, she added, 'Oh dear, I hope I'm not wasting your time...' her voice trailed off.

So do I thought Gayle. 'Doug here will take down the details and we'll check him out. Don't worry about wasting our time. You've done the right thing in coming to us. If it turns out not to be him, that's ok. Your intentions are good. Thank you for your time.'

On the short journey back to the station, Doug was apologetic. 'Sorry if it's been a waste of your time, boss. I should probably have dealt with this myself after all. She doesn't seem very sure, does she?'

'No, but no worries. Check him out and let me know what you find,' said Gayle. She felt weary but knew there would be no let up until Eva was found.

CHAPTER TWELVE

Talking through progress with her team, Gayle went through all the steps being taken. 'Eva has now been missing for nearly twenty-four hours. Let's look at what we've got. We know from the photo taken by Mrs Townsend that Eva was in Richardson-Dees Park at four thirty yesterday afternoon, holding hands with a man, apparently being led along by him. The response from the public following publication of the photo supplied by Mrs Townsend is very good and keeping you all busy. All the information you are gathering is being followed up, but so far nothing concrete. We've put out another appeal for the public to check on their phones for any other photos taken in and around the park. Let's hope someone comes forward with a better image.' Gayle wiped her hand over her face.

'The team searching the park haven't found anything yet. They started checking the lake early this morning but have drawn a blank so far.'

'That's a blessing,' commented one of the DCs. 'We don't want her to be in there.'

'That's true, Jill. But where is she? What has he done with her? Did he take her out of the park? Was she taken to his car and whisked off somewhere? Or is she still somewhere in there? That's looking less and less likely as the search goes on. They're going over every square inch of it again.'

Perching on the front of a desk, legs outstretched, she continued. 'If he took her out of the park, there must be some CCTV coverage somewhere. We've located a lot of cameras, and there's a team double-checking every building in the vicinity of the park, and a half-mile radius around it, to see if any more exist. I know some of you are painstakingly combing through what tapes we've got already. We need to find a man matching the one in the photo, with or without a little girl. If we get more tapes, I want more manpower allocated to checking. He didn't just disappear into thin air.' She took a breath.

'We've increased the numbers out searching throughout the town, and they're going over areas already covered in case anything has been missed and knocking on doors to re-interview the occupants.' She stood up. 'Keep up the good work. I'll be in my office if anyone needs to see me.'

Feeling exhausted and a bit dizzy, she got herself an extra strong coffee and took it to her desk. Despite the caffeine shot, she could barely keep her eyes open and eventually gave in, putting her head down on her arms, telling herself it was just for a few minutes.

When the shrill ring of the phone sounded in her ear, she jerked awake, knocking over her mug and its remaining contents. 'Shit,' she exclaimed as the by now cold coffee ran off the desk, spilling on to her skirt. Jumping up and wiping her skirt with one hand, she cursed loudly again before picking up the receiver, 'Yes?' she barked.

'It's me boss.' Dave's voice was quivering with suppressed emotion and excitement. 'We've found her.'

'Alive?' asked Gayle, holding her breath.

'Yes, she's alive,' Dave confirmed and Gayle sank to her chair, sighing with relief. 'She's hurt, not sure how badly. We found her at the west end of the park, towards the Arboretum. Bound and gagged. Shoved out of sight in the undergrowth. Poor little bugger. The dogs picked up her scent. I've got the area cordoned off and SOCO are on their way. She's being taken to Cramlington hospital as we speak. I assume you'll be going there. Do you want me to pick you up?'

'Yes, do that right away,' said Gayle, relief still flooding through her. 'You can fill me in on the way to the hospital. I'll inform the parents.'

'The father knows already. He was in the vicinity when she was found. He's on his way to the hospital now. He's in a bit of a state, ready to string somebody up with his bare hands.'

'Get a couple of uniforms to stay with him. He's a volatile sort, we don't want him causing any problems,' said Gayle. 'I'll get Georgia to take the mother there. Oh, and I'll make sure Social Services are informed. Good work, Dave.'

'I'll be there in five, boss.'

On her way into the MIR to update her team, Gayle quickly rang Georgia. 'We've found Eva, in the park. She's alive. Dave's team found her bound and gagged, hidden in undergrowth. She's injured and on her way to hospital. That's as much as I know at the moment. Take Rachel straight down to Cramlington Hospital. I'll meet you there. Tommy knows already and he's on his way.'

'Oh, what a relief, boss. Thank God,' said Georgia. 'I'll tell Rachel and we'll set off straight away.'

'Listen up, everyone. Good news...' announced Gayle as she entered the room. She looked round at the sea of expectant faces. 'Eva has been found, alive.' There was a stunned silence for a second before the room erupted with whoops, cheering, and clapping. Gayle held up her hand for silence. 'She was in the park. She's been assaulted and is injured. We don't know how badly, as yet. I'm on my way to the hospital now.'

As a flurry of questions ensued, Gayle again held up her hand. 'There'll be a briefing here as soon as I return from the hospital. I should have more information by then.'

'Oh, thank God she's alive. Thank God. I just can't bear it when it's children.' It was Wendy, the Office Manager who spoke, tears in her eyes. A warm, motherly type, when she wasn't running the office with a rod of iron, she tended to wear her heart on her sleeve and felt a strong empathy for all victims, but especially children.

Gayle looked at her, 'Wendy, can you advise social services. They'll need to go to the hospital.'

'I hope we find the bastard quickly.' This from a scowling DC sitting behind one of the desks.

'Well, that's down to us, Colin, isn't it?' said Gayle raising her eyebrows as she looked at him. 'I'm off to the hospital now. There'll be a briefing when I get back,' Gayle repeated. 'Keep searching through the CCTV footage of the area surrounding Woodbine Avenue and the park. Look for anything that looks remotely suspicious. DS Fairbairn's team is still doing house to house, double-checking if anybody saw anything suspicious. Let's find him.'

On the twenty-minute drive, Dave described what had happened. 'The guys in the air actually pinpointed the heat spot at about four o'clock this morning,' he confessed. 'When the lads searched that area, apparently a fox emerged from the undergrowth, and they assumed that was the reason for the heat spot and moved on.'

'They missed her?' Gayle was incredulous.

'To be fair, we were finding wildlife all over the place in the dark. Unfortunately, the crew who did the initial search at that location didn't have any of the dogs with them. Sod's law.' Grimacing, Dave ran his hand over his head, sighing.

'At daylight, the Underwater Search Unit arrived and, once I'd got them underway, I ordered the search team to go over the whole park once again, and that's when we eventually found her. The guys who missed her are devastated. I take full responsibility, and I'm not making excuses, but she was extremely well hidden, in dense undergrowth. I was with the lads when the dogs found her, and I had to crawl on my belly to get to her. Without the dogs, we'd never have found her.' He took a deep breath. 'Oh man, the terror in her eyes. I never want to see that again. She was gagged, with a sock and her mouth taped over. She'd clearly taken a beating. Seemed to be in a lot of pain,' he said, shaking his head. 'The paramedics had to administer pain killers before they could move her. Her clothing was disturbed... looks like sexual assault, I'm afraid.'

'Fuck.' Dismayed but not surprised, Gayle realised she had been hoping Eva had been spared that.

'She was conscious,' Dave continued. 'In shock. Shivering. I peeled the tape off her face and got the gag out. Tried to reassure her. She didn't say a word. Not a word. Just made little mewling noises.' He sounded emotional. 'The ambulance crew were on the scene very quickly.'

. 'So, she wasn't able to tell you anything?' asked Gayle.

'No. Poor little bugger was traumatised.' He was silent for a moment before spluttering 'I hate these fucking child molestation cases. Bastard pervert...'

'Stay detached, Dave. We need to concentrate on catching him. Cool heads needed.' Truth be told, Gayle was having to work hard not to let her own emotions get the better of her. They sat in silence for a little while, each lost in their own thoughts.

Dave parked in the drop-off bays fronting Northumbria Specialist Emergency Care Hospital. As she got out of the car, Gayle spotted Georgia beneath the tent-like awnings at the curved glass entrance. She was making her way into the building, holding the arm of a visibly distraught Mrs Simpson. Hearing their footsteps, Rachel turned and caught sight of Gayle. Shrugging off Georgia's arm, she rushed towards Gayle, clutching at her sleeve, and shouting hysterically.

'Who would do this to her? She's only eleven. What kind of monster attacks an eleven-year-old kid?'

'We'll find him, Rachel,' said Gayle in a firm voice, patting her hand and guiding her back to Georgia. 'I promise you; we'll find him.'

CHAPTER THIRTEEN

'This korma's good,' observed Sandra, tucking hungrily into her curry and rice. She'd slept in that morning and skipped breakfast, so was feeling particularly ravenous. The canteen food used to be dire, but they'd recently got a new head guy in, and things had improved dramatically. 'I'm going to have to watch my weight.'

Sitting opposite her at the small Formica-topped table, Anne, engrossed in her phone, was clearly not listening to her. Sandra shrugged and took another forkful, thinking to herself *Oh really Sandra? So glad you're enjoying it.*

Suddenly, Anne jumped excitedly to her feet, waving her phone in the air. 'Girls,' she shouted. 'Listen up. The girl that went missing, they've found her.'

'Thank God,' said Sandra, surprised by the feeling of relief that washed over her. Her voice was drowned out by the chorus of responses, everyone asking questions at the same time.

'It's on AOL... Apparently she was found in Richardson-Dees Park,' said Anne, reading through the article on her screen. 'A police search team found her late this morning...' She looked up, 'So that means the poor little bugger must have been there all night.'

'Is there any more detail?' one of the girls asked. 'Is she ok? I hope she hasn't been hurt.'

'It says she was assaulted and left in some bushes... It must have been that bloke, the one in the photo,' speculated Anne. 'Bet she's had a hell of an ordeal.' Murmurings abounded of what the girls would like to do with the dirty bastard if they could get their hands on him.

On the bus home, trundling through the Battle Hill estate, all Sandra could think of was the little girl. She hadn't heard anything further from the police, and she fervently hoped and prayed that meant that Ian Cooper had been ruled out, but she still had an uneasy feeling in her gut. She was impatient to see Marek and talk it all through with him now that he was back from his latest trip. As she gazed out of the window at the bright, sunny evening, it seemed impossible to believe that such evil could take place, right in the heart of the community. Her thoughts inevitably turned to her own daughter, who would be about the same age as the girl who'd been attacked. The familiar waves of self-loathing and guilt washed over her. How could she have neglected her? How could she have been so selfish? Same old questions, same old lack of answers.

Marek was already in the flat when she let herself in. She was pleased to have him home for a couple of days before he had to go back to work. The unmistakable aroma of fried garlic and onions greeted her as she hurried up the stairs.

'Spag bol,' he announced. 'Hope you're hungry? It's nearly ready.'

She gave him a peck on the cheek as he leaned over the sink, transferring spaghetti into a colander. 'Smells great sweetheart. I'll just get changed.'

'No, you won't' he teased, 'not until you've given me a proper kiss and cuddle.'

Once seated at the table, she showed him the photo on her phone and told him about talking to the police about her suspicions.

'What? You think this man is your ex?' He snatched the phone, peering at the image on the screen. 'You should have rung me. Why you not call me?'

'It's not something I could have explained properly over the phone sweetheart... besides I'm not certain... I mean, it's just his stance, the way he's walking... I didn't want to bother you when you were at work.

You couldn't have just dropped everything and come home. I talked it over with Katie and she said if I had even the slightest suspicion it could be him, I should tell the police. So, we rang them. They promised to keep my name out of it. They won't mention me. They said they'll just check him out.'

'Well... but I don't know how you can be sure it's him from that picture,' he said, taking another look before putting the phone down on the table. 'You can't even see his face.'

'I know... I'm not at all sure, really... I'm probably wrong. Anyway, I haven't heard anything further, so they've most likely ruled him out.' Sandra picked up her fork. 'It's just, I can't help thinking... the girl, she's the same age my Chloe will be now. It... just brings everything back...'

'I knew that's what you were thinking about, sweetheart. Come on, don't start beating yourself up again.' He leaned over and squeezed her hand. 'Besides, your considerate partner has been slaving over a hot stove all afternoon. I produce this banquet for you, so eat up my lovely or I'll be the one that's upset.'

Sandra attempted a smile and began to pick at her food. She knew she was lucky to have found Marek. Even knowing all about her past, he never judged her or criticised her, and he understood her sadness and regret at things that couldn't be changed.

'You know, since I saw that photo, I've been thinking... it's all I can think about actually... If it is him, then that makes him a paedophile. A bloody paedophile, Marek. I never saw any sign of that, when I was with him, but it makes me wonder... did I miss anything?' she gulped. 'Could Chloe have been at risk? I feel sick at the thought of him doing anything to her. Do you think he could have been doing something to her? Please God, no... please...' She dropped her fork and put her head into her hands, shaking it from side to side. 'I'll never know...' she choked. 'She was under three years old when they took her...' Her voice sounded strangled.

'Sandra, stop it...' began Marek. 'You don't even know it was him.' His voice went unheard, as her anguish escalated.

'Oh God, this makes everything worse.' She raised her head and looked at him, her eyes wild. 'The poor little bugger had such a shit start in life... but if she was being abused as well... Oh God, what sort of a person does that make me? Not only neglecting my own daughter but not even noticing if she was being abused. Because I was drunk. And stoned. How bloody selfish could I be?'

The self-loathing, always just under the surface, was palpable. The thought of the possibility of Chloe being sexually abused made her feel physically sick and added to the guilt she felt at the neglect she'd heaped upon her helpless little girl. From her current sober and clean state, she could barely believe how low she had sunk. What a terrible, evil mother she had been. She would give anything to go back in time and put things right. If only she could... As it was, she knew she had to live with the guilt and regrets for the rest of her life. She didn't deserve to be happy. She didn't deserve anything.

'Sandra,' Marek raised his voice. 'You are too dramatic. You must bloody stop this. This pervert is probably not Cooper. You imagine too much.' He grabbed her hands and squeezed them tightly to emphasise his point. 'Chloe was only a baby when she was taken away. The girl he attacked, even if it was him, which it probably wasn't, was eleven. There is big difference. It doesn't mean he would abuse a baby, so you've got to stop thinking like that or you will drive yourself mad.' He clasped her hands tighter, shaking her.

'And another thing. You were just a kid yourself. He made a junkie out of you. He's the bad person in all this. Not you.' He let go of her hands. 'Now, come on, you have to stop this. Eat up.'

'I know. You're right. Sorry... I am overreacting. I'm probably mistaken. It's probably not him at all.' Sandra smiled sadly at him, shaking her head. 'I don't deserve you. Any other man would have run a mile, hearing about my past.'

'Don't be silly, sweetheart. Now, stop letting your imagination run away with you. Ok?' And eat your spaghetti.'

'I'll try,' said Sandra sighing heavily as she picked up her fork.

CHAPTER FOURTEEN

At five o'clock, Gayle addressed the team in the Incident room. The mood was clearly much lighter now that Eva was safe. Finding the perpetrator was their only goal and every person in the room was focused on doing their bit.

'As you know, DI Chapman's team found Eva Simpson earlier this afternoon. Alive but hurt. We've just come back from Cramlington hospital where she's being assessed by the medical team. Naturally, we haven't been able to speak with her yet, but depending upon Eva's condition, we may be able to interview her tomorrow.' Pacing back and forth as she spoke, as usual playing with the locket at her neck, Gayle continued. 'Her parents, Rachel, and Tommy are staying at the hospital with her. Georgia and another officer are there to support them and to keep an eye on Tommy. DI Chapman was concerned about Tommy's volatility, but far from causing any trouble, all the fight seems to have gone out of him. At least for now. Let's hope it stays that way.' She turned to DI Chapman, 'Dave, will you brief the team on how and where she was found?'

As Dave got slowly to his feet, rubbing the back of his neck, Gayle noticed he looked even more exhausted than she was feeling. Lack of sleep, combined with the stress of searching for the child all night, and missing her first time, had drained the colour from his face and deepened the shadows under his eyes.

'Just after noon today, some of the team searching in Richardson-Dees Park found Eva Simpson... here,' he said, turning and pointing to a spot on the map of the park. 'More or less in the middle, not far from the lake and quite near the Arboretum She was well hidden beneath dense shrubbery at the top of a steep wooded rise. Tied up and gagged... with one of her own socks. We found her after the helicopter reported a heat spot and the dogs dug into the undergrowth to pinpoint her exact location. She was conscious, in some pain and unable to speak.' Gayle noticed his brief summary did not include any mention of Eva being missed first time round. 'Her clothing was ripped, and her body exposed. It looks very much as though she's been sexually assaulted.' Several groans could be heard from the squad. Dave promptly resumed his seat, his face grey.

Gayle took over again. 'Thanks Dave, excellent work.' She turned back to the assembled team. 'Until we get some feedback from the medical team, we don't know how badly hurt Eva is, nor how serious the sexual assault was.' She looked at the sea of faces before adding, 'We'll have to wait and see, but there's no doubting she's had one hell of an ordeal.'

Noting exhaustion on the faces of some of the team, those who hadn't yet taken a break, she glanced at her watch. 'Right, everyone, it's five thirty pm now. It's been a long haul for most of you. Thanks for your support – you've all been amazing. Those of you who haven't had a break, go home, and get a few hours rest.' There were a few protests from some of the squad. Gayle put her hand up, 'I know, I know, we urgently need to find the person who did this, but you won't be any good to anyone if you don't get some rest. Come back refreshed and raring to go. We'll find this perp. If he can do this to one eleven-year-old child, he can do it to others. We will stop him.'

Back in her office, Dave joined her. 'You need to go home, too,' she told him. 'I can see you're all in.'

'You don't look so chipper yourself, boss,' he laughed. 'Have you looked in the mirror recently?'

‘Cheeky bugger,’ she said. ‘Actually, I’m planning to get a few hours myself. I’m going to go home, grab a coffee have a bite to eat, then a quick shower. In that order. Then I’m going to get some shut eye.’

CHAPTER FIFTEEN

Exhausted, Gayle finally got back to her flat at about seven. Kicking off her shoes, she popped an Americano Intenso pod into the machine, deciding she couldn't face food after all, and waited impatiently for the coffee to finish trickling through. She carried it to the coffee table, sank gratefully on to the settee and put her feet up. *Just for a minute* she thought. An hour later she was jolted awake by the sound of her phone, and the feel of it vibrating against her thigh. Fumbling to get it out of her pocket, she eventually succeeded, peering at the screen through bleary eyes. It was the station.

'DCI Gayle Jones,' she responded, swinging her legs to the floor, and trying hard not to sound too groggy.

'Boss, A new development.' Doug's voice penetrated the fog. 'A woman rang to say she has a photograph she took in the park at the relevant time. I got her to send it to me. It's definitely of a man holding Eva's hand, only this time he's facing the camera. We've got a clear head shot.'

Gayle felt her pulse quicken. 'We need to get that in front of Sandra Howard pronto,' she said to Doug. 'Check that she's at home, then we'll go up together. At the very least, it will definitely rule out her ex, but if it's him... Can you pick me up and we'll go and see her together. She's only five minutes from here.'

'No problem boss. I'll be there in fifteen.'

Gayle dashed to the bathroom and after a quick wee, splashed her face with cold water and ran a comb through her hair. *God, what a mess* she thought, examining her reflection in the mirror, noting the dark circles under her own eyes. Fuelled by adrenalin, she impatiently waited for the confirmation that Sandra was home. Could this be the breakthrough they needed? Her phone buzzed. "She's home" the text read and for the next ten minutes she paced the floor, thinking through the possibilities. If Sandra ruled out Ian Cooper, they would immediately circulate the new photo. Someone would recognise him.

After leaving the flat, she hurried to meet Doug as soon as she saw his car turn onto the quayside. Once inside, Doug handed her a photocopied picture. It showed a good-looking man, probably early forties, shoulder-length dark brown hair. He didn't look evil. *They rarely do* she thought. He was walking alongside Eva, whose eyes and nose looked red, as if she'd recently been crying. *Bet you thought you were so clever, preying on a young girl's misery, you nasty piece of shit,* she thought. If she had her way, all paedophiles would be castrated, if not hung, drawn, and quartered. There was an air of excitement in the car. They both knew that if Sandra confirmed the photo to be that of Ian Cooper, they had their man. Hard evidence would still be needed of course, but if Sandra confirmed it was him, she had no doubt it would be there for the finding.

Doug put his foot down as they sped towards Walker. 'I'm not building my hopes up,' he said. 'She didn't seem all that sure when she looked at the other photo, did she? And when we checked out the guy, he had a strong alibi, so we didn't take it any further.'

'Yes... his wife provided the alibi, didn't she?' said Gayle, recalling Doug's report following his visit to Ian Cooper's house.

'Yeah, that's right. The wife told us he had a day off and they'd spent it together, chilling out in the back garden. If this does turn out to be him, she'll have some explaining to do.'

'Well, we'll soon find out if it's him. And if it's not, we'll immediately circulate the new photograph. We're nearly there,' said Gayle pointing ahead as they neared the turn off for Sandra's street. 'What did you tell Sandra when you rang?'

'Just that we had a clearer photograph and wanted her to take a look. She sounded apprehensive, seemed a bit flustered. Said she hoped it wasn't him. She's very worried about any possibility of having to see him again. Very much in fear of him,' said Doug, swinging into the street, drawing up in front of the red door.

'Well, that was evident when we last spoke to her. It's the same with the majority of abused women. It's sinister how these men continue to instil fear and exert emotional control, long after the woman has escaped their clutches.' Gayle had her seatbelt undone before they'd come to a halt. 'Right, let's find out what she has to say...'

Sandra's face looked flushed as she greeted them at the door. After a muttered greeting she hurried ahead of them up the stairs with an air of urgency. Once in the sitting room, Gayle explained that another photo had come to their attention that they'd like her to take a look at.

'Yes, yes, I know. Doug told me,' said Sandra, wringing her hands, watching as Doug removed a print of the photograph from a folder and held it out to her. Taking it with shaking hands, Sandra seemed to steel herself with a deep breath before looking at it. She gasped audibly. 'Oh my God, it *is* him... It's him.' The colour drained from her face, as she slumped into a chair, still gripping the photograph in both hands. She continued to stare at the image, clearly having difficulty accepting what the photograph was telling her. 'Oh my God... oh my God... he's done this... Oh the poor little girl...' She closed her eyes, tilting her head back against the chair before taking another look. 'The wicked bastard... I can't believe it...but this is definitely him...' her voice trailed off. She looked from one to the other. 'I thought I was mistaken... That it wasn't him in the other photo... I hoped... but it is.' Her face crumpled.

'You're absolutely sure, Sandra? No doubts at all?' asked Gayle. Bit of a rhetorical question she thought to herself, given Sandra's reaction, but one that had to be asked.

'No. None at all. I wish I had,' she said. 'It's him. Oh my God, I feel sick to think I once lived with him...' She momentarily closed her eyes again, wincing.

'Ok, thank you Sandra. Now, what can you tell us about him? We need everything you know. We are aware that you escaped from him and went to a Refuge.' When Sandra looked surprised, Gayle explained, 'We work closely with the Refuge, Sandra, especially with Linda and with the founder, Carol Barrington. We only know that you left an abusive relationship. Can you tell us a bit more about what he was like and what happened between you?'

Sandra nodded. 'Oh God, where do I begin...?' she sighed, absentmindedly tugging at a strand of hair at the nape of her neck. 'I was fifteen when I first met him. Only sixteen when I moved in with him. My dad was furious... but I was determined. I was young and daft, as you are at that age...' she said. 'He was five years older. Very controlling. He got me into drugs... Used to beat me up...' She hung her head. 'He even pimped me to his so-called friends for extra money...' She went on to tell them about the drugs, his temper, the violence and how she eventually made her escape.

'Did you ever have any reason to suspect him of being a paedophile?' asked Gayle.

'Never...' Sandra whispered, shaking her head, putting a hand over her mouth. 'He was a nasty piece of work... perverted, but not with kids. Nothing like that... we had a little girl... he wasn't very nice to her, shouted at her a lot and stuff like that, but... my God, you don't think he could have...?'

'I wasn't aware that you have a daughter. Does she live with you?' asked Gayle, surprised, automatically looking round the room for evidence that a child lived there. There'd been no mention of a daughter in the conversation she'd had earlier with Linda.

'No... Social Services took her... she was adopted. I haven't seen her since she was three...' Sandra welled up as she looked at Gayle, seeming to gauge the effect of her words. 'You have to understand... I was scared of him... I was living under the threat of violence all the time. It hardly took anything to start him off, sometimes nothing at all. He put me in hospital a few times... It took me a long time to find the courage to get away from him. I should have left years earlier, taken Chloe... but... I couldn't... I wasn't strong enough...and I needed the drugs...' Taking a deep, shuddering breath, she wiped tears away with her fingers. 'God, this is bringing it all back.' She looked stricken, the lines in her face appearing to be etched even deeper. 'I'm so ashamed...'

'I appreciate it must be hard for you to tell us all this, Sandra. But we are not here to judge you, and I'm sorry to hear that you lost your daughter,' said Gayle. 'You've been very helpful. We know where he lives now. He was questioned after you first brought him to our attention, although he provided an alibi for the day in question. We'll be looking into that. Anyway, he'll be arrested and brought in for further questioning. Don't worry, we'll keep your name out of it. You won't be implicated. And as to your concerns about whether he could have sexually assaulted your daughter, you say she was three when social services took her?' Sandra nodded. 'Under the circumstances, the violence, the drugs, the child will have been thoroughly examined by the authorities at the time. If any evidence of sexual abuse had been found, I'm sure it would have been investigated there and then, and you would both have been questioned about it. So, if you weren't, I really don't think you need to worry about that possibility. Alright?'

'Thank you,' whispered Sandra. 'That helps put my mind at ease. I couldn't bear to think...' Her voice trailed away.

'We'll be in touch. Thank you so much for your help. And try not to worry.' They left Sandra fumbling to light up, her hands trembling so badly she could barely flick the lighter.

CHAPTER SIXTEEN

'Did you have much trouble finding Ian Cooper after our first interview with Sandra?' asked Gayle. They were on their way back to the station following Sandra's confirmation that the man in the park with Eva was Ian Cooper.

'Nah, piece of cake,' said Doug. 'He hasn't tried to hide. Just moved up to Chester le Street to live with his girlfriend. DCI Chapman went to see him. He mentioned a ten-year-old daughter living with them,' he added meaningfully.

'Oh shit! There's a ten-year-old girl living in the same house as him?'

'Fraid so,' confirmed Doug, nodding his head. 'We'll need to check her out.'

'Let's make absolutely sure he's the perp first, before we cross that bridge,' said Gayle. 'I'll bring everyone up to date once we're back at the station.'

'Right, listen up everyone, we've got a positive ID on the man in the photograph. One Ian Cooper. Identified by his former partner, Sandra Howard, who I believe to be a credible person. She identified him even from the first photo where his face wasn't visible, and then confirmed it when she saw the second. We need to keep her name out of it. She was a victim of abuse and escaped with the help of the refuge, Sanctuary.' She gestured to Dave. 'DI Chapman paid him a visit following Sandra's first ID. He was eliminated from the enquiry because he had a strong alibi. Supplied by his partner,' she added, pulling a face. 'Dave, what do we know about him?'

'Ian Cooper. He's thirty-four. No previous. The Met had him on their radar around two thousand and seven, as a dealer, but no charges were ever brought. He moved north to Chester le Street three and a half years ago to move in with Maria Clements, a nurse at the James Cook Hospital in Middlesbrough. She has a ten-year-old daughter living with her, from a previous relationship. Cooper is currently working as a sales rep for an electronics company based in Leicester, J C Woodward's. His address is,' he glanced at his notes, 'Weldon Terrace, Chester le Street. He works away from home on a regular basis, but he's at home this week. On holiday, according to his boss.'

Gayle took over. 'Now we need to find corroborating evidence. Take a good look at Cooper's mug and find him on CCTV. He must be there somewhere. He had to enter and exit the park. Find him. I want to hold off picking him up until we have more evidence.'

Her phone rang, 'DCI Jones'. She listened for a while, before saying 'Thank you, I'll be right there.' She looked at the assembled faces as she ended the call. 'We've got permission to speak to Eva. She wants to tell us what happened.' She got to her feet. 'While we're at the hospital, keep searching. Redouble your efforts. Find me some evidence before we get back. Let's get this bastard good and nailed.' Picking her jacket up, she called for Dave.

'I gather the doctors are not too happy about it,' she told him once they were en route, 'but Eva's insisting, and Rachel is backing her up. I'm surprised she's well enough to talk so soon, but hey, let's see what she has to say.'

'You've got five minutes, DCI Jones. If it was up to me, she wouldn't be speaking to you at all just yet, but she wants to tell you what happened. She's agitated and needs to get it off her chest. She's a brave kid.' The grim-faced doctor had just given her a brief update on Eva's condition and emphasised Eva's need to talk. 'I don't think she will settle until she's talked about what she's gone through. I'm hoping she'll be less agitated once she's seen you. That's the only reason I'm allowing you to see her today.'

'I understand, Dr Mason,' said Gayle. 'We won't keep her long, I promise.'

'Five minutes,' he repeated. 'She's in here.' He gestured towards nearby door. 'Be gentle with her.' As he walked away, he turned back. 'Five minutes. Max.'

Gayle knocked lightly before grasping the handle and pushing against the door. She tentatively put her head around it before entering. Rachel, sitting at the far side of the bed, looked up as Gayle came into the room and acknowledged her with a slight nod before returning her gaze to Eva, whose hand she was holding.

Behind Rachel, through the half-open vertical blinds, Gayle could see a small courtyard, with rustic benches and potted plants. Somewhere for the patients to relax and recuperate, weather permitting, she supposed. Her heart skipped a beat as she turned to look at Eva. She looked so tiny and fragile, propped up against snow-white pillows, a pale blue coverlet pulled up to her neck. Her eyes looked sunken, giving them a haunted look and dark shadows and bruises stood out sharply against her pale skin. Gayle's heart went out to her.

'Hello, Eva,' she said in a gentle voice. 'I'm Gayle,' she began tentatively. 'I'm a police officer and the doctor has told me you want to tell us what's happened to you? Are you sure that you feel up to talking to us now?'

'She says she wants to talk to you.' Rachel answered for her, putting a protective hand over Eva's. 'She wants you to find the man that did this to her.'

'Well, I think that's very brave of you, Eva,' said Gayle, pulling up a chair near the bed, opposite Rachel. 'If you're sure you're well enough?' She looked anxiously at Eva, who gave a slight nod. 'Ok then. I won't keep you long. Do you want to start by telling me what happened after you left Sophie's house?'

Eva gave another small nod and began to speak, her voice thin and wavering. 'I started to walk home... past the park. I was going to go straight home,' she turned with pleading eyes to her mother. 'Honest, mum, I was...'

Rachel squeezed Eva's hand, stroking it reassuringly, 'I know you were, darling. It's alright,' she told her daughter. 'Just tell the police lady what happened.'

Taking a tremulous breath, Eva turned back to Gayle. 'Two of the older girls from school stopped me outside the gates. They told me to go with them into the park. I didn't want to... but they said they wanted to make friends with me 'cos they thought I was cool. They said I should hang out with them for a bit... I didn't want them to think I wasn't allowed... wasn't cool... So, I went.'

'Were these girls friends of yours, Eva?' asked, Gayle.

'No, they're in the year above me. Everyone knows who they are. They're the popular girls. I was surprised they'd bother with someone like me.' She bit her lip. 'They tried to get me to smoke cannabis,' she said, 'up a hill, behind some bushes. But I don't smoke... so I couldn't... They made me try, and it made me cough and I felt sick. They laughed... said I was useless and pathetic 'cos I couldn't get high. They called me a baby.' She hung her head. 'After that we went back down to the path... kept walking towards the far exit. I wanted to go home, but they held on to my arms. When I started to cry, one of them pushed me away and told me to run back home to my mum and dad... she said I was too much of a baby to hang out with them. They were both laughing. Then they just turned and walked off and left me.'

'That wasn't very nice of them, Eva,' said Gayle, shaking her head. 'What happened after they left you?'

'I started to walk back the way we'd come... I was late and knew I'd be in trouble if I didn't get home soon. I was still crying, and this man started to walk beside me. He asked if I was alright... He said he'd seen me being bullied and told me not to take any notice of nasty girls like that. He said if he found anyone bullying his little girl, he would sort them out. He said I was a lovely girl, just like his daughter... and he was smiley and nice, and I thought he was kind...' Eva turned to her mother again. 'I know I shouldn't have spoken to a stranger, mum... but I was upset, and he seemed to care that I was upset...' She began to cry, and Rachel gently stroked her hair, shushing her, telling her she understood, and everything was alright.

'I told him about them making me try to smoke weed,' said Eva, sniffing and wiping her eyes with the tissue her mother had pressed into her hand. 'He asked where... I said behind some bushes, up the bank, further on. He asked me to show him, and sort of put his arm around me. He said we should look for evidence... maybe a cigarette butt that I could use to make a complaint to the school.' Eva stopped speaking for a few moments, wincing as she changed position slightly, trying to get more comfortable. Gayle waited patiently, letting her take her time. She was doing well. Eventually, the small voice began again. 'He kept his hand against my back... I didn't really like that, but he acted like it was normal... I didn't want to make a fuss...'

Almost whispering, Eva went on to describe her ordeal. It made harrowing listening, and the misery etched on Rachel's face as she listened to her daughter was something Gayle would never forget.

'He said he would kill me if I didn't keep quiet and do what he wanted,' she sobbed, burying her face in her hands. 'He hurt me, mum. He hurt me so much,' she whispered through her fingers. 'Then he said I had to stay there after he left and not make a sound, or I would never see you or dad again,' she said, turning to her mother, her voice breaking. 'I was so scared. Then it got dark, and I was cold. And

I could hear the helicopter and sometimes voices nearby... but nobody came...'

'Oh, sweetheart...' Tears coursed down Rachel's face as she tried to comfort her daughter, gently cupping her face, dabbing at her tears.

Gayle gently patted the child's hand. 'Eva, you've been a star, telling us about all this. You are a very, very brave girl,' she smiled reassuringly. 'I wonder if there's one more thing you could do for me? I've got a photo here of a man with you in the park. It was taken by a lady who was photographing someone else, and you were in the background,' she explained, taking a copy from her wallet. 'Can you just look at it and tell me whether this is the man who hurt you?' She held out the photograph to Eva. Rachel gasped and leaned forward to look at the picture.

Eva studied the image for a few seconds before whispering, 'Yes, that's him.' Gayle was astonished at how calm the girl was as she handed the photo back to Gayle.

'Thank you, Eva. Now, I want you to rest and get better. We'll make sure we get this man, and we'll send him to prison for a very long time.'

Rachel followed Gayle out of the room. 'I want to see him,' she hissed. Her voice was shaky, rising in hysteria as she tried to snatch the photograph from Gayle's hand, digging her nails into her arm as Gayle held the photo out of reach. 'Do you know who he is?'

'Nothing is confirmed yet, Rachel,' said Gayle, gently prising Rachel's hand from her arm. 'Look, you just concentrate on getting Eva better. We'll let you know as soon as we make an arrest. Ok?' Rachel started to protest, then nodded, reluctantly, before turning and wordlessly going back to her daughter.

CHAPTER SEVENTEEN

On the drive back to headquarters, Gayle relayed the conversation to Dave who had stayed with Tommy during the interview. 'So that supports Sandra's evidence. She's a brave kid. She's had a hell of an ordeal. By the way, how is Tommy taking this?'

'Quietly. He's in shock, I think. It's like knowing what was done to his kid has knocked all the stuffing out of him,' said Dave. 'At one stage he broke down and cried like a baby. But I think once he comes out of shock he might react violently. I've asked a couple of uniforms to keep an eye on him.'

Back at the station, Gayle brought the team up to date with the significant developments. Recounting her interview with Eva, Gayle described the role of the two girls. 'Normally, Eva wouldn't figure on their radar, but they decided to have some fun with her. They pretended they wanted to be her friends and persuaded her to go into the park with them. They kept her in the park for more than an hour, taking her behind some bushes, where they tried to get her to smoke weed. But she couldn't inhale without coughing, so it had no effect on her. After a while they abandoned her, telling her she was useless and pathetic as she couldn't even get high.' She looked around the room. 'Nice girls. We'll need to speak to those two and their parents. They must have known Eva was missing but didn't bother to come forward. We need to follow up on this.'

Gayle sat down on the edge of a desk and went on to describe how the man had persuaded Eva to retrace her steps, purportedly to look for evidence. 'Before she knew what was happening, he'd pulled her deep into the undergrowth and had his hand over her face. He told her he would kill her if she made a sound. He removed one of her shoes, pulled her sock off and stuffed it into her mouth. She said he took a roll of silver tape out of his pocket and taped up her mouth. He bit the tape to cut it and she said he grinned at her while he did it, like he was enjoying himself. Then he undid his trousers and made her touch him. He told her what he was going to do to her. She started to struggle at that, terrified, and that's when he punched her, several times, fracturing three ribs. He then removed her lower clothing, spent some time examining a small birthmark on her tummy, in the shape of a butterfly, tracing it with his finger and kissing it. Then he raped her.

'Her consultant confirmed to us that she was raped both vaginally and anally, causing some internal physical damage.' Gayle paused, 'Eva has a clear memory of the appearance of her attacker. She said when he first started talking to her, she thought he had a kindly face, nice teeth when he smiled. Brownish hair, wavy, shoulder-length. I showed her the photo from the park, and she has confirmed that it's him in the photo.'

Getting to her feet, Gayle looked at her team. 'Now, where are we with the CCTV coverage?' she asked. 'Anything new?'

DC Donna Morrison, nicknamed Shorty for obvious reasons, blurted, 'Yes boss.' Looking pleased with herself she explained, 'As you instructed boss, we checked for CCTV over a mile radius from Richardson-Dees Park. Looking in particular for someone matching the photograph. We've found some footage of a man getting into a car at eight fifteen pm on the day the girl went missing.' She checked her notes, 'A dark coloured saloon, Ford Mondeo. It was parked on Northumberland Street, just off the High Street. It looks like the same man who's in the photographs taken in the park. Same face. Same clothes. I've got the footage here...' She swivelled her chair round and adjusted her computer screen, so it could be more easily be seen by the team.

They all crowded round and watched as the grainy footage played out on the monitor. 'Definitely looks like him...' said Dave, pointing at the screen.

'Yes, it's the same guy,' agreed Gayle. 'What about the car, Donna?' she asked, leaning over to take a closer look at the screen. 'Is the registration plate visible?'

'Yes, it can be seen briefly as he drives away, but it's not very clear... there.' Donna froze the screen, and they could see the number plate. It was fuzzy and difficult to read. 'Not sure if that's HR something? Fifty-one?'

'No, it looks like BR to me,' said Dave. A few other voices chimed in, all giving different interpretations.

'I've already asked the tech guys to take a look, boss,' said Donna, turning to Gayle and looking even more pleased with herself. 'They're looking at it now. Said it won't take long.'

'Well done,' said Gayle. 'Nice to see you using your initiative.' She nearly added *for a change* but decided not to show Donna up in front of the whole team. That pep talk she'd recently given her must have paid off.

The phone on Wendy's desk jangled. She picked up, making notes as she listened. 'Boss,' she called out, 'sorry to interrupt, but we've got the results from the tech guys.' She waved her notebook in the air. 'They've recovered the full number plate and run a check on the car. It's registered to a company in Leicester, J C Woodwards.'

'This is good,' said Gayle. 'We've got a positive ID that puts Ian Cooper in the park, holding the hand of the victim, and later that evening we've got him in the vicinity of the assault, getting into a car that's registered to the company that employs him. That gives us reasonable grounds to arrest him on suspicion and to search his house.

I want to find the clothes he was wearing on the day of the assault. Then I want his DNA.' Gayle was pacing back and forth in front of the evidence board. We've got plenty of DNA from the crime scene for comparison.

'Hold off circulating the new photograph on social media. If he is the perp, we don't want to alert him to the fact that we're on to him. We need to bring him in. We'll leave in twenty minutes. Dave, you come with me. Kris, bring some uniforms, the usual back-up. Wendy, inform Durham force we'll be making an arrest on their territory, but doubt we'll need to involve them.'

They set off for Chester le Street, heading south on the A19, making their way through the Tyne Tunnel, before turning off to join the A1(M). Gayle had butterflies in her stomach, feeling her excitement mount. She was always this way before an arrest, as the adrenalin kicked in. Dave drove along the A167, took a right at the next roundabout on to Ropery Lane. A left turn at the roundabout would have taken them towards the Emirates Cricket Stadium, where many of Gayle's cherished memories resided. As a keen cricket fan, her father frequently took her there in her childhood to watch Durham play. *Wish dad had lived to see me become DCI* she thought. *He'd be so proud of me leading a serious investigation.*

'Park further up the street,' she instructed Dave, giving the same instruction over the radio to the back-up team. She didn't want to spook Cooper before they'd gained entry to the house. They were in a street of old terraced houses. Tiny front gardens fronted by low brick walls. 'Four of you round the back,' she instructed. Flanked by Dave and Kris, she pushed open the low wrought iron gate and walked up the short path to a blue-painted front door. After pressing the bell, she stepped back to observe the facade. To the right was a square bay window, with slatted white blinds, and Gayle noted the paintwork was clean and the glass sparkling. A well-kept little house. *Let's hope he's here,* thought Gayle. The door was opened by a slim attractive woman of around thirty-six, wearing pale blue jeans, with a red tee-shirt tucked in. She looked startled when Gayle held up her ID and introduced herself, and her two colleagues.

'Ms Clements? We need to speak to Ian Cooper. Is he at home?' asked Gayle. 'Can we come in?' Without waiting for a reply, she stepped over the threshold, followed by the other two officers.

'What's going on...?' Maria Clements began, taking a step back in alarm.

'Ian Cooper. Is he here?' interrupted Gayle.

'Yes...' the woman stammered, turning towards the stairs she shouted 'Ian.' Just then, Cooper appeared, coming down the stairs barefoot. Gayle's pulse quickened as she recognised him. There could be no mistake; this was the man in the photographs. Surprisingly attractive in the flesh, he was wearing dark blue joggers with a pale blue sweatshirt and looked unperturbed at the sight of police in his home.

'Ian Cooper,' said Gayle, stepping forward, holding out her ID. 'DCI Jones, Northumbria Police. I'm arresting you on suspicion of serious sexual assault and rape.' Addressing Dave she instructed, 'DI Chapman, cuff him and read him his rights. Then put him in the car.' She turned to Kris; 'Get the team in.' Cooper had nothing to say in response to the caution, just nodded to indicate he had understood it.

'What's going on? What's this about?' Maria Clements looked perplexed. 'Ian hasn't done anything... There must be some mistake.' She was frantically looking back and forth between her partner and Gayle, as the handcuffs were put on. She grabbed Cooper's arm, shaking it in agitation. 'Tell her, Ian. Tell her she's making a mistake.' Ian Cooper just looked at her, wordlessly, before roughly shrugging off her arm and going with the officer to the door.

Maria made to follow him, reaching out to grasp his arm again. 'Step away Ms Clements,' Gayle commanded. 'Ian Cooper is under arrest.

He's being taken to Northumbria Police Station for questioning. We need to search the house now.'

'What? You can't... I mean, why? What are you looking for?' her voice rising. 'Have you got a warrant?'

'A warrant is not required where an arrest has been made, Ms Clements. We will be looking for evidence relating to the offence for which Cooper has been arrested. We'll need to take a statement from you, too, but for now please let my officers do their job.' Gayle gestured to the team.

Wearing gloves, the uniformed officers spread out, ready to begin a systematic search of the house, two of them moving towards the staircase. They were looking in particular for the clothing Cooper had been wearing in the photographs and in the CCTV footage. All his electronic devices were to be taken for examination too.

'But my daughter's in her bedroom up there,' shouted Mrs Cooper, inserting herself between the two officers and the staircase, spreading out her arms and holding tight to the banisters. 'She'll be frightened.'

'Hold it, guys,' instructed Gayle. 'One of you go upstairs with Ms Clements and bring the girl down here.' She turned to Maria, 'When you've got her, take her into the kitchen and keep her beside you for now. She'll be quite safe. It might be an idea if you get a relative to look after her. Do you have anyone nearby?'

'I'll ring my mother.' Maria Clements bit her lip, her eyes filling with tears. 'She'll come over.'

After being processed through the Custody Suite, Cooper was taken to a cell and left to cool his heels. 'We'll let him stew for a while,' she told Dave. 'Can you get me a coffee? I'm going to put my feet up for half an hour. We'll start the interview in an hour or so.'

In the interview room, an hour and a half later, Gayle began by asking Cooper where he had been on the day that the assault had taken place.

'I was visiting clients in Northumberland, in and around the Hexham and Corbridge areas,' he asserted. 'I made a mistake when I told your officers the other day that I was at home with my wife. Sorry about that, I got my day off mixed up. I'd been off the day before.'

'Really?' commented Dave, straightening his notepad, and readying his pen. 'Ok, just give me the names of the companies and clients you visited.' He waited, pen poised, looking expectantly at Cooper.

'Look,' Cooper said, leaning forward and spreading his hands, 'I was supposed to have been working that day, but to tell the truth I didn't feel well, so I cancelled my appointments... I decided to go for a walk instead.'

'So, when you told us you were seeing clients, you were lying?' asked Dave.

'No, not really. I didn't mean to mislead. I was supposed to be seeing clients but changed my mind at the last minute. I had a headache and decided to go for a walk instead. I drove to Tynemouth. Thought the sea air would do me good. I walked from there to St Mary's Island and back again.'

Smooth, lying bastard thought Gayle. 'Did you visit anywhere else that day?' she asked.

'No, I eventually just drove back home,' he told them with confidence.

'We're now going to show you some photographs, taken on that afternoon,' said Dave as he extracted two pictures from the substantial file in front of him. 'Is that you?' he asked, pointing to the man holding hands with the girl? And here?' indicating the second picture, with Cooper's face clearly showing. There was no response, and he continued. 'We also have CCTV coverage of you returning to your car.' He pressed the 'play' button on the recorder. As Cooper watched, Gayle studied his face. It gave nothing away *Cool customer this one.*

'Well?' said Gayle when there was no response.

Cooper continued to attempt to lie his way out of it. 'I must admit it looks like me, but it's not me. Where were these photographs taken?'

'Is that your car?' asked Gayle, indicating the photo of the car, frozen on the screen.

Cooper peered closely at the monitor. 'No, I don't believe it is.'

'I see,' said Gayle evenly. 'Our technical people have enhanced the number plate so it's now legible, Mr Cooper. Do you see?' She showed him a still photo, clearly showing the full number plate. 'Ring any bells? And just to prompt your memory, the car is registered to J C Woodwards in Leicester. Your employer.'

Blustering, Cooper blurted, 'Someone must have taken it while I was walking on the beach. I was away for a long time. Someone could have used the car and put it back where they found it, to put suspicion on to me.'

'So, you're really asking us to believe that someone looking remarkably like you took your car from Tynemouth, drove to Wallsend, committed a serious offence, and then went to the trouble of returning the car to Tynemouth? All whilst wearing your clothes?' asked Dave.

'Yes. I mean I know it sounds crazy. I don't understand why, or who would do this. But, yes, that's what must have happened.' He sounded sincere and confident. 'And those are not my clothes he's wearing in the photos. Grey is really not my colour.'

'Can you explain why these items of clothing were found in your wardrobe, Mr Cooper?' asked Gayle, retrieving several packages from a nearby chair. 'They were found right at the back of the wardrobe, in a heap, underneath a blanket. I'm showing the suspect Items 321, 322 and 323,' she added for the benefit of the tape. Lifting the packages one by one, she held each out to show him the garments through the clear evidence bags.

'That's just some old stuff I was going to throw out,' he said, apparently unperturbed. 'Haven't worn that stuff for ages.'

'Hmm, white shirt, grey trousers, dark trainers? Well, if you haven't worn them for some time, then we won't find any of Eva Simpson's DNA on them, will we?' she asked. There was no response from Cooper who was trying desperately to maintain his cool, nonchalant facade. 'Let me tell you what I think happened, Mr Cooper,' said Gayle, leaning over the desk towards him. 'I believe that *is* you in the photos. I think you have a predilection for little girls, and I think you deliberately went looking for one. Maybe you spotted Eva walking in the direction of the park and decided to follow her? Am I right so far?' she asked.

'No. I wasn't there,' Cooper almost shouted. 'I've told you I was on the beach.'

Gayle continued, 'You watched Eva being bullied, then as soon as she was on her own and visibly upset you took your chance to play the kind stranger, offering sympathy and support. Then you got her to go with you back to where the other girls had made her smoke, on the pretext of helping her. And when you were out of sight of any by-passers, you viciously attacked and raped her. A defenceless little girl, not much older than your partner's daughter.'

'No, no... You've got it all wrong,' he protested. 'I've told you I was on the beach. I'm not a child molester, for God's sake.' He dropped his head into his hands.

The duty solicitor, a young, bearded guy, who up to that point had been quiet, spoke up. 'I'd like to ask for a break at this point to confer with my client in private.'

'We're done for now,' Gayle told him. 'Confer away.' Turning to Cooper she said, 'We're remanding you in custody, pending further investigations.' When the duty solicitor began to protest, she held up her hand, 'I'm well aware of the regulations. We're expecting DNA results very soon which I believe will result in your client being charged with serious offences.' She stood up. 'Interview terminated, 02:15.'

CHAPTER EIGHTEEN

It's been six months. On waking, I keep my eyes closed and I'm transported back home to Wallsend. In a few minutes I'll get up, late as usual, take a quick shower and grab some breakfast. I'll check my backpack; make sure I have what I need for the school day. Then I'll hurry down Kings Road to meet up with my bestie by the park gates, and we'll walk to school together, swapping secrets, laughing, and joking...

At some point during the day Matt will give me a sneaky hug if we're lucky enough to find a moment alone together... I think I love him... Then I open my eyes... and with a sickening jolt reality hits me all over again and I groan.

I think back to what happened in the aftermath of... the attack. As soon as I was well enough to be taken home from hospital, and before I really knew what was happening, I was taken away from everything I knew. My home, my friends, my school, my life. We came down to Walton Bridge, in Surrey, to start again where nobody knew me. We changed our name. I'm no longer Eva Simpson. Now I'm Emma Jackson. I've lost so much... I've lost everything...

Quite why my parents chose Walton Bridge I'm not sure. I think they probably just stuck a pin into a map. I had no say in it, but to be fair I was not in any state to have an opinion. All I know is things were arranged very quickly and I was relieved to get away from Wallsend and everyone there who knew me. Mum and dad told me they hoped, in time, we would be able to resume a normal life away from everyone who knew us. Where no-one would know what had happened to me. A normal life? I know that nothing will ever be 'normal' again for me after that terrible day.

There wasn't any choice about leaving I couldn't bear to face anyone. Couldn't ever face going back to see my school friends. The newspaper coverage was fairly graphic, and I knew I must be the talk of the whole school. The whole neighbourhood. The papers may not have named me, but word always gets round. How could I ever face any of them again? I still feel unbearably, deeply ashamed. Dirty, soiled, unworthy.

The old nightmares about the woman screaming have given way to nightmares which are so much worse. Every night, I see him. I feel him and smell him and hear his whispered threats. Just as though it happened only yesterday. My physical wounds are almost healed but inside my head I am lost. Counselling sessions are not helping me. I don't want to talk about what happened. I want it all to go away. I just want the pain to end. I've started cutting myself and at those times, the pain I inflict on myself pushes the anguish away, just for a little while. Please, God, when will it all end? They say I've got Post Traumatic Stress Disorder and they're trying to treat me for it, but so far none of the medication is making any difference.

There's been some talk about me starting a new school, but that's not something I can deal with any time soon. It's too early. All I want to do is curl up in my bed and pull the duvet over my head. How can I ever even begin to feel normal again?

All our lives have been changed forever. Dad is angry all the time, not just some of the time as he was before. Mum tries to be upbeat for me, but I can see that she's heartbroken and constantly worried about me. And my brother. When Sam was told what had happened to me, he took it very badly. They all did, of course, but I'm sure that something in my brother was fractured. After rushing back from Oxford, he came straight to my bedside. Sat with me for hours at a time, willing me to get better. There was a lot of anger. I remember overhearing him and my dad arguing loudly, on several occasions, about what they'd like to do to Cooper if they could only get their hands on him. My brother has returned to university now, but he rings me every day to check up on me, making sure I haven't done anything stupid. I'm so miserable, there are times that I really don't want to go on.

CHAPTER NINETEEN

Before all this happened, PTSD was something I thought only soldiers got, when they'd been in war zones. I now know differently. Although not as all-consuming as it was in the first year, when I felt I'd been to hell and back, I still experience times when out of the blue, a black cloud descends over me threatening to totally engulf me. At those times, I can't cope, and my life is put on hold and I start cutting myself again. My arms are now criss-crossed with scars. When I'm in the grip of the darkness, I can barely function. I cower in my bed, bury myself trembling and sobbing under my duvet.

Sometimes flashbacks and nightmares still overwhelm me and when that happens, I wake in terror, screaming, reliving the horror all over again. At those times, my mother hurries to my room, holds me, talks to me, comforts me. Despite all the psychiatric and counselling sessions, the different drugs and therapies, I understand the emotional damage is so deep that it's going to take a long time to come to terms with.

It took a full eighteen months before I felt strong enough to join a new school. When it came time to start, I felt sick with nerves and apprehension. The night before my first day, I was throwing up, didn't sleep at all, and nearly refused to go. What if someone had found out about me? What if they could tell just by looking at me? What if they talked about me behind my back? Felt sorry for me? Sniggered? What if I got a panic attack at school?

In the end, my fears of going to school were groundless. School isn't so bad. Nobody knows anything. At first, I was just treated like any other new girl on the block and was able to pretend to be normal, just like everyone else. I reinvented myself. Now, I'm just one of the girls. They're a friendly enough crowd, and one of them, Lucy, took me under her wing from day one. She's nice, and we've become good friends. But I've never confided in her about my past. I feel that as long as it remains hidden, I can fit in to my new environment and get away with it. I remember thinking that if I pretend for long enough, I might even be able to convince myself I'm normal, and I just about have.

My friends are all into boys now, in a big way, and some of them aren't even virgins anymore, at fourteen. I know they think I'm strange because I'm not interested. There are rumours, which I don't discourage, that I'm a lesbian, but that's alright. I would rather they think that than know the truth, that I can't bear the thought of being touched by a boy. Ugh, they freak me out.

Waving Lucy goodbye, I turned into my street, hitching my heavy backpack further up on to my shoulders, grumbling to myself that considering we live in a digital age, it amazes me how many books we need for A Level study. Our house is right at the end of the road, up quite a steep incline, and today as I trudged up the hill, my thoughts returned to the first time I saw our new home. I hated it on sight. To be fair, I was so badly traumatised back then that I hated everything. I particularly hated Walton Bridge and southerners. I missed my friends, especially my bestie, Sophie. Missed my old school and the warmth of the Geordie people. And I missed Matt. I still do. But I'm not the same person anymore and I couldn't bear to see any of them again. Matt wrote to me once, but I didn't reply. What could I say? I don't ever want to see him or anyone from my past. I just couldn't face them...

After pushing through our front gate, I made my way up the drive to the side entrance and slid my backpack to the ground, fishing in my pocket for my key. First stop, the fridge to get a chilled Seven UP, before grabbing a packet of cheese and onion crisps and heading upstairs to my room. Might as well get the homework out of the way. My computer pinged as I entered the bedroom, and I slung my bag on the bed and idly looked at the screen. 'Can't stop thinking of the day I'll see that little butterfly again'.

What? I stared at the message in disbelief. As its meaning sank in, my stomach lurched. I could feel my heart began to thud faster and faster until I could hardly breathe. Whoosh. In a second, I was back in the park in Wallsend, feeling the weight of him pressing me into the ground, smelling his nauseating breath acrid with tobacco. I could feel his finger tracing the outline of the birthmark in my groin and hear his chilling voice, "Oh, a little butterfly, just waiting for me to set it free with a kiss". I felt faint and found myself clinging to the edge of the desk, my legs shaking so much I could hardly stand. How could this be happening? How could he know where to find me?

I don't know how long I stood there staring at the screen, but at some point, my mother must have returned home from work, because she was suddenly there in the bedroom, shaking my arm, asking me what was wrong. I couldn't speak, just pointed wordlessly at the screen. My mother's hand went to her throat as she peered at the computer, taking in the vile message.

'How on earth...?' she whispered, turning to me, her face ashen. 'But you've changed all your settings... your name... and he can't have access to a computer, surely?'

'It can only be him. It's got to be... Who else could know about my birthmark... who else could know? He... he...' I couldn't go on.

As she sank down on to the bed, I could see the disbelief registered on mum's face.

'God, Emma, this can't be happening. It must be a hoax. A nasty hoax. I mean it can't be from him... how could he even have your email address? We've changed our name... and you changed all your settings,' she repeated. 'And we've moved and everything...' She got to her feet and put a hand on my shoulder, gripping it tightly. 'I'm going call your father, and then we're going to call the police.'

The fear that had never completely gone away since the attack, returned with a vengeance, overwhelming me. With a groan, I doubled over, slowly sinking to my knees as I vomited over the duvet.

Within an hour the police arrived. They expressed concern about the message and said they'd investigate it. Said they were taking very seriously the possibility that it could have been sent by a serving prisoner. A few days later, a Family Liaison Officer came to see me, sent from the police. She told me they hadn't been able to trace the source of the message. She told me that Cooper did not have access to the internet, except under close supervision and they don't believe that it could have been sent by him. She told me they have questioned him at length about it, but he denies all knowledge.

'Of course he'll deny it,' I screamed at her when she told me. 'He's not going to bloody admit it, is he?'

The police know he's part of a paedophile ring... sick perverts who share their filthy photos and videos around. They found hundreds of them on his computer after he was arrested. Including a video of what he did to me, which thankfully didn't need to be shown to a jury once he pleaded guilty.

'He could have got one of his sicko friends to send it for him,' I yelled, panicking as I realised they weren't going to do anything about it.

They just dropped the matter. No evidence to link it to Cooper. They suggested it must have been some kind of hoax and I should try to forget about it. Forget about it? I felt hopeless and terrified. All the self-confidence I'd managed to build up over the five years since the attack just evaporated. I felt as though my life had been destroyed all over again. I couldn't face going to school and began self-harming again, something I hadn't done for some time.

My parents kept trying everything they could think of to get me to go back to school. But I just couldn't face it. They kept telling me how proud they were of the nine straight A's I got in my GCSE exams, but nothing meant anything to me anymore. I told them I no longer had any interest in studying for my A Levels. All my plans for a career in forensic science suddenly didn't matter. I didn't want to do anything but hide in my bedroom. I knew my mum and dad were distraught and at a loss as to how to help me, but I didn't care.

For a week after getting the vile message I hardly left my bedroom, barely got out of bed. Then my brother, Sam, arrived. He told me he had come to stay for a while, taken some overdue leave from his company. I'm not sure exactly what he does, but I know he's based at GCHQ in Cheltenham, and there's a veil of secrecy about his work. Anyway, he came back home to be here for me, so I realised he must be pretty worried. I think my parents turned to him for help, as Sam's always understood me better than anyone. I think they were hoping he would instinctively know how to get me functioning again.

It worked. The first thing Sam did was to make me get up, take a shower and get dressed. After noticing the fresh scars on my arms, he sat with me for a long time, getting me to talk to him about why I felt compelled to cut myself, trying to understand what made me do it.

'I don't really understand it myself,' I told him, embarrassed, biting my lip. 'It makes me feel more in control and when I do it, it seems to lessen the anxiety a bit.'

'Next time you have the urge to do it, why don't you ring me instead?' he asked. 'Talking will help to lower your anxiety levels. Will you at least try to do that, Emma?' After extracting my promise, he changed the subject. 'Right, we're going for a long walk now,' he informed me. 'And I'm not taking no for an answer.' Once outside, I must admit I found it quite pleasant to be in the fresh air, walking along the Thames Path with the sun glinting on the river. We walked for a fair way before he suggested we sit on a bench overlooking the water. Firmly he told me I needed to find a way to take back control of my life.

'Moping around and being a pathetic passive victim isn't going to get you anywhere, Emma,' he said. 'You need to buck up your ideas and stop wallowing in self-pity. Enough is enough.' My brother had never spoken to me harshly before and I got quite a shock.

'But, what about that message, Sam? What if he did send it... what if he's watching me...'

'Emma, he's in prison and he's going to be there for a very long time. He can't be watching you. Maybe, just maybe, he's told one of his 'friends' on the outside about your birthmark and they've sent the message to upset you. Computer geeks have their ways of tracing people. I don't know. But I do know that instead of hiding away like a frightened animal, you should take positive action. I've been thinking, how would you feel about enrolling in an intensive fitness course? It will do you the world of good to get yourself super-fit and acquire some self-defence skills, combat skills even. Getting fit would get you into a more positive frame of mind. Think Lisbeth Salander in The Girl with the Dragon Tattoo. You'll be equipped to deal with any aggressor in the future.'

We recommenced walking and as we passed under Walton Bridge, we found ourselves almost surrounded by a large bevy of swans, and Sam threw them some bits of bread that he produced from a bag in his pocket. 'And' he added, 'after that, you are going back to school.'

Already quite sporty, the idea of getting fitter and stronger did appeal to me. Sam had already done his homework and found a course for me. So, I found myself enrolled in an intensive twelve-week warrior training course. It was full time and intensive and to say it was hard would be an understatement. However, I soon found that the more gruelling the sessions became, the more I thrived on them. Having told my trainer that my goals were to become fitter and stronger, he tailored my sessions accordingly and day by day I could feel my body getting stronger. The peak of the training was an arduous overnight hike across the Brecon Beacons, which I managed to complete in record time. Just as my big brother had known would happen, as my body gained in strength, so did my mind. At the end of twelve weeks, I was in a much better place mentally. More positive and optimistic.

My father was delighted. 'If you're so much better now, you can go back to school and get on with your A Levels,' he gruffly told me, and to his surprise I agreed.

CHAPTER TWENTY

2022

'Emma, visitor for you,' my mother called up the stairs. Curious, as I wasn't expecting anyone, I closed my computer and hurried from my room.

'Hello Emma, how are you?' Mrs Pearson asked as I made my way down the stairs. I could tell she was trying to sound upbeat and chipper and something about her tone made me begin to feel uneasy. A feeling of dread began in the pit of my stomach as I looked at her false smile. 'I hear congratulations are in order,' she gushed. 'Two A stars and one A? Very good results. Which university are you thinking of?'

'Haven't made my mind up yet,' I said quickly. 'Why are you here?'

'Can we talk?' she asked brightly, smiling.

'Come on up,' I said, turning and going back up the stairs, leading the way to my bedroom.

She followed and again asked, 'How are you, Emma? I haven't seen you for a while.' When I didn't respond, she had the grace to look a bit flustered, her face reddening. 'I've come to give you an update on what's happening with Ian Cooper.'

'Oh, yeah?' I stared at her. I instinctively knew what Marilyn Pearson, my Victim Support Officer, was going to say, and I didn't want to hear the words come out of her mouth.

'He appeared before the Parole Board last week and they've confirmed that he is to be released, on Licence. In six weeks.'

She continued talking and I watched her fat lips moving, fascinated by a bit of spittle at the corner of her mouth. I concentrated on that as it glistened and formed a little bubble. Anything but listen to her words. Through the pounding in my ears, all

I could think was he's getting out. Oh God, he's getting out. I could feel the familiar panic building up in my chest, restricting my breathing and making me feel breathless.

'... condition of the offender's licence that he's not to make any contact with you, nor come within a proscribed distance from you. If any of the conditions are breached, he'll go straight back inside...'

'But he will come for me,' I shouted, as her words registered. 'You know he will. He said he can't wait to see the butterfly again. They can't let him out. They can't.' My barely suppressed panic was threatening to spill over into hysteria.

'I'm sorry, Emma. I know how worried you'll be, but...'

'No, you don't. You can't know,' I screamed. 'None of you know. It didn't happen to you.' I was hyperventilating, gasping for breath. Mum must have heard the commotion because she hurried into the room, demanding to know what was going on. When she saw the state I was in, she fussed around, making me sit down and take some deep breaths.

'They're letting him out, Mum,' I sobbed. 'What am I going to do?'

'Surely this can't be true?' Mum asked, standing beside me, one arm protectively around my shoulders, staring at the woman. 'He can't be eligible for release already, Marilyn?'

'The Parole Board has decided that he's no longer a threat to children and approved his release. With conditions, of course,' she said to mum. She at least had the grace to look shamefaced about the information she was imparting. To be fair, it wasn't her fault. She was only the messenger, but in that moment, I hated her and all the system with a vengeance. The victim doesn't matter when decisions like this are taken.

'You know, Emma, there was no evidence that the email came from Ian Cooper. And he strenuously denies having anything to do with it. The parole board was therefore not able to take it into consideration.' She shrugged, spreading her hands in front, palms up.

'The justice system stinks,' I screamed, shrugging off Mum's arm and stamping my foot. 'What about me? What am I supposed to do now? They don't care. They just don't fucking care.'

'Language, Emma,' Mum admonished.

'Oh, shut up, Mum.' I yelled. 'You too,' I said, turning and glaring at Ms Pearson. 'Just leave me alone. Go on,' I yelled. 'Get out. Both of you.'

Mum tried to put her arm around me again, but I pushed her away, more violently than I intended to. She looked hurt and turned on her heel, taking Marilyn Pearson with her. Once alone, I sat on the bed, put my head in my hands, and sobbed and sobbed. Over the years since the attack, I've become adept at hiding my true feelings, masquerading as a normal person. Only I know that inside, I'm broken and will never get over what happened to me. Nobody looking at me would guess. They see an ordinary teenage girl, slightly built, long fairish hair, quite pretty, confident.

But, oh God, they're letting him out. What am I going to do?

I crawled under my duvet and lay there, shivering. I'd never felt so alone in all my life. Nobody understood. None of the counsellors, psychiatrists, and other do-gooders I've seen over the years has been any real help to me. I just can't let them in. All they want to do is listen to me talk about my feelings and that's the last thing I ever want to do.

I can't rely on my parents to protect me. I blame Dad. It was his fault that it happened to me in the first place. He's such a control freak. If he'd only let me have a mobile phone, they would have been able to trace me. Or I might have managed to call them. I wouldn't have lain in terror and pain, in the dark, for hours and hours, not knowing if anyone would find me in time. And as for my mother, she was weak. She should have stood up for me and insisted that I be allowed a phone. All my friends had them at that age. But no, she'd backed up my father. I know if it was up to mum alone, I would have been allowed one, but as usual she'd given in and allowed my father to rule the roost.

A tentative tap on my door. Mum's voice, the door slowly opening. I screamed at her again to go away and leave me alone. Hours later, I made my way down the thickly carpeted stairs. I could hear raised voices, getting louder as I neared the kitchen door. Pausing, I listened to my father, ranting, my heart hammering.

'It's not bloody right. That evil bastard roaming the streets again,' he yelled, the last word accompanied by a loud bang, which sounded like something being slammed down onto the marble worktop.

My mother's softer voice, 'Careful, you'll break that...'

'Supposed to be fucking rehabilitated,' he raved on. 'Scum like that are never rehabilitated. A leopard never changes its spots. Mark my words, he'll do the same to some other poor bloody kid.'

'Keep your voice down, Tommy,' my mother hissed in a loud whisper, 'I don't want Emma upset any more than she is already. I don't know how she's going to deal with this as it is.' She sounded distraught, her voice wobbly.

'Has she said anything to you?' he asked, belatedly lowering his voice.

'Not a word. Not since the Pearson woman left. She won't speak to me. I tried to talk to her again earlier, but she screamed at me to go away. I know she's terribly upset, but she won't let me near her.'

I pushed open the door to see my mother mopping up coffee from the bench. There was a mug nearby and I noticed it was the one with "Best Dad in the World" on the side. And it now had a crack running up from the base to the rim. They both looked up, sharply, as I came in.

"Upset?' I yelled, looking from one to the other. 'Upset doesn't come close. Try bloody horrified, terrified, scared out of my sodding wits, and you won't even come close.' I turned at that and ran sobbing back up to my room, back to the safety of the duvet. I must have drifted off because suddenly he was there with me, the tip of the knife cold and sharp against my throat again, his hushed voice at my ear, "Don't make a sound or you'll never see your mother again..." Faint voices in the distance... mothers calling to their children... snatches of conversation... laughter. I want to cry out for help but don't dare... not with the knife at my throat and the thought of never seeing my mother again... I feel grit digging into my cheek and smell the sharpness of damp earth as he presses my face into the ground, his body a dead weight on top of me. I taste the nicotine on his breath and smell the acrid aroma of his sweat. And I feel the pain. Oh, the pain. I'm terrified. I wet myself.

I jolted awake, looking around my familiar room, at the dressing table with the bulbs around the mirror, just like those you find in a star's dressing room, the exercise bike in the corner with my jeans hanging over the handlebars. Just another dream; I could relax. I was safe. Then I remembered the fat lips and the conversation. It all came flooding back, and I was hit all over again by a fresh wave of panic.

Sitting up, I pushed the duvet to one side and thrust my hand between my legs, checking. Thankfully, I hadn't wet the bed this time. Even after all these years, to my shame and embarrassment, it sometimes still happens when the flashback comes.

I sat on the edge of the bed, head in hands, elbows on my shaking knees, waiting for the trembling to ease. I needed to make plans. Knowing that he was going to be free, I couldn't stay. I knew I had to go away, somewhere he couldn't find me. Where could I go? One thing I knew for sure is that he would make it his business to trace me. And if I stayed put, I was certain he'd find me.

CHAPTER TWENTY-ONE

'You ready, Matt? C'mon man. The lads are waiting.' Yusef was hopping from foot to foot with impatience.

'Coming,' said Matt, grabbing his keys and debit card. Stuffing them into the back pocket of his jeans, along with his phone, he quickly followed his mate from the small room, along the corridor, down the uncarpeted stairs and out of the block of flats that was home for this academic year.

Cheers and ribald comments greeted him as they emerged from the block. They were a good bunch, these lads, Matt thought, a couple of them real comedians.

'What've you been doing Matt?' shouted one voice in a strong Liverpool accent.

'Doesn't take that long to have a wank,' shouted another, eliciting jeering as well as several more obscene remarks. Matt grinned ruefully, punching the Liverpudlian playfully on the shoulder, as he joined the group.

They were heading for Hoochie Coochie, one of the trendiest bars in Newcastle upon Tyne, where Matt had been looking forward to seeing Jazzy Jeff, one of the best DJs on the circuit. Despite knowing that Newcastle was the best city in the world for student nightlife, Matt hadn't really sampled much of it before coming to uni, tending to socialise around the bars in Wallsend where he lived, or sometimes travelling down to the coast, to Tynemouth or Whitley Bay. Once here and part of student life, he had been blown away by the vibrancy of the scene. You could literally go out any night of the week and find something going on. It was mind blowing. In addition, he had looked anew at the majesty of the Quayside area with its Millennium and Tyne Bridges, and on the opposite bank, the sight of the huge slug-shaped silver building that was the Sage, and the tall, iconic former flour mill, now a state-of-the-art Gallery for modern art. He felt a sense of proprietary pride when his mates praised the city and told him how impressed they were with all that Newcastle had to offer.

Walking down the top part of Grey Street, past Grey's Monument, they were five typical students in a city teeming with them. Just a few steps further on they walked under the portico of the impressive Theatre Royal, currently running a production of The Rocky Horror Show. The grandeur of the architecture in this street had made a big impression on Matt the first time he saw it, as a boy. Now he enjoyed showing off his city to the other lads. Soon they turned into Shakespeare Street, past the side entrance to the theatre, making their way towards Pilgrim Street and Hoochie Coochie.

Matt hung back, unusually quiet. Deep in thought, tonight he was oblivious not only to the beauty of the buildings but even to the legs on the group of mini-skirted girls sauntering down the street in front of them. Typical Newcastle girls, scantily dressed even on a cold winter's night. Normally, Matt would have enjoyed the sight and probably struck up a conversation with the girls, but not tonight.

Fuck me he thought. *That fucker gonna be back on the streets. Hard to fuckin believe.* It had felt like a physical punch to the guts when he'd come across the news article on the Tab. He'd literally gasped in shock. How could they let such an evil bastard out of prison so early? How? There was no fucking justice anymore.

The thought of Eva's reaction when she heard the news was distressing him more than anything. Poor Eva. How would she cope? He fervently wished he could see her. He wanted to so badly, but despite all his efforts over the years, she never answered his letters.

'What's with the long face, Matt?' Yusef asked, hanging back, and putting his arm around Matt's shoulders. 'Dizzy's waiting for you. Cheer up.'

Matt forced a smile to his face, 'Can't wait.' He punched Yusef playfully on the arm and they strode on.

***

He was running blindly through dark woods, desperately trying to find Eva. She had screamed once, a blood-curdling sound that made the hairs on the back of his neck stand on end. But now she was silent, and with no sound to guide him, he didn't know which direction to go in... Still, he kept on running. Stumbling over uneven ground, his boots crunching on dry bracken, his breath coming in painful gasps, he called her name over and over. He was becoming more and more frantic... he had to get to her... he took a deep breath and screamed at the top of his voice,

'Eva...'

Matt woke in a sweat, his heart hammering, an out-of-control metronome pounding inside his chest. He sat up, disorientated in the semi-gloom of his room, put his head in his hands and took a few deep breaths, trying to dispel the panic the dream had created. Realisation dawned...

'Just a dream...' he muttered. 'Thank fuck... Just a dream.'

Wide awake by then, and stone cold sober despite the six pints he'd drunk earlier, he flicked on his bedside light, before stumbling out of bed. In his boxers, he headed along the short corridor to the communal kitchen shared with the other five students on this floor. After making himself a mug of steaming Nescafe, he padded back to his room, propping himself up in bed to sip his coffee. Holding it to his lips with shaking hands, he inhaled the welcoming aroma, gradually feeling his heart rate returning to normal.

He often had disturbing dreams about Eva, but none so vivid or upsetting as tonight's. He knew why, of course. She had been on his mind constantly since he'd read about Cooper's impending release. His thoughts went back to that night, seven years earlier, when Eva had gone missing. Just a kid himself, he'd followed his mother to the front door when the policewoman knocked. He'd listened as she asked if Eva was with them or if they had seen her. He remembered his father telling his mother he was going out to help in the search for her. And he remembered his mother crying in the kitchen the next day, after she returned from taking a casserole to Eva's mother.

Piecing together the whispered conversation of his parents then and in the following days, he knew Eva had been found, but gathered by their solemn faces and his mother's tears, that all was not well. Suddenly, Eva had been whisked away by her parents, and he hadn't seen her again. He was only eleven years old, but he knew that he loved her even then... just as he did now. The papers had told him what his parents would not; the details of what had happened to Eva. Though not comprehending all the implications at his young age, he'd been horrified and broken hearted for his childhood sweetheart. It had been the hot topic for discussion amongst the kids at school for quite a while, but then Eva was gradually forgotten.

But not by him. Never by him. He'd written to her many times, after finding out her address by sneaking a look at a letter his mother had written to Eva's mother. He knew she had changed her name to Emma, but to him she would always be his Eva. But all his letters went unanswered. One day during uni holidays, Eva's parents paid a visit to see his mother. They were visiting relatives in Wallsend and called in on their old friend. Eva's father asked if he could have a word with him, and they'd gone for a short walk. Any optimism he may have felt in anticipation of what he was about to say was soon quashed when he started to speak.

'Matt, I know you mean well... contacting Eva, or Emma as she is now. You two were great friends and I know we took her away without even giving you the chance to say goodbye to her. But I must ask you to stop contacting her. She's trying very hard to put the past behind her and build a new life. Anything that brings back memories of her old life just upsets her. It reminds her of the horror she endured. Please, for Eva's sake, forget about her. She's not the same person anymore, and I'm afraid she never will be again.'

He was devastated, and had reluctantly promised to stop writing, a promise he failed keep. He managed to desist for a while, but within a few weeks, resumed sending his letters. Communicating with Eva made him feel that she was still part of his life, and he didn't want her to think that he had stopped caring. There was also the forlorn hope that one day she would answer. Over the years, he would often find himself pausing in whatever he was doing, thinking of her, wondering if she ever thought of him, if she was alright, if she was happy.

And now this. All the anguish came flooding back. That bastard had served just seven years for defiling an innocent young girl. Not only had he robbed Matt of having her in his life, but from snippets he overheard, she had become a completely different girl. A shadow of her former self, no longer gregarious and fun-loving, but a little ghost (that description had come from one of her cousins who'd come to the house to see his mother). Matt had a talent for making himself invisible, as he strained to hear any bit of news about Eva.

As he thought about Ian Cooper walking free, getting on with his life, a slow, cold rage began to build up in Matt. He punched the wall in his fury, bruising his knuckles in the process. The bastard couldn't get away with it. He had to do something.

He yearned to see Eva. She must know about Cooper's early release. Victims had to be told these things, didn't they? He wanted to go to her, comfort her, be there for her, protect her. He had to keep her safe from Cooper.

CHAPTER TWENTY-TWO

'Have you heard; they're letting that bloody paedo out of prison already?' Anne asked, taking a sip of tea. They were in the canteen having lunch. Fish pie today.

'No, what paedo?' asked Sandra, idly wondering what gossip Anne had gleaned now.

'You remember? That little kid that was raped in the park in Wallsend. Bastard was put away for fifteen years, now he's getting out in a few weeks. He's only done seven years. Seven fucking years. They call that justice? Fucking joke.'

Sandra momentarily froze, before commenting, 'Yes, I remember... but surely he can't be getting out already?' She could feel her heart thumping. Looking down at her plate, she concentrated hard on not letting her feelings show. 'Are you sure? How do you know?' Her mouth had dried up.

Anne, who had just put a large forkful of fish pie into her mouth, chewed for a while before mumbling 'It's all over the internet.' She delicately dabbed at the corner of her mouth with a paper napkin. 'Everybody's up in arms about it. God knows how the girl will feel about this.' She took a gulp of juice, swallowing noisily. 'She'll be, what, eighteen now?'

'About that, I should think,' commented Sandra. 'I remember she was only eleven when she was attacked. And he's getting out of prison already? That's shocking.' She casually picked up her knife and fork and returned to the remnants of her meal, appetite suddenly gone.

'They'll have to tell her he's being released. Imagine how the poor little bugger's going to take that.' Anne's lips were set in a straight line. 'I don't know what this country's coming to, I really don't. Bloody judges want locking up if you ask me. They're far too lenient with dirty paedophiles.'

'Awful,' Sandra responded, pushing her plate away and getting to her feet. 'Time to get back.'

'No doubt the bastard will be up to his old tricks in no time. A leopard doesn't change its spots,' observed Anne as they made their way back to their machines. 'Just mark my words.'

Throughout the rest of the afternoon Sandra was on edge. It was all she could think about, and she couldn't wait for four o'clock to come around. The second the buzzer sounded, she was up and out of the door, muttering something about an appointment. The bus journey seemed to take forever, and then she was almost running down the street towards Katie's house.

'Oh Katie, something dreadful...' she began as soon as Katie answered her door. 'He's getting out. He's being released...' Her breath was coming in great gulps. 'I can't believe it.'

'For goodness' sake come in,' Katie said, taking Sandra's arm and almost propelling her through the hallway, towards the kitchen. 'Sit down Sandra, calm down. Here, have a fag...' Katie lit two cigarettes before handing one to Sandra. 'It does seem quick,' she said, exhaling a long stream of blue smoke. 'What did he get? Fourteen years, wasn't it? Course these days they just do half their bloody sentences if they behave themselves inside, don't they?' She took another drag. 'But why are you so agitated? He doesn't know it was you who identified him, does he? He has no reason to connect you with him going to prison. And he doesn't know where you live. Even if he wanted to, he wouldn't be able to find you. You've got a new name, a new life. And it's been such a long time since you left... There's nothing for you to worry about, surely.'

'I know... I know,' said Sandra, taking a deep drag, her hands shaking. 'It was just such a shock... hearing his name again after all this time. He's an evil bastard, and now he's going to be back on the streets. He's only done seven years. Seven years for what he did to that poor kid. And they call that justice? They should bring back hanging.' Sandra went on smoking, lost in her thoughts, thinking through the implications of his impending release. 'I wonder where he'll be allowed to live. Do you think they'll let him go back to the area he used to live in before?'

'I'm not sure. He won't be allowed to go anywhere near the victim, that's for sure, but I've no idea where he'll end up. Some bail hostel at first, I suppose. That's what happened with my ex. Come to think of it, he did eventually end up not that far from where we'd lived. Course, I was miles away by then, or he wouldn't have been allowed.' The kettle came to the boil and Katie put a spoonful of Nescafe into each of two mugs, pouring as she spoke. 'Your ex was living in Durham when he was put away, wasn't he?'

'Yes. And it was a shock to find that out at the time. I moved up here to get away from him. Finding he almost lived on my doorstep was scary. Well, thirty miles away, but that's still too close for comfort. I hope the swine won't be allowed back there. I mean, the victim doesn't live here anymore... so he might be. Oh, I wouldn't like to know he was that close again.' Sandra's frown deepened as she tugged furiously at a strand of hair.

CHAPTER TWENTY-THREE

Well, good as their word, they let the bastard out just a few weeks after the visit from the Victim Support Officer. The day following her visit, I packed a bag and took the 11.55 from Walton Bridge to Waterloo. A half-hour journey, but hopefully a start in getting a world away from him. My father tried everything to stop me from leaving, even threatening to leave me out of his will. My mother, more pragmatic, understood that I had to go, but tearfully begged me to take care and to keep closely in touch.

Sitting on the train, I felt panic-stricken. What would I do? Where would I live? First things first, I told myself. I found that I was talking to myself more and more, trying to make sense of my life. I'd already found a cheap hotel on-line which I hoped would give me a base for a few days until I could sus out things out and look for a job. It was in Sidcup in the London Borough of Bexley, a place I'd never heard of let alone been to, but the hotel looked ok online and was the cheapest I could find, barring staying in a hostel or dormitory which I really didn't fancy. I'd withdrawn all my savings, such as they were, and so had a bit of cash to tide me over. Too afraid to use a credit or debit card in case he could trace me, I wanted to use cash for as long as possible.

I wasted no time in finding a job in a bar. With no experience of bar work I was surprised to be taken on almost as soon as I walked in off the street. The shortage of bar staff and hospitality workers worked in my favour, and I soon got the hang of pouring the perfect pint and learned about the various craft beers on offer. Even managed quite quickly to mix good cocktails. Gerda, one of the other barmaids, took on the task of showing me the ropes and we soon hit it off and got along like a house on fire. A week or so into the job, knowing I was looking for somewhere affordable to live, she told me one of her housemates was leaving and asked if I would be interested in renting the vacant room. It was the ideal solution, so of course I jumped at the chance.

I couldn't think about my longer-term future but feeling relatively safe in the anonymity of the bustling capital, I found I rather enjoyed working in the bar. I liked the lively atmosphere, the buzz of the place, the laughter of the groups of young women on girlie nights out. Gerda was easy to work with and good fun and on our rare nights off, we would hit the clubs and dance all night. I was able to temporarily put my troubles to one side and take one day at a time. But, as the date of Cooper's impending release approached, I found myself dreading each day, trying outwardly to carry on as normal, but inside coiled like a spring. Then the night before his release, unbidden, my carefully constructed mask slipped and suddenly the emotional barriers I'd so carefully constructed, came tumbling down. I was at the house, with Gerda, adding lime juice to some avocado I was crushing for our supper, and breaking up walnut halves to add. Gerda was toasting some sourdough. I'd been on edge all day, knowing that Cooper was being released the next morning. It was all I could think about but didn't think I'd let anything show. Picking at my food, I became aware that Gerda was watching me.

'Liebling is there something wrong?' she asked. 'You haven't been yourself all day. 'Sitting by me at the tiny breakfast bar, she put her hand on my cheek, turning me to face her. She peered at me, frowning. 'What is it? What is the matter?'

'Oh, it's nothing...' I said, attempting to smile. 'Really, I'm fine.'

'I can see there's something very wrong. Emma,' she said, her gaze steady.

'Well... it's hard to talk about... I've never told anyone.' I began welling up and quickly lowered my eyes. 'It's a long story...' The words wouldn't come, they were stuck in my throat. I took a deep breath, and I could feel her looking at me intently.

'Emma, if you don't want to talk about it, that's fine. But you know Liebling,' she said, stroking my cheek, 'sometimes it helps to talk.' She reached for the wine. 'Why don't I top up our glasses?' she suggested, pouring as she spoke. 'Then we'll make ourselves more comfortable.' Picking up the two glasses, she said softly, 'Come through here.'

I followed her through to the sitting room where, after depositing the two wine glasses on a nearby side table, she insisted on me taking a seat on one of the small settees, plumping up a couple of cushions and placing them behind my back.

'Now,' she said, settling herself near me on the sofa, 'what is it, Emma? What happened to you? You can tell me, Liebling. It just might help.' She placed a glass in my hand.

I took another deep breath, a sip of sauvignon, and began to talk. 'A few days after my eleventh birthday, I went to see a friend, not far from where I lived...' I went on to describe exactly what had happened. Every detail. The terror. The pain. The revulsion. It was the first time I had ever described in such graphic detail the ordeal I'd been through, and I found it strangely cathartic.

When I'd finished, Gerda was silent for a few seconds, before exclaiming 'Oh mein Gott. Mein Gott. Liebling. Du armes Ding. You poor thing...'

'He went to prison for fourteen years,' I told her. 'But he's got early release. They're letting him out tomorrow.'

'Tomorrow?' her eyes widened in astonishment. 'Tomorrow? And that is why you are so upset today. Mein Gott. No wonder.' She leaned over and squeezed my hand.

'I'm scared, Gerda. I think he'll try to find me. That's why I left home.' I then told her about the message on my computer. About the butterfly.'

'But... how did he know how to get in touch with you? What did the police have to say? What did they do?'

'Nothing. Oh, they said they'd investigate it, but they got nowhere. They said it was impossible for him to have sent the message from prison. But he was the only person who knew about my birthmark. The police know he was or is part of a paedophile ring. I suppose he could have got one of the others to send it. God only knows how they found my new email address after I changed my name.'

'And now he's going to be released tomorrow,' Gerda said. 'No wonder you are in such a state.' She shuffled closer and put her arms around me. We sat in silence for a little while, Gerda patting my back and murmuring soft words in German, before sitting back on her haunches.

'Did you get any help, Emma? After it first happened?' There were tears in Gerda's eyes.

'Oh, loads of bloody psychiatrists, counsellors, and therapists. But you know the more I was told it wasn't my fault that he'd done that to me, the more I believed it was. I thought I must have done something to make him choose me. When I was younger, I used to think maybe it was a punishment? I'd disobeyed my parents and gone into the park when I should have gone straight home.'

'No, no, Liebling. How could it be your fault? Du warst nur ein Kind. You were just a child.'

'Before that,' I continued, unexpectedly feeling a great sense of relief to be able to unburden myself, 'the last normal, happy day I remember was on my eleventh birthday. My mother had suggested a ten-pin bowling party, but I told her that was naff. Did she want me to be a laughingstock at school? I wanted a group of us to see a movie, go for a pizza, and then have a sleepover. Just my closest mates, four girls and two boys.' I closed my eyes, remembering.

'Go on Liebling,' Gerda urged.

'We were so excited. At the movies, one of the boys, Matt, arranged things so that he was sitting beside me, and when he saw my tears at the sad bits, he held my hand, under the armrest so no-one could see. He was my hero. I was in love. I found a note from him, tucked into my schoolbag the next day. I've kept it all this time. Here, I'll read it to you,' I said, climbing off the settee and reaching for my phone lying on a nearby chair. 'I keep it inside my phone cover... a reminder of how life used to be. "Dear Eva, You are a lovely girl, inside and out. You have a big heart and a pretty face. I'm glad we're in the same class so I can look at you all day. I love you, Matt". I look back on that as the last carefree day of my life. Two days later, everything changed. Nothing has been the same since.' I carefully re-folded the note before tucking it safely back inside the phone cover and resuming my place on the settee.

'Eva? Was that your name then? It's a nice name... tell me what happened... afterwards. When you came out of hospital?'

'We moved away from the area, three hundred miles south, to Surrey. We changed our name, so no-one could associate me with what had happened. I used to be Eva Simpson. I left all my friends behind. To be honest, I didn't want to see them any more anyway. They all knew what had happened to me and I didn't want them

looking at me and talking about me. I couldn't stand the shame. I couldn't bear it. I never saw my friends again or went back to my old school.'

We sat in silence for a while, then Gerda asked, 'So, tell me how it was when you moved away? Did you go to school in your new place? Did you make new friends?'

'Eventually. When I was well again. I was diagnosed with PTSD, Post Traumatic Stress Disorder. I was in a very bad place for a long time. But after about eighteen months, I was able to start school in Walton Bridge. With my changed name I felt anonymous. No-one knew about me, and I never breathed a word to anyone about what had happened to me. I got on well with most of the girls. I was friendly enough with boys, but I'm not comfortable getting close to men. I'm sure my friends thought I was a lesbian and I was happy to let them think that.' I told her.

She smiled. 'What about Matt? Did you ever see him again?'

'No... He managed to find out my new address. His mother kept in touch with mine and I think he got it from one of her letters. He wrote, saying how much he cared for me and how distraught he was at what had happened. He wanted to know how I was. But I never replied. I did try, but I just felt overwhelmed with shame, and I couldn't think of anything I wanted to say. I felt dirty, soiled, beyond redemption. Why would he want to have anything to do with me? Anyway, I didn't hear from him anymore, so he must have moved on with his life and forgotten about me.'

'Mein Gott, darling, but nothing was your fault. You had no need to feel dirty or ashamed.' Gerda gripped my arms and shook me. 'Listen to yourself. You are the victim here. This evil Fotze is the one to blame.'

'What does that mean?' I asked, amused despite my distress at the ferocity in her voice.

'I don't know the English,' she said, letting go of my arms. 'Very bad word.'

'He pleaded guilty. Didn't have much choice, really, there was so much evidence against him. He was sentenced to fourteen years in prison... but then a few weeks ago they came to tell me he was being released. He'd only done seven years...' I closed my eyes, remembering. 'I was completely gutted; couldn't believe he was being freed so early.'

'So, when I first met you at the pub, you had only just found out that this monster was to be released?'

'Yes... That's why I had to leave home. He'd have found me there. I know he would. I don't know how he managed to get my email address, even after I'd changed my name... but there could be hackers amongst his bloody paedophile friends. They're everywhere you know, from all walks of life.' I felt exhausted and emotional, all of a sudden. I began to cry then, quietly at first, building to noisy, raw, guttural sobs. My whole body was wracked with them, partly I think at the relief of being able to tell someone the whole sorry story at last. Gerda took me in her arms, wordlessly folding herself around me like a comfort blanket. We sat like that for a long time, Gerda gently patting my back and muttering comforting sounds in German.

Once all the pent-up emotion had been released, and my sobs finally subsided, she wiped my tears with her fingers and thumbs.

'Liebling, you needed to get all that out. You'll feel much better now.' She pushed my unkempt hair back from my face, looked into my eyes and suddenly, very gently, kissed me on the mouth. She drew back, gauging my reaction, and we just looked into each other's eyes. Suddenly we were passionately kissing. It felt so right, and I didn't resist when she took my hand and led the way up to her bedroom. For the first time in my life, I experienced exquisite, tender lovemaking.

Life felt better with Gerda in it. Unburdening myself to her had lifted much of the dark cloud that hung over me. Just to have someone on my side who knew what I'd been through, who understood and accepted me as I was. My mood lightened and I found myself relaxing in a way I hadn't been able to since that awful day. The spectre of Cooper free and walking around receded a little, and I felt safer in the anonymity of London.

But, as the saying goes, all good things must come to an end. Sitting in a trendy little coffee bar in Notting Hill one morning, I picked up my latte to take a sip, and as I did so, a creepy feeling came over me. A feeling of being watched. My seat faced the window and as I looked past Gerda sitting opposite, I froze. On the pavement across the road, a man in a dark hoodie was standing stock-still, staring right at me. I gasped and the cup slipped from my hand, spilling its contents over the table, running down onto my lap. It was him. Cooper. I felt Gera's hand on my arm, shaking me.

'What is it Emma?' She was on her feet, trying to mop up the coffee with a napkin. Following my gaze, she peered out of the window before turning back to me, frowning. 'What? What are you looking at Liebling?'

'It's him...' I spluttered. 'Cooper.' I pointed to where I'd seen him, but he'd gone. There was no sign of him. Just a normal busy street in London, people hurrying about their business. I blinked. 'He was there... watching me... he was staring at me. Oh God, he's found me...' I reached for my phone with shaking hands. 'I need to tell the police.'

Two police officers arrived quite promptly, took details, and said they'd be in touch. They seemed to take me seriously, but a couple of days later informed me by phone that after making enquiries they'd established that Cooper was fitted with an electronic tag, which on examination showed that he was nowhere near London, let alone the Notting Hill area that morning. They told me I must have been mistaken. Logic told me they had to be right, yet... could he have slipped his tag somehow? Gerda did her best to reassure me, saying the police would know if he'd removed the tag, but the incident completely unnerved me. I felt myself slipping back into paranoia after that day. Everywhere I went I looked for Cooper, unable shake off the feeling of being watched.

I knew Gerda was worried about me and my deteriorating mental health. I could feel myself regressing, convinced he was watching me and waiting for his chance to pounce. Part of my brain, the logical part, told me that I had not seen what I thought I'd seen, but it couldn't override the fear which dominated every waking moment.

'Liebling, I have a suggestion,' Gerda said as we walked home from work one night, a few weeks after the incident in the cafe. 'I've given this a lot of thought. You can't go on like this, seeing Cooper everywhere. I think you need to get out of London. How would you feel about moving with me to Germany? To Berlin? We could get a cheap little flat there and find jobs.'

We met up with Sam the following week when he was in London for work and told him of our plans. 'I need to get away from here, Sam,' I explained. 'I can't bear living like this, seeing him everywhere.'

'I can see that, Emma,' he responded. 'I've been thinking along the same lines since your "sighting" of Cooper.' He turned to Gerda. 'And you think it'll be fairly easy to find work and somewhere to live in Berlin?'

'Yes, I'm sure, but in any event my parents live in Berlin and will help us if we have any difficulty. They're already looking out for a flat for us to rent and I know there'll be no problem getting bar work.'

'Well, I agree it could be a good move for now. Look, Christmas is going to be here in three weeks. Why don't you both come up and stay over for a few days or so?' He looked from Gerda to me. 'Mum and dad will be there too, and it'll give you a chance to see them and to say goodbye?'

When I hesitated, he continued. 'You won't need to see anyone else, Emma. No-one but family. Olivia's parents will be there and possibly Cousin Craig, at some point as Aunty Rebecca is doing the Salvation Army stuff on Christmas Day. Nobody else needs to know you'll be there. And it'll be good for mum and dad to see you again before you go. They do miss you, you know? And they'd really like to meet Gerda.'

'I think that's a great idea,' Gerda responded. 'We could fly out to Berlin after Christmas direct from Newcastle. And Sam, could I ask... would it be alright if my cousin Eric comes too?' Eric, who also rented one of the rooms in our house, was great fun and the three of us often went clubbing together.

It was all agreed and I couldn't wait for Christmas to come. I began to look forward optimistically to the move to Berlin. Another fresh start, away from all the memories and him.

CHAPTER TWENTY-FOUR

The alarm beating into her brain woke Sandra with a start. *Oh God, is it that time already?* Scrambling out of bed, she couldn't help wishing that Marek hadn't been working last night. At least, he would have woken her up in good time, with a nice cuppa. They'd been living together for a long time now and although she knew that Marek would like them to be married, she was still cautious. Although she loved him, her independence was hard-won and precious to her, and she wasn't yet ready to relinquish it. But maybe soon. Cleaning her teeth, she thought he was everything she could ever want, kind, good sense of humour, generous. And profane. She smiled, thinking of the colourful language he was prone to use. It made him sound gruff and belligerent, but underneath his rough exterior, she knew he was a decent person with a good heart.

In the bus to work, she thought about their plans for Christmas, coming up in a couple of weeks. They would both be off work, and they fancied a quiet one at home. Katie was coming over on Christmas Day, with the kids. Sandra would cook, and they'd watch the Queen's speech and all play games. Have a few glasses of wine. Then Boxing Day, she and Marek would just chill, maybe go for a walk. She alighted at her stop, still thinking about Christmas plans, when her arm was grabbed from behind, and an arm linked through hers.

'Hey, Sandra, how's things? Did you have a good weekend?' It was Anne. Without waiting for a response from Sandra, she went on to describe her weekend. 'We had the neighbours and Antonia and Declan over for supper on Saturday night. You know, the social worker and the ex-cop. You've heard me mention them before. The ones that moved here from London?'

Sandra made a non-committal grunt in response, secretly amused as she mentally christened Anne's visitors "Ant & Dec". Anne was always going on about people she had never met and most of it went straight over Sandra's head. 'They're great fun,' Anne was saying, 'I cooked my speciality, chicken in creamy tarragon sauce...' She continued, regaling Sandra with every detail of what they'd had to eat, to drink, and what they had all talked about. They reached the factory entrance and Sandra, who was only half-listening, was fishing in her bag for her security pass, when she became aware of what Anne was saying.

'... and another thing,' said Anne, lowering her voice conspiratorially, 'I got some insight into that poor girl. You know, the one found in Richardson-Dees Park. Well, it turns out the girl was adopted. She was apparently taken away from her real mother when she was just a baby. She's had a tragic life, poor thing.'

'How do you know that?' asked Sandra, her voice more strident than she'd intended. 'I mean, social workers aren't supposed to give out that sort of information, are they?'

'No, but this Antonia knows the social worker who was involved at the time, and she told us. In the strictest confidence, of course,' she said, completely oblivious of the irony. 'Apparently, the father and mother were druggies, always fighting and the kid was taken away for her own safety.'

At her words, Sandra felt a stab of guilt. A physical jolt at the reminder of her unforgivable past. Jostled as the other workers piled in, accompanied by a cacophony of greetings and banter, there was no further conversation with Anne until they were sitting next to each other at their workstations. Sandra was still feeling shaken and troubled, but Anne continued chatting as soon as they'd taken their seats, unaware of the impact of her words,

'Of course, I'm only telling you because I know you're discreet, Sandra. You're not like this lot here,' she said, waving her arm to indicate the rest of the girls. 'You're different. They would spread it around like wildfire if they got wind of it.' Her complete lack of self-awareness never ceased to amaze Sandra.

'Antonia said the girl initially went to her grandparents, but then they were killed in a head-on crash on the motorway. The kid was brought out alive, but both grandparents died.'

At Anne's words, Sandra froze. Time stood still. Her brain could not believe what her ears were hearing. *No, no, it can't be...* Shocked beyond belief, she fought hard to try to keep her distress from showing. Her brain was whirling, and she felt dizzy.

'...and then she was adopted, and brought up here to live... Hey, are you alright, Sandra? You've gone as white as a sheet... Sandra? What's wrong?' Concerned, Anne got to her feet and went over to Sandra, touching her shoulder.

'It's my head,' improvised Sandra, groaning and holding her forehead. 'I've got such a headache. It's really bad... kept me awake most of last night. Think I've got a migraine coming on...' She needed to get out of there.

Anne made sympathetic noises, fussing around, and getting her a glass of cold water, telling her she should go home if she felt ill.

'I'll take some tablets and see how it goes,' said Sandra, getting to her feet. She needed to be on her own to absorb the enormity of what she'd just heard. 'I'm going to the loo, and then I might sit in the First Aid room for a while, 'til the tablets take effect.' *This has got to be a coincidence* she told herself. It wasn't possible... surely to God it wasn't possible for this nightmare to be true.

Rushing into the ladies, she staggered into a cubicle, retching. She was violently sick, cramps assaulting her stomach as she crouched over the toilet bowl. Afterwards, drained, she wiped her face and rinsed out her mouth, before leaning against the wall, taking deep breaths trying to calm down. After a few minutes, feeling slightly less disturbed, she ran her fingers through her tousled hair, touched up her lipstick, took another deep breath and went to sit quietly in the First Aid room. Fifteen minutes later, her feelings tightly under control, she returned to the factory floor and told Anne she was feeling much better.

Not wanting Anne to make any connection between her not feeling well and what they'd been discussing, Sandra did not broach the subject of the girl again. She would bring it up tomorrow, when she'd had time to process the information and would be able to affect an air of nonchalance. In the meanwhile, she got on with her day, behaved normally, even laughed and joked with the other girls over lunch.

'Marek, I need to talk to you,' she gasped as soon as he came through the door that evening. She'd meant to discuss things calmly and dispassionately with him, but as soon as she started to speak, the tears came, and she began to shake.

'Hey, hey, sweetheart, what has happened?' Marek was all concern and kindness. He put down the jacket he was carrying and went straight to her, putting his hands on her shoulders. 'What is it?'

'I... I... don't know how to tell you… I think... I think the girl that...' she couldn't go on.

'What girl, Sandra? What is it?' Marek asked again. 'You're shaking.' He put his arms around her, holding her close for a few moments, before holding her at arm's length so that he could look at her. 'Sandra, tell me what's wrong.'

Taking a deep breath, she lowered her eyes as she said, 'I think the girl he raped is my daughter... his daughter.' She hung her head.

'What are you saying? What are you talking about?' asked Marek, gripping her shoulders. 'Look at me, Sandra,' he urged.

‘My ex, Ian Cooper,’ she explained. ‘I think he raped his own daughter.’ Seeing his incomprehension, she added, ‘The girl in Richardson-Dees Park.’

‘What? I don’t understand. Why you think that piece of shit rape your daughter?’

Sandra could see he was perplexed, unable to follow what she was trying to tell him, noticing his English became less fluent when he was upset. Haltingly, as calmly as she could, she explained what Anne had told her. ‘It’s too much of a coincidence, Marek. This kid was taken away from her parents when she was three, and then her grandparents were killed in a car accident. And she was in the car and brought out unscathed. That’s exactly what happened with Chloe. My parents were both killed outright, and she was brought out unhurt. There can’t be two cases like that. There just can’t...’

‘But... my God, how could he have found her? If you are right, and he attack his own daughter, did he know she was his own child?’ His voice carried a note of incredulity. ‘No. Nobody could be so sick?’ He was staring at her.

‘I don’t know, Marek. I don’t know,’ said Sandra. ‘I can’t believe he knew... but what a hell of a coincidence if he didn’t?’ She began pacing backwards and forwards, one hand over her mouth.

`I think we could both do with a drink. Come on, sit down, let’s talk this through calmly.’ Marek took a bottle from the fridge and poured two large glasses of white.

CHAPTER TWENTY-FIVE

'Where's dad?' asked Sam, coming into the lounge and flopping down on to the settee by the window, one leg dangling over the arm. 'Olivia wants to put the supper out soon. I thought he said he was going for a walk, but I see the car's gone?'

'He did say he was going for a walk,' said Emma. 'Needed to clear his head.'

'He's been acting oddly lately,' said Rachel. 'I don't know what's got into him.' She walked to the window, peering out into the darkness in a futile attempt to see Tommy. 'I mean, where on earth can he have gone? It's pitch black out there now.'

'I've noticed he's been extra grumpy this holiday,' said Sam. 'He's always a cantankerous sod, but he seems much worse than usual. I know he's worried about you, Emma, with that paedophile being back on the streets. But we all are, and we're not acting like him. There seems to be something else bothering him. Any idea what?' He unwound his legs and stood up. 'Hey, Emma, you don't think he's upset that you and Gerda are an item, do you? You know how homophobic he can be.'

Emma, who had joined her mother at the window, turned around hands on hips. 'Well why don't you call a spade a spade brother?' she chortled. Turning to Gerda curled up on one of the velvet easy chairs, she said, 'Honestly, Gerda, only a brother would ask that. Take no notice of him.' She addressed Sam again, 'If you must know, Dad's been very nice to Gerda and to Eric. He's pleased I've got some good friends to support me.'

'It's nothing to do with that, Sam,' added Rachel. 'He just wants her to be happy after everything she's been through.' She headed for the kitchen. 'I'll tell Olivia not to wait for him. We can eat now, and his meal can always be heated up when he finally decides to come home.'

'Great. I'm starving,' muttered Eric.

'When he does get back, I'll see if I can get to the bottom of what's bothering him. He might talk to me, you know, man to man,' suggested Sam.

'Well, good luck with that. He won't speak to me about what's wrong. He just gets angry and shouts at me to leave him alone.'

Rachel could tell by Olivia's demeanour that she was annoyed at Tommy's absence. She didn't blame her. She'd prepared a tasty supper, delicious teriyaki chicken with fried rice and a Greek salad with avocado and feta cheese. After they had eaten and were busy stacking the dishes in the dishwasher, Rachel's phone rang, and she walked into the hall to take the call.

'That was your dad,' she said, worry etched into her face as she came back into the kitchen. 'He says he's not coming back tonight. Says he's fine but needs some space. We're not to worry; he'll be back in the morning. He won't even tell me where he is.' She looked from Sam to Olivia. 'What on earth is going on?' she asked, beginning to chew at her nail again. 'He's never done anything like this before. Just stayed out and not told me where he is or what he's doing? It's all very strange. You don't think he could be having an affair do you, Sam?'

Sam laughed harshly. 'Who would want a grumpy old git like him?' he asked. 'No, I'd rule out another woman. But wish I bloody knew what's in his head,' said Sam, his face darkening. 'Let's see if I can find out. Where's my phone?' Picking up his mobile from where it was charging on the nearby dresser, he stabbed at the keypad and put the phone to his ear. Freeing it from its anchor, he paced the room, and Rachel could hear the muffled sound of the ringtone, then the automatic voice telling him to leave a message. 'Dad, it's Sam. Call me when you pick up this message. You've got us all worried about you, and for God's sake it's Christmas and we're all supposed to be enjoying ourselves. This is really not fair on mum or any of us.' Sam disconnected the call and threw his phone on to the worktop. 'Bloody switched off,' he growled. 'What the fuck is he playing at? He's acting like a bloody moron. All the work you've put into this Christmas, Olivia, and he has to go and do something like this. It's not bloody well on.'

CHAPTER TWENTY-SIX

January 2023

Standing in front of the white board in the Murder Investigation Room, Gayle prepared to address her investigation team of twenty, hastily assembled that morning. Many had interrupted their weekend to come in. Observing them, she saw a diverse bunch, all shapes, sizes, colours and gender. Most were detectives she knew well and worked with regularly, but she'd also drafted in a few uniforms to help with the groundwork. As usual, there were a couple of civilians on the team. One of them, Wendy, who had been office manager it seemed forever, was a real gem. Gayle knew she could rely on her to make sure all the paperwork and documentation was in order, everything cross-checked and ship-shape, and the white board kept updated, all so vital in a complex murder enquiry.

'Right, everyone. For those of you that don't know me, I'm DCI Gayle Jones. I'm heading up this enquiry into the murder of an unidentified male found in Rothbury yesterday afternoon. Before we start, I'd like to thank those of you who've given up your weekend to come in and help on this investigation.' She perched on the edge of a desk, pushed up the sleeves of her black sweater, and continued.

'The body was found by a dog walker. A former colleague as it happens, former DI Joe Barnes. Some of you will know him.' There were a few murmurs of assent. 'The body was located at the bottom of a hill at the end of Hillside Road, in Rothbury.' She half turned to point to the map pinned to the White Board, on which the location had been highlighted with a red marker. 'The victim's body was hidden under the snow, but the dog sniffed it out and began pawing at the snow, exposing a foot. Joe Barnes immediately contacted us and protected the scene until forensics got there.'

Gayle got to her feet and turned to scoop a pile of photographs from the desk. 'These are the crime scene photos,' she said, beginning to distribute them amongst the team. 'Some of them are pretty graphic. As you can see, the face has been extensively mutilated; criss-crossed with slashes. He's unrecognisable. There's a stab wound to the abdomen too, as you can see... and the genitals have been almost hacked off.' There was a gasp from one of the younger members of the team.

As the photos were passed around, the team got their first look at the body. They could see that the victim, still surrounded by piles of snow, was dressed in a heavily bloodstained dark blue hoodie, wet with melting snow, a tear just visible where the knife had been thrust through the fabric. Faded jeans, and Calvin Klein boxers, also covered in dark blood, were pulled part-way down, almost to his knees, blood-soaked grey trainers on his feet. Wide gashes, black with blood, where the knife had done its work stood out starkly against the pale skin of his face, one of his eyes just a mangled mess. More blood around the genital region, which resembled a pile of bloody offal. The last few photos, taken after the medical examiner had pulled up the top to expose the chest, showed a wide gash to the abdomen, surrounded by dark wiry hair matted with blood.

'DNA samples were taken late last night and are being processed as we speak,' said Gayle, once everyone had had a chance to study the prints. 'And the PM is being carried out later this morning. In the meantime, we need to try to find out who he is. There was no identification on him, but you might have noticed there's a small tattoo on his right shoulder.' She held up one of the photographs, pointing to a colourful snake on the shoulder, about seven centimetres long. Picked out in vivid purple, pink and green, it was poised as if to strike, its forked tongue protruding from its open jaws.

Gayle continued. 'Whoever did this seems to have been fuelled by rage. Why? This might become apparent, once we've identified the victim, but, if necessary, we'll get a psychological profile done. Could help identify some characteristics of the perpetrator.' She checked her notes before continuing. 'The victim's clothing was designer. Expensive. He was wearing a gold Tag Huer watch and a heavy gold necklace. His age is estimated to be around early forties. He's five feet eleven and a half, and as you can see in the photos, thinning, dark brown hair, medium build.' She looked around at her team, 'Let's hope he's on the DNA database.

'We urgently need to know who this guy is. If the DNA doesn't produce a result, we'll put out an appeal – someone will recognise that tattoo.' Gayle was pacing backwards and forwards as she spoke, playing with a locket at her neck. 'Georgia, see if you can find out anything about the tattoo. If we can find out who did it, we could get a name...'

There were no questions, and Gayle left the room, her mind buzzing. She hadn't slept much last night. It was always the same at the start of a murder enquiry, the adrenalin would kick in and her energy levels would soar. Her mind went into overdrive and sleep was out of the question.

The next morning, by the time she arrived at the mortuary and donned protective clothing, David was already working on the body, assisted by a young male technician. Two more white-coated assistants were working in the background. As Gayle entered the autopsy suite, David looked up, peering at her over his glasses.

'Morning, Gayle. You got here then?' he queried. A rhetorical question. Without further preamble, he went on, 'I can tell you I was right, he wasn't killed where he was found. Livor clearly shows the body has been moved; also, there wasn't enough blood in situ.'

'So, he was killed elsewhere, and the body dumped in the field then?'

'That's right,' said David, bending his portly frame further over the body to check something. 'Found one stab wound to the abdomen, as well as several slashes to the face and of course the genital mutilation.'

Gayle quickly adjusted her mask, as the familiar, cloying smell of formaldehyde hit her nostrils.

David continued, 'Three spinal fractures, inflicted post-mortem.'

'The spine was broken after he was already dead?' she asked, approaching the gurney, where she could see that the Y incision had already been made. Slippery intestines, gleaming red and blue, were lying in a large stainless-steel dish on a side table. The ribs had been prised apart, revealing the heart still in place within the vast cavity. 'How can you tell it was post-mortem?' She was intrigued.

'The features of the fractures in 'dry' or post-mortem bone differ from those in 'fresh' bone. The edges have different characteristics and are more jagged in appearance. Also, there's no adherence of bone fragments or radiating or concentric fracture lines. So, definitely broken post-mortem. At first, I thought the body could have been dropped as it was being moved, but the damage to the spine and extensive bruising to the back, is too severe for that sort of scenario. Three vertebral compression fractures, two of them in the cervical spine, one in the neck area,' he explained, indicating the back of his neck. 'I've seen these types of fracture following road traffic accidents, where the body experiences high velocity impact.'

Gayle rubbed the back of her neck. 'Hmm... Interesting. What about the genital and facial mutilation? Please say that was inflicted post-mortem too'

'Again, definitely post-mortem, I'm pleased to report.' David nodded.

'Well, that's a relief,' said Gayle. 'What about the head injury? Was that the cause of death?'

David grunted in mock exasperation. 'No. Be patient, Gayle, I'm coming to cause of death soon. The head injury was also sustained post-mortem... probably at the same time the spine was broken. Something traumatic happened to his body after he'd been killed. Now... let me take a closer look at this heart.' He turned back to the gurney.

Gayle watched him as he lifted the heart out of its dark cave, using both hands, and carefully placed it in a metal dish, before carrying it over to a nearby table. 'If I'm not mistaken,' he said, placing his hands on the table and peering into the dish, 'I think we'll find the cause of death here. Looks like the stab wound penetrated the heart. I'll be able to confirm it when I've taken a closer look,'

Gayle glanced at the muscle, glistening red in the dish. It amazed her that she was able to observe post-mortems so dispassionately these days. Her first experiences in the autopsy suite had made her throw up. Once, to her shame, she'd actually fainted. *What a cliché* she thought.

'We found a cut in the top the victim was wearing, consistent with a blade being pushed through, and fibres from the top are present in the external part of the incision. Inflicted with a four-inch-long serrated blade, I'd say.'

Gayle watched as he lifted the heart from the dish and placed it carefully on to the slab, before commencing a detailed examination, peering at the organ, photographing, prodding, measuring, cutting, and calculating. Once he was satisfied his examination was complete, he placed the organ back in the dish, and Gayle listened carefully as he dictated his report.

'Dissection of the thorax cavity revealed two wounds in the chest wall. The upper wound was present in the fourth inter-coastal space near the left anterior axillary line, directed upwards, backwards, and medially, perforating the upper part of lower lobe of left lung. The second wound was present in the fifth inter-coastal space.'

Two wounds? thought Gayle, surprised. *But surely there was only one entry wound on the chest?*

'The fatal injury was a vertically placed stab wound on the chest at the level of left anterior axillary line. After carefully reconstructing the direction of stab... it was found that the blade of the knife entered the chest at an angle directed from a lateral aspect.

'Externally there was a single wound of entry, but internally there were two separate tracks entering the chest cavity through two separate inter-coastal spaces. Hence it indicates the weapon was first thrust in, partially out and in again in a different direction.' He turned to his assistant. 'I'm taking a break now, Monty,' he said. 'You finish up here and put him back in the fridge when you've finished.'

As they left the suite, David simplified his findings, 'In other words, Gayle, he was unlawfully killed by a stab wound to the heart. Knife thrust in...' he mimed stabbing Gayle, 'then partially withdrawn,' he demonstrated, pulling his hand slightly back, before thrusting the imaginary knife back in, at a slightly different angle, 'then thrust hard into the abdomen with a more upwards trajectory.'

'So, there was just the one external stab wound. I wondered what you meant when you mentioned two wounds. Why would someone do it like that?' asked Gayle, trying to envisage the stabbing.

'Could be there was a struggle and the victim moved away a bit. Or the perp hadn't realised how tough the skin is and hadn't thrust hard enough at first. Got a better grip and finished the job properly.'

'Any idea of timescale?' asked Gayle, bending over and balancing on one leg as she removed her protective overalls.

'Difficult to tell with any precision,' said David, putting his overalls into the bin. The body has been preserved in the snow; therefore, normal decomposition timescales don't apply because insect activity is curtailed. Makes it much harder to be precise about the date of death.' He paused, 'However, there were a couple of inches of snow spread evenly on the ground beneath the body, therefore I believe it was put there on the first day the snow fell. I've looked it up and established that was on the twenty-seventh of December. You might recall on that day there were blizzards and very heavy snowfall. That was three weeks ago, and my best guess is that he was killed no more than a day or two before his body was dumped.'

'So, if you're right, we're looking at date of death being around the twenty fifth of December?'

'As I say, it's hard to give a definitive date,' he spread his hands, 'but my best guess is sometime between the twenty-fifth and the twenty-seventh of December. To be on the safe side, probably best to work on, say, twenty-fourth to the twenty-seventh.'

'Could the body have been buried in the snow after the twenty-seventh?' asked Gayle.

'I don't think so. It's very unlikely in those circumstances that the snow would be so evenly distributed under the body. There was nothing to indicate that either the snow or the ground around the body had been disturbed.'

'Ok, that gives us something to work on,' said Gayle. 'What about the fractures to the spine and the head injury? How could those have been sustained?' she asked, scratching her head.

'Well, Gayle, this is quite interesting,' said David, looking at her over the top of his rimless glasses. 'Because the spinal fractures are consistent with the body being thrown against something with great force, I returned earlier this morning to take another look at where he was found. I'm pretty sure the fractures, including the head injury, were caused by the body being flung against the oak tree beneath which it was found. There are gnarled bits on the trunk of the tree which correspond with marks on the flesh of his back, as well as bits of bark embedded in the victim's clothing and hair.'

'Bloody hell,' exclaimed Gayle, still scratching her head. 'Let me get this right. He, or rather his body, was thrown against the tree with enough force to fracture his spine in three places?'

'That about sums it up,' said David with a wry grin. 'Come into the office and I'll show you the evidence.' Walking ahead, he pushed the door, holding it open for Gayle to enter. Going to his computer sitting on the desk, he deftly brought up images of the victim's back, pointing out purple marks and lesions at intervals down the spine. 'Now, if you look at the tree,' he said, bringing up a close-up showing the trunk of the oak, 'you can see where these gnarled bits protrude...' He pointed out the relevant bits, before putting the two images side by side on the screen. Gayle could immediately see how the marks on the body corresponded to the contours of the tree trunk.

She frowned, peering closely at the screen. 'So how the hell was that done?' she muttered, talking to herself, trying to picture the scene. 'It would need to be thrown with some force... one person couldn't do it... maybe more than one could...?'

'Possibly, but it would take two very strong people to propel it with enough force, to produce such severe injuries,' he said, picking up his plaid jacket from the back of his chair, and shrugging into it.

'But how else could it have been done, I wonder,' said Gayle running her fingers through her hair, now tousled from wearing the cap.

David chuckled. 'That's your department, I'm afraid... but I will be extremely interested to know what your findings are.' He opened the door and stood back to allow Gayle to go ahead. *Ever the gentleman* thought Gayle.

'No theories then David? Not like you to be backward in coming forward,' she teased.

'Not this time, I'm afraid. Bit of a mystery. Good luck in solving it, Detective Chief Inspector.'

CHAPTER TWENTY-SEVEN

'Cause of death was a stab wound to the heart,' began Gayle, before describing what the pathologist had told her about the knife being thrust in twice. 'And the pathologist has found that he was killed elsewhere, and the body moved to where it was found.

'The mutilations to the face and genitalia were carried out post-mortem,' she said, leaning against the desk, hands gripping the edges. 'Interestingly, there were other significant injuries, also caused post-mortem. The victim's spine was broken in three places, the result of a substantial impact. As you can see from the crime photos,' she half turned and waved towards the white board behind her, 'the body was found lying at the bottom of a large oak tree. The surgeon believes the injuries are consistent with the body being thrown with great force against that tree.' She had the full attention of the whole room. 'We need to find out how that happened.'

'Is there evidence to confirm the body hit the tree?' asked one of the team.

'Just coming to that,' said Gayle. 'Look at this.' She stood up and passed around a photocopy of the split screen showing the injuries to the spine alongside the profile of the bark of the tree. 'According to the pathologist, the injuries to the spine exactly match the profile of the trunk of the tree. He took detailed measurements to establish that as a fact. Also, there were bits of bark embedded in the vic's clothing and hair. So, the pathologist is in no doubt that the fractures were caused by the body colliding with the tree with some considerable force. The question is, how?'

Pacing around, worrying her locket, she went on. 'Let's put that to one side for now. What we do know is that the vic lay there from the first day the snow fell. There were two inches of snow underneath the body. If you recall, the blizzard came suddenly and unexpectedly, a really heavy snowfall. That was on the twenty seventh of December. Met records show that several inches fell that night and it continued to snow, off and on, over the course of the following two weeks. The body will have very quickly become covered.' She resumed her seat on the desk. 'So, he was killed on or before the twenty-seventh, probably within two to three days, so we're looking at date of death twenty-fourth, fifth, sixth or possibly twenty-seventh of December.' She paused, 'Nice Christmas present.'

Gayle glanced at her phone as it vibrated. 'Hold on a sec...' she put her hand up, palm forward. 'Hi David,' she said, 'You got something for me...?' She listened for a while, her excitement building. 'That's great... thanks.' *Bloody hell,* she thought, feeling the familiar surge of adrenalin. Running her fingers through her short, spiky hair, she raised her head and surveyed her team.

'This is great, everyone. We have a positive ID on our John Doe from the DNA results. He's already on our database,' she announced. 'Now we can really get moving.' A murmur of excitement rippled through the team. 'His name is Ian Cooper. He's a convicted paedophile. Some of you will remember him. He was found guilty of raping an eleven-year-old girl in Richardson-Dees Park, around seven years ago?'

'I remember that case. You worked on that one yourself didn't you, Boss?' asked DS Kris Peterson.

'I did, Kris. I should have been able to recognise him, but with his face in that condition, there wasn't much chance of that.' She grimaced before turning to Wendy, 'See if you can find a fairly recent photo.' She continued, 'He was given fourteen years, and served seven. We were notified of his early release a few weeks ago. So, he served only seven years for a horrific attack on a child. No wonder people are upset.' She looked around the sea of faces. 'Now, I wonder who would want to murder and mutilate a paedophile. Let's find out.'

She stood up and resumed pacing. 'We need to find out where he was living – no doubt probation will know,' she said. 'Georgia, find out who his probation officer was. The sooner we can check out his accommodation, the better... If that's where he was murdered, we'll at least have a crime scene. It could possibly be a bail hostel or ex-offender place. Find out when he last reported in.'

She came to a halt in front of Kris. 'We'll have to notify his family, get a formal identification. Kris, see if you can trace any relatives. And we want to know everything he's done; everyone he's seen since he got out of prison. Go to it, we'll reconvene at four. Buzz me before then if there's anything significant.'

Back in her office, Gayle was deep in thought when her mobile lit up, belting out her ringtone. 'DCI Jones,' she answered automatically, before noticing it was her mother calling. 'Hello Mum, what's up?' Silence. 'Mum, it's Gayle. Are you ok?'

'Yes... I just wondered if you'll be calling in to see me tonight... on your way home?' Her voice sounded thin and reedy to Gayle.

'Oh mum, I'm in the middle of a big case. Not sure I can make it tonight. No idea what time I'll get home. Can it wait til the morning? I'll swing by on the way to work?'

'Oh dear... well... alright then, if you're busy...' Her mother rang off, leaving Gayle feeling worried and unsettled. It was unusual for her mother to call her at work and Gayle knew she wouldn't have done so without a good reason. She made up her mind and went in search of Georgia. Finding her at her desk, phone to her ear, she waited until she finished the call. 'Georgia, I've got a family crisis. Need to dash off. Hopefully I won't be long, but if I'm not back for the briefing, can you take over for me please?'

'No problem, boss,' she said, looking up at her. 'I hope everything's ok.'

Driving towards Heaton, Gayle chewed her lip, thinking about her mum. Since her diagnosis of cancer seven years ago, and its apparent eradication with radio therapy, her mum had been able to live a fairly normal life, until the last three years or so. Although the doctors had told Gayle that a recurrence of cancer was likely at some stage, her mum had seemed so well in the aftermath of the treatment that Gayle had begun to hope the prognosis was wrong. Despite being warned that the improvement would in all probability be temporary, Gayle had not passed this information on to her mother, believing it would upset her and make her less optimistic about the future.

The radiotherapy had shrunk the tumour significantly, giving her mum a new lease of life. Gayle had been able to move out of her mother's house and into her new flat, as her mum's health improved dramatically. For about three years, her mother had been able to resume living a normal life, back to her happy, energetic self. But, over the last few years, Gayle had noticed a gradual deterioration in her. She seemed to be tired a lot of the time and her skin had lost its healthy glow. Never one to complain about how she was feeling, Gayle hadn't realised just how significant the deterioration was until her mum collapsed one day at home. That had been a couple of weeks ago, and now the results of various tests were awaited. Had the cancer spread? Gayle had begun to suspect that it had. *Oh, please, please, please don't let it be cancer again* she prayed, unshed tears blurring her vision as she drove.

A couple of harrowing hours later, hurrying back to the station, her mother having been admitted to hospital with breathing difficulties, Gayle sighed deeply, the anxious knot always present in her stomach, tightening. *At least she's safe for the moment. In the best place for now* she told herself, knowing that big decisions would soon have to be made as to her mother's future care. Forcing herself to park her worries for the time being, she turned her attention to the case. Her thoughts went back to the last time she'd seen Ian Cooper, seven years ago. It seemed like yesterday. It had been a harrowing case. *Always is when a child is involved*, she thought. She remembered her mixed feelings when Cooper cynically changed his plea to guilty at the last minute. The overwhelming evidence against him left his counsel little choice but to encourage a guilty plea. Cooper was no doubt hoping pleading guilty would earn him some brownie points with the judge. Later, when pronouncing sentence, the judge told Cooper he needed to be taken off the streets for a long time, to keep children safe. He gave him fourteen years, knowing Cooper wouldn't have to serve the full term. What a bloody farce. Out in seven. How was that keeping children safe? And now Cooper was dead. Funny old world.

She rushed in just as the briefing was getting started. 'I'm back Georgia. Thanks for getting things underway,' she said, flashing her a smile. Having the newly promoted Georgia as her second in command was working out well although she still missed Dave. He'd been promoted to DCI, as she knew was inevitable, accepted a post with the Met, and moved to London. Pity really, they'd made such a great team, but nothing stays the same forever and she knew that Dave was destined to be a high flyer.

'No bother, boss. I'm just about to give my update.' She raised her eyebrows and asked sotto voce 'Everything ok?' Gayle nodded before taking a seat to listen to Georgia, who tucked some of her unruly curls behind one ear before walking around to stand near the white board. 'We have an address for Ian Cooper,' she informed the team. Glancing down at her notes, she continued. 'Not a bail hostel or half-way house, far from it. He lived in Julian Court, South Shields. The penthouse suite, overlooking the sea front. He's owned it for the last four years. Very nice. He had it as a buy-to-let but didn't renew the tenancy once he knew he was to be released. We've got it secured, pending forensics going in.

'I've spoken to his probation officer, Gillian Shaw. She's been concerned that Cooper's been out of contact. She last spoke to him, on his mobile, on the twenty-third of December, but has been unable to get in touch with him since. She visited his flat on the twenty-eighth of December, but there was no response when she rang the bell and banged on the door. She didn't notice anything untoward on her visit. There's an outstanding warrant for breach of bail conditions.'

'Thanks Georgia,' Gayle said, turning to Kris. 'What about family, Kris?'

'We've been unable to trace any family, boss. His parents are deceased and there are no siblings. His partner abandoned him when he went to prison, and he has no children. No close friends have been found yet. Seems he was quite a loner.'

'Gillian Shaw is prepared to ID him in the absence of anyone else who can do it,' interjected Georgia.

'We'll take her up on that, Georgia,' instructed Gayle. 'Right now, we need to check out the flat. See if we've got ourselves a crime scene. We'll need to speak to all the other residents. Joe,' she turned to a DS standing nearby, 'can you organise door to door enquiries around his flat; find out when he was last seen? And check if there's any CCTV.

'Kris, check his mobile, computer, iPad, whatever forensics find. All the usual stuff.' Gayle ticked off each action, using her fingers. 'In due course, we'll need to interview the parents of Eva, the eleven-year-old who was attacked. And Eva herself; she'll be eighteen now. They moved away from Wallsend after the attack; we need to find where they're living now. Wendy, see if you can get an address. I'm sure she has a brother too. Find out where he lives. Close family would have a strong motive. It's possible that one of them may have been so pissed off at Cooper getting out of prison early, after what he did to Eva, they decided to do away with him. Right,' she said, easing off the desk and looking around the room. 'Any other ideas at this stage? Ok, let's get to it. You come with me, Georgia; we'll start with his flat. Kris, you follow with a couple of the team.'

CHAPTER TWENTY-EIGHT

'You spent a lot of time with the Simpsons when you were their Family Liaison Officer,' said Gayle, glancing at Georgia as she deftly steered the car through road works at the exit to the Tyne Tunnel. 'Do you think the father, Tommy Simpson, would be capable of killing and mutilating Cooper?'

'Well, I remember he was a bad-tempered bugger, but...'

The shrill ringtones of Gayle's mobile interrupted the conversation, a loud booming voice filling the car.

'Gayle? Joe Barnes here.'

'Joe? Hi. To what do I owe this pleasure?' Joe and Gayle went way back, since she first returned to Newcastle after transferring to the Northumbrian force, as a young Detective Constable. Still smarting from the break-up of her previous long-term relationship, she found a sympathetic ear from Joe who had taken her under his wing. She had got hammered one night at a session in the local after work and had become maudlin, crying over her ex. Joe was sympathetic and offered a shoulder to cry on. He ended up taking her home and had to literally carry her into her flat and put her to bed. When she woke up the next day, with the mother of all hangovers, she vaguely remembered wrapping her arms around his neck and asking him to get into bed with her. To his credit, he refused and quietly left after putting a glass of water on her bedside table, alongside a strip of Anadin he must have found in the bathroom cabinet. She could barely face him the following day at the Station, and avoided being near him, but eventually he cornered her in the tearoom.

'Don't look so embarrassed, DC Jones,' he'd said to her, with a twinkle in his eye. 'Look, I was very tempted last night, you're a beautiful girl, but I don't take advantage of inebriated, upset ladies.' He winked at her, before adding 'And besides, I'm old enough to be your father... also my wife wouldn't like it.' He laughed.

After that, they'd formed an unlikely bond, with Joe taking a paternal interest in her career progression at work. When he retired, some six years ago, she'd been lost without him. At first, they'd kept in regular contact, but this had dwindled over time. When his wife died, a couple of years ago, she'd gone to the funeral and visited him once or twice afterwards, but she hadn't seen anything of him recently.

'I've been thinking,' Joe said. 'I heard about the injuries to the body Jess found... the fractures to the spine corresponding to the profile of the tree...'

'Still keeping a keen an interest in the force then Joe? Who's been telling you about our investigation? You're supposed to be retired.' Gayle grinned to herself. She knew that Joe kept his finger on the pulse and liked to keep himself up to date with interesting cases.

'I've got a theory, Gayle. Could help. You might not have heard about it, but the night of the big snowstorm, there was a car accident in Rothbury. Car went into a skid in the snow on Hillside Road, missed the hairpin bend and went over the top. It ended up in the field below. The field where the body was found.'

'I wasn't aware of the accident, Joe. Go on,' said Gayle, intrigued.

'The driver managed to get out before the car went over the top. No injuries or fatalities, so no reason to involve the police,' he explained. 'It made the front page of the Rothbury Gazette, but I don't imagine that's a paper you would ever see in your neck of the woods?'

'True...' she said.

'Well, the farmer who towed the car away the next day happens to be a neighbour of mine, and he told me what a mess the car was in.

Complete write-off. That's quite a steep drop there, and he told me the car will have bounced off boulders and probably rolled on the way down. He said the boot lid was almost ripped off, just attached by one corner.' He paused before getting to the point and a little frisson of excitement passed through Gayle as she realised where this was going. 'Is it feasible that the body was in the boot and was flung out as the car descended?' He paused again. 'A long shot, but worth looking at. It could account for the force with which the body hit the tree? And the blizzard was so dense, and went on all night, that come daylight the body would be completely covered.'

'I suppose that's possible, Joe... there was a couple of inches of snow underneath the body, so it had to have been put there on the night of the blizzard ... as you say, worth following up. Let's see where it takes us.'

'If I turn out to be right, you'll owe me a pint or two, mind,' he said, and Gayle could hear the laughter in his voice. 'Time we had a little catch-up girl.'

'As much as you can drink, Joe. This could be a good line of enquiry.' She was beginning to feel optimistic at having a possible breakthrough this early in the case.

'I'll hold you to that, young lady,' he teased. 'Now, go find your car driver. Could be an open and shut case for you. I'll text over the farmer's contact details; his name is Bill Dawson. Good luck.'

'I'll let you know how we get on,' said Gayle, noticing that it had begun to rain quite heavily. 'And Joe,' she added, 'thank you.' She disconnected the call and within a few seconds it pinged as Joe's text came in. She turned to Georgia, 'Had you heard anything about that accident?'

'Come to think of it, I did hear something about it at the time,' said Georgia, braking carefully on the wet road as they approached a bend. 'But I never gave it another thought... I suppose if the accident took place the same night the snow started, it would seem to be too much of a coincidence for there to be no connection?'

'Exactly... and I don't like coincidences... So, let's picture the scene,' said Gayle. 'The perp is driving in Rothbury, perhaps looking for a suitable place to dump a body... Hillside Road is a dead end for vehicles, with dense woods at the far end. For some reason, he doesn't dump the body in the woods – could be there were people around or something. He drives back along Hillside Road, the car goes into a skid, hits the embankment, but he manages to get out. Then the car goes over the top, crashing down the incline. On the way, the boot's ripped open and the body is flung out, hitting the tree before falling beneath it... it's soon covered in snow. Feasible, I suppose. David used the word 'propelled' to describe the body hitting the tree...' She picked up her phone and tapped in a number.

'Yes, definitely possible,' muttered Georgia, leaning forward the better to concentrate. The rain was now pelting heavily against the windscreen, the wipers working overtime like a noisy metronome in a futile attempt to cope with the deluge.

'Kris,' said Gayle when the phone was answered, raising her voice above the monotonous thud of the wipers and the drumming of the rain on the roof. 'Can you hear me ok? It's pissing down here. Listen, I need you to investigate a car accident that took place on the night of the twenty-seventh of December, in Rothbury. It might be connected to the investigation. A car went over the top at the hairpin bend on Hillside Road. Take some of the team. Find out what happened to the driver, and if there were any witnesses. In particular, find out what happened to the car. I'm told a local farmer towed it to a nearby garage. I'll forward his details. We need to examine that car urgently.' She ended the call, sent him the details, and put the phone in her pocket.

'Here we are,' announced Georgia, pulling into a small car park at the side of a smart three-storey block of flats. 'And the rain seems to be easing up a bit, thank God. Looks like forensics are already here,' she added, nodding towards the van used by the forensics team.

To the front of the building were landscaped gardens, with grassy areas and raised flower beds. Brick walkways led to small seating areas, with cast iron benches overlooking the sea. Gayle thought it would be a pleasant space to sit with a book on a sunny afternoon.

Georgia had spoken too soon. As they left the car, the heavens opened again. The kind of rain that soaks you to the skin in a few seconds. But the weather wasn't going to dampen Gayle's spirits today. She pulled up her hood, feeling optimistic. Her gut was telling her that she'd just been handed a significant lead. Looking at the facade, her eyes strayed to the windows at the very top of the building as she wondered what they would find there. Is this where he was killed?

Entering the foyer, Gayle greeted the officer on duty before looking around. To the right was a staircase, beside which Gayle spotted a lift. To the left, against the wall was a console table on which a vase of silk flowers provided a splash of coral against the subdued tones of the light grey walls and darker grey carpeting.

'Forensics are already here, ma'am,' the constable informed her. 'Top floor apartment. There's a lift over there.'

'Let's take the stairs, it's healthier,' said Gayle. Ignoring Georgia's grimace, she led the way up the four short flights to the top floor. The door to the flat was wide open, a stocky uniformed officer slouching in the doorway.

'Morning, ma'am,' the PC said, straightening up and picking up two sets of protective clothing for them. Gayle could see the white-suited forensic team at work within.

As they entered the narrow hall, their shoe covers made scuffing noises on the wooden boards. Her nose wrinkled in distaste at the stale air tinged with the unmistakable rusty smell of blood. From the first doorway, Gayle examined a spacious living room. An impressive space, its ceiling rising to an apex with dark wooden beams forming a high arch. French doors opened onto a spacious balcony, beyond which she could see a panoramic view of the North Sea, looking cold and grey in the rain and liberally speckled with white horses. The room was sparsely furnished, minimalist Gayle decided. A large black leather corner settee with bright geometric scatter cushions, a black wrought iron coffee table with a thick glass top and a huge television resting on a polished black stand.

They walked on, along the passageway towards the kitchen where a lot of activity seemed to be taking place. Passing a large bedroom on the way, she could see one of the forensics team on his knees bagging the contents of the bedside cabinet.

'Found anything interesting, Martin?' she asked him.

'Got an array of bloody sex toys in here,' he muttered. 'What the hell's this?' he asked, holding up a black object shaped a bit like a large baby's dummy.

'Butt plug,' announced Georgia.

They both stared at her. 'A what?' asked Gayle. 'No, don't tell me. I've obviously led a very sheltered life.'

Martin grunted. 'Me too,' he said, shaking his head. 'Bloody butt plug indeed. We've bagged quite a bit of stuff. There's a phone and a laptop... be interesting to see what's on there. Hard-core kiddie-porn magazines under the bed.' He pulled a face, muttering, 'Filthy ponce,' as he got to his feet. Coming into the hallway, he gestured towards the kitchen. 'Half-eaten sandwich in the kitchen area... full cuppa left on the bench. Looks as though his snack was interrupted. Pretty clear that's where he was killed. Blood everywhere,' he said. 'There's been an attempt to clean it up, but there's plenty in between the tiles and up the units and the bit of the floor that's carpeted is saturated.' He stood near the doorway, pointing out the carpeted area. 'We'll know for definite when we get the blood analysed.'

Gayle peered into the kitchen, a huge rectangular space, pale grey floor tiles at one side, carpeting to the right delineating the dining area.

'Ok if we go in?' she asked.

'Stick to the tiled area and you should be ok,' said Martin, glancing down at their shoe covers.

Gayle stepped over the threshold and looked around. An enormous lantern light in the roof lent an impressive height to the room, flooding the kitchen with light, despite the dullness of the day. To the left, a vast number of white, high gloss units, black marble worktops and an impressive range cooker. To the right of the doorway, a dining area incorporating a large, horseshoe-shaped, built-in bench with black cushions forming a semi-circle around a large, oval shaped white marble table with a black wrought iron pedestal. Four black wrought iron chairs completed the effect. These were presently stacked on top of the table, under which a technician was busy removing samples from the dark grey carpet. Gayle could hear squelching noises as he moved, his overalls red with blood at the knees.

'You can hear that bit is wet,' Martin said, indicating the carpet. 'Someone bled out there. We'll get the analysis done as soon as possible.'

'What's through here?' asked Gayle, crossing the tiled area towards a door on the far side of the room. It opened easily on to a short corridor leading to a staircase. 'Let's take a look down here Georgia.' They descended the stairs, which they found led to a communal fire exit. 'Shoe covers off,' she instructed as they reached the bottom, before pushing open the door into the driving rain, and finding herself in a car park devoid of cars. 'It's quiet here,' she said, pulling the hood of her parka further around her face as the rain drove straight at them. 'Wonder where the residents park their cars?' Heads down, they battled to the end of the block where the question was answered. There was a second parking area there, marked out with the numbers of each property.

'Must be an overspill car park at the back,' said Georgia. 'Maybe for visitors.'

'Yeah. Let's get back inside out of this bloody rain.' As they hurriedly retraced their steps, Gayle looked up at the rear edifice. 'A vehicle could leave this area without being seen by anyone in the block. Those windows look too high.'

Once back in the kitchen, Georgia looked around. 'You're right, boss,' she said, looking up. Apart from that bloody big roof-light thing, the only other windows in here are those narrow ones, high up. More like skylights, just to let more light in rather than provide a view out.'

'Go and check a couple of the flats on the lower levels,' Gayle instructed. 'Just to confirm all the kitchen windows are as high as these. If they are, it would have been easy enough to get a body through the fire exit and into the boot of a car without anyone seeing anything.' Gayle walked through to the living room, where Martin was dusting the door frame for prints. 'Martin, make sure you check the rear exit,' she said, pointing her thumb towards the back door. 'That's probably the way the body was taken out. Quiet. Out of sight.'

'Yes, ma'am. Coming to that next,' snapped Martin.

Realising he'd taken offence, Gayle grinned, and put her hand up. 'Trying to teach my granny to suck eggs again.' She got a rueful grin from Martin in return. 'Ok boys,' she called out, 'we'll get back to the ranch and leave you guys to finish off here.'

CHAPTER TWENTY-NINE

'Briefing in ten,' called Gayle, ducking into the ladies. *This place could do with a coat of paint* she thought for the umpteenth time, looking around at the dingy green walls and scuffed vinyl flooring. As she washed her hands, she leaned forward and studied her face in the speckled mirror. The dark circles beneath her eyes didn't look too bad today and the product she'd used on her freshly washed hair was holding the spiky urchin look in place. A touch of lip gloss and she was ready to address her team.

In the corridor, she almost collided with DS Kris Peterson, as he hurried through the door, wiping the rain off his face with one hand, 'Just got back from Rothbury...'

'Anything interesting?'

'Yes,' said Kris, now mopping his face with a handkerchief. 'God, it's wild out there.'

He started to give Gayle a brief summary of his findings, but she interrupted. 'On second thoughts, Kris, we're going to start in about five minutes, so why don't you get yourself dried off and grab a coffee. You can bring me up to speed in the briefing along with the others.'

He nodded, 'Ok, see you there.' A tall, fair-haired chunky sort of guy, he was an object of desire for most of the female contingent in the station, and probably some of the guys too. Despite that, there was no hint of conceitedness or arrogance about him, characteristics which were all too prevalent in the force.

Entering the room, Gayle could feel the energy coming from her team. They were buzzing, waiting for the updates. She wasted no time in getting down to business.

'I've just come back from Ian Cooper's flat. The Forensics team have found a large amount of blood in the kitchen. Soaked into the carpet. Traces on the units and floor. Amateurish attempts had been made to clean it up, but there's a large amount soaked into the fitted carpet. So, it's looking pretty certain that he was killed there. Just waiting for confirmation that it's definitely his blood, but we'll proceed for now on the basis that it is. No weapon found at the scene. The team are still there, so we'll see what else they come up with.

'There are twenty three luxury flats in the three-storey block, ten on the ground floor, twelve on the first, and one penthouse on the second floor, which was Cooper's. All the upper flats are accessed by a communal staircase, and lift, both leading off the entrance hall. Behind the hall are some storage facilities for the flat owners, boiler room and caretaker's room. There's CCTV coverage at the front, covering the entrance, but none at the back.' She turned to look at a plan of the building that Georgia had just pinned up on the Board. 'As you can see, there's a rear entrance here,' she said, pointing to it. 'Used as a communal fire escape.

'Cooper had been living there for three and a half weeks, since early December, following a short stint in a bail hostel on his release from prison. The other residents in the block said he was quiet, kept himself to himself. Not surprising, since he wouldn't want to advertise the fact that these respectable people had a convicted paedophile living in their midst.

'The caretaker remembers seeing him on the twenty-third of December, when Cooper sought him out to report a blocked sink. He went into Cooper's flat later that day, at four twenty-five pm to clear the blockage and Cooper was at home then. He told me the fire-escape stairs at the back are virtually never used, which confirms it would have been relatively simple to get a body out of the building without being seen. The kitchens of all the flats face the back, but all have windows designed just to let light in, too high up to see out of. There's vehicular access to the rear, so a car could easily have been brought to the back door. Forensics are checking out that area too.

'I've got the stick with the CCTV footage covering the period twenty-third to twenty-seventh December for analysis,' she picked up a fire stick from the desk and held it up. 'Bob, as our IT guy, I'd like you go through this please? We need three sets of photos of every visitor.' She handed it to him. 'Georgia, once the photographs are ready, I want you to take two others and interview each resident. Show each of them all of the photos. Let's get names and addresses for each visitor, matched to the person they were visiting.' Toying with the locket at her neck, she added, 'Then we'll need to interview each visitor, find out if they noticed anything.' She looked around at the sea of faces. 'Any questions or observations so far?' she asked.

'Boss, I was reading an article last night about Fair Justice, the Tyneside-based vigilante group who trap paedophiles. I'd be surprised if Ian Cooper wasn't on their radar. Might be worth a word with them?'

'Yep, definitely worth following that up, Holly. Good thinking. Now,' she said, pausing until she had the full attention of the group, 'this is very interesting. I had a call from Joe Barnes earlier. He suggested a theory for how the victim got those spinal fractures...' She went on to describe the conversation she'd had with the former DI.

'Sounds like a pretty logical explanation,' commented one of the DCs when she'd finished. 'Can't think of any other way the body could have hit the tree with such force. I mean otherwise, it would have taken at least two people to swing the body against the tree, in the middle of a blizzard, and that doesn't make sense. Can't think why anyone would even do that? Even assuming it could be thrown hard enough to do the damage the pathologist describes.' There were a few murmurs in agreement.

'I agree, Natalie,' Gayle continued. 'So, we are going with that theory for now. Kris here,' she indicated Kris sitting nearby, 'has been up to Rothbury where he's been making some enquiries about the accident. And getting a good soaking into the bargain, right Kris?'

He grimaced. 'Too bloody true. It was chucking it down. Anyway, I spoke to a local farmer that Joe Barnes put us in touch with. Bill Dawson. He confirms that a car went over the top at the end of Hillside on the twenty-seventh of December.' He paused and looked at Gayle. 'Now, do you want the worst news first or the bad news?' he asked. 'I'll save the good news until last.' Without waiting for a response, he continued 'I'll give you the worst first. Get it out of the way. I'm afraid the car has been destroyed. It was extensively damaged. The garage said the state it was in suggested it must have rolled several times and hit obstacles on its way down. The bodywork was in a hell of a state, boot ripped open, and all the windows broken. The insurance company wrote it off and the garage sent it to the scrap yard in Blaydon. I checked with Blaydon, and they confirmed it was crushed on the seventh of January.'

Gayle's heart sank and there was a collective groan from the team. That was what she'd been hoping not to hear. 'No evidence there then. That's a bugger,' she said. 'What's the bad news?'

'We got a description of the driver from some of the local residents, though not a very clear one. After the car hit the fence, but before it went over the top, the driver managed to crawl out. People came out of the nearby houses and a couple at number five, the Taylors, took the driver into their home and gave him a brandy. They said he seemed pretty shaken up.' He consulted his notes, 'Male, possibly late-thirties but estimates vary. Approximately six feet, medium build, wearing a grey woollen hat with red Fair Isle design. He didn't remove his hat, so hair colour not known. He kept the hat pulled low, scarf obscuring part of his lower face, kept his head down and hardly spoke. They put it down to shock. Black North Face jacket, black jeans, and dark brown hiking boots. Without the hat and the scarf, they didn't think they'd be able to recognize him again.' Kris shrugged.

'Right. And the good news?'

'I'm coming to that, boss.' He ran his fingers through his still-damp hair, before continuing. 'The driver gave his name as Smith; very original. Mr Taylor rang the County Hotel and booked "Mr Smith" in for the night. He also contacted a local farmer, Bill Dawson who collected the driver, and gave him a lift down to the village in his four by four. The night manager at the County says he paid cash, stayed overnight, and left very early the next morning without anyone seeing him.

'Bill Dawson told us he towed the car to Peterson's Garage the morning after the accident. I went to see the proprietor at the garage who told me he didn't meet the driver himself, just spoke to him on the phone before he left the hotel. "Mr Smith" told him the car belonged to a friend and said he would get him to contact the garage. He never did, so the garage ran a check on the registration and found it was registered to a Nick Davis They contacted Davis and he said he'd loaned the car to a friend. Guess who?'

Gayle, swinging her legs back and forth beneath the desk, ankles crossed, asked, 'Ian Cooper?'

'The very one,' responded Kris, grinning.

'Great. So, this confirms we're on the right track,' she said, getting to her feet. 'That's reassuring.' She began to pace. 'So, Cooper's body was dumped using his own car? Or rather, the car he'd borrowed. That's a nice touch.' Gayle's tone was dry. 'Carry on Kris, did the driver say what he was doing up on Hillside?'

'No, he didn't have much to say at all. As I said, the Taylors' put it down to shock.' Kris took another look at his notes. 'We have the car registration, and a picture of it from the Rothbury Gazette. They had it as front-page news the next morning. One of the residents took a picture of the car perched nose-down on the edge, just before it went over, and sent it to the paper. The headline read "THE DRIVER OF THIS CAR WILL NEVER BE SO LUCKY AGAIN" 'He handed Gayle a photocopy of the front page.

'How did the driver manage to get out of that?' asked Gayle, looking at the photo. It showed the front end of the car hanging over the void, back wheels high in the air.

'The Taylors said they saw him scramble out of the back door on all fours, just before it tilted further over. Presumably he couldn't get out of either of the front doors. Must have clambered into the back.'

'Hmm... He was bloody lucky. Can you get the artist up there and get a photo fit done from the residents' description?' she asked.

'Already arranged. Not sure how much help it will be mind, bearing in mind what the Taylors and the other residents had to say. According to everyone who saw him, he kept his head lowered most of the time, and his hat pulled down over his eyebrows. They all assumed shock, but with hindsight he must have been trying to avoid too much scrutiny.'

'Great,' muttered Gayle. 'Still, worth a try.'

'Yes sir,' grinned Kris. It was a private joke. Kris always said Gayle had more balls than any of the men at the station.

CHAPTER THIRTY

'Gayle?' Rachel Jackson's face registered her surprise. 'And Georgia too?' she said, looking from one to the other. 'What are you two doing here? It's been a long time.' Her surprise turned quickly to alarm, 'Has something happened to Emma?'

'Emma...? asked Gayle. 'Oh, you mean Eva?'

'Emma's her name now,' explained Rachel. 'Emma Jackson. The family name is Jackson now.'

'Of course. No, no,' Gayle was quick to reassure her. 'It's not about Eva... Emma. Is Tommy in? I need to see you both.' She was shocked to see how much Rachel had aged in the seven years or so since she'd last seen her. Deep lines etched around her mouth and eyes, hair peppered with grey, dull and lifeless.

'Oh... yes. Come in.' She stood back so that Gayle and Georgia could step into the narrow hallway. 'Tommy's in the kitchen. Come on through.'

'How are you both keeping?' asked Gayle to Rachel's back, looking around as they walked down the hallway. The house was smaller than the home they'd had in Wallsend and Gayle supposed the north to south move must have been difficult for them financially, with the disparity in house prices. 'What's it like, living in Walton Bridge?'

Rachel paused, turned to face them, her hand on the door handle. 'It's alright. But it's never felt like home to me,' she said quietly. 'I'm a Geordie lass. I really miss living in Wallsend.' Rachel's face looked bleak, almost as though she was going to cry. 'But there was no choice. We had to get Emma away from there.'

'And how has she been?' asked Georgia, joining in the conversation.

'She's never been the same since that day,' said Rachel. 'But she's coped. Made some nice friends. Got some good GCSE results and A levels... got a place at university, but now...'

'She took it badly, Cooper getting released?' asked Gayle, briefly touching Rachel's arm.

'We all did. He should never have been let out so soon.' Her mouth set in a grim line. She opened the door and led them into a small, modern kitchen. Pale grey painted units, white granite worktops, stylish brushed chrome lights above a tiny central island.

'Tommy, we've got visitors. You remember Gayle?' asked Rachel.

Tommy, sitting at the island, looked up from his computer. He quickly closed the top but not before Gayle noticed that he was playing poker. He twirled round on his stool to face them.

'What are you doing here?' he asked, without preamble, getting to his feet and leaning back against a cupboard, arms crossed.

You've aged too, thought Gayle, registering the change in his appearance. She remembered him as quite well-built, nothing like the slimmer, older man she saw before her. *Still as pleasant as ever, though. The years haven't mellowed you one bit, have they Tommy?* Why Rachel had stayed with this odious man for so long was beyond Gayle. 'Hello, Tommy, how have you been?' she asked, smiling. 'Long time, no see.' He grunted in response, and she continued. 'How's life been for you since the move?'

'I don't think you've come all this way just to ask how I am,' he replied. 'Why don't you just tell us why you and your sidekick are here, and be done with it?'

'I'm here to inform you that a body recently found, in suspicious circumstances, has been identified as that of Ian Cooper. He was murdered.' Gayle watched their reactions as the news sank in. 'I'm leading the enquiry.'

There was silence for a few seconds before Rachel gasped, 'He's dead? Ian Cooper? He's really dead?' There was hope as well as surprise in her voice, as her hand flew to her mouth. 'But... how... what happened?'

'Somebody done the bastard in, have they?' asked Tommy. 'Thank fuck for that.' His face broke into a wide grin as he unfolded his arms. 'Calls for a celebration.' Grabbing a bottle of Bells from the bench behind him, he found a glass and poured himself a large measure, adding a couple of ice cubes from a dispenser on the front of the fridge/freezer. 'Cheers,' he said, raising his glass towards them.

'What happened?' Rachel repeated, wringing her hands. 'I mean how did he die?'

'Before we go any further, Rachel is Emma here?' asked Gayle. 'She needs to be told.'

'She's gone...' began Rachel.

'As soon as she knew that bastard was going to be released, she was so bloody scared she ran off,' growled Tommy. 'Went to London. Hasn't lived here for months now. We saw her at Christmas at Sam's but haven't seen her since. She went to Germany. With her girlfriend.'

Gayle turned to Rachel, 'Do you know exactly where she is? Are you in contact with her?'

'She gets in touch from time to time. She's ok, but she doesn't want to come home. She's too frightened... she thinks he'll come looking for her. Won't even give me her number in case he could trace her through her phone. Just uses the throw-away ones. Won't tell me where she lives either. All we know is it's somewhere in Berlin. A few weeks ago, she thought she saw him in London, staring at her... The police said it couldn't be him as he was tagged. But she couldn't shake off the feeling that he was watching her. She was paranoid. It was making her ill again.' Rachel was anxiously pacing around the kitchen then came to a sudden standstill as the news began to sink in. 'He can't watch her now though, can he? Oh, thank God,' she said, clasping her hands to her chest.

'When do you expect to hear from her next?'

'I'm not sure. I just wait until she contacts me, but sometimes I go for a week or more without hearing from her. As Tommy said, we just saw her at Christmas. I've heard from her twice since, so I'm not sure when she'll ring again but it shouldn't be too long.' Rachel's words came out rapidly and Gayle noticed her hands were trembling. 'I hope she calls soon; I can't wait to tell her about this.'

'Ok, thanks. We'll try to find her ourselves, but if she gets in touch in the meantime, please let me know,' said Gayle. 'Now, we're making a few routine enquiries and I need to ask you both some questions, if you don't mind?' Without waiting for an answer, she continued.

'Have either of you seen Ian Cooper since he was released from prison?'

'No, we bloody haven't,' grunted Tommy, resuming his seat at the island. 'Why the hell would we want to see that pervert?' He took a large gulp of whisky. Looking at him, Gayle noticed he was developing a drinker's face, with the tell-tale red and purple nose, mapped with broken veins.

'Have either of you been up north recently?' asked Gayle.

'Why are you asking that?' he demanded, glaring at her. 'Do you think one of us has done away with the bastard?' He laughed, taking another mouthful of whisky.

'I'm simply making routine enquiries in order to rule people out of our enquiry. Could you please just answer the question, Tommy?'

'We often go up north. We've still got family up there, you know, in Wallsend.' He took another gulp, emptying the glass, before grabbing the bottle and pouring himself a generous refill. 'And our son has a place at Edmundbyers. We stayed there over Christmas, along with some other family.'

'I need the dates of your stay. And details of where you went during the period twenty-fourth to the twenty-seventh December. And the names of the other guests and their movements as far as you can remember them,' Gayle informed them.

Tommy got to his feet and leant over the island, pointing a stubby index finger at Gayle. 'Why the fuck do you need all that?' His tone was becoming more belligerent as the alcohol entered his bloodstream.

'Sit down Tommy.' Gayle's tone was dismissive. She turned away and addressed Rachel. 'Can you give us those details, please Rachel?'

Rachel shot Tommy a look and nodded. Gayle wondered afresh why she was still with this unpleasant man. She often heard women say they have no choice but to put up with an abusive partner, but in her experience, there was always a way. Especially these days, when at long last domestic abuse was beginning to be taken seriously and a lot more help was becoming available.

'I'm simply trying to rule people out of our investigation, Rachel,' said Gayle. 'We need to establish where everyone was during that period of time. It hasn't been possible to determine the exact date of death, so we need to look at that four-day period.'

'I understand...' Rachel began, before being interrupted by Tommy's raised voice.

'Well, I bloody don't understand,' he boomed. 'Why don't you go and find the real murderer, instead of hounding innocent people like us? We are the victims here too, you know.'

'Mr Jackson,' said Gayle, with exaggerated patience. 'I'm asking the questions. I'd like you and your wife to answer them. The sooner we can establish the facts, the sooner I can leave you both in peace. Now, please be quiet and let Rachel continue.' She turned to Rachel again. Georgia had her notebook in her hand, pencil poised.

'We stayed with our son, Sam,' she began. 'They live in Northumberland, in Edmundbyers. We drove up the day before

Christmas Eve, so that would be the twenty-third. Must have taken us about six hours, with all the Christmas traffic. It would be about six o'clock when we got there.'

Rachel went on to give her statement, detailing their stay with Sam and her daughter-in-law, Olivia She explained there were several people staying at the property and there was a lot of coming and going amongst the guests over the time they were there.

'Emma came with a friend, a German girl called Gerda, and her cousin, Eric. They were all going off to Berlin straight after the holiday. Emma just wanted to get out of this country, as far away from him as possible. She's terrified he'll come after her.' She suddenly smiled, softening the deep lines a little. 'She's going to be so happy when she knows he's dead.' Apparently realising how that must sound, Rachel quickly added, 'I mean... you know what I mean. Not that she'll be glad he's dead, but glad she doesn't have to worry any more about him finding her.'

'I know what you mean,' said Gayle, nodding. 'Did either of you go to South Shields whilst you were up there?'

'No, we went to Wallsend one day, to visit relatives,' said Rachel, 'but we didn't go to South Shields. We had no reason to. Is that where he was murdered?'

'Can either of you think of anyone who would want him dead?' Gayle asked, looking from one to the other.

Rachel looked startled, but Tommy had no qualms about sharing his opinion on this question.

'I can think of at least fifty,' he said, 'starting with me. Any one of Emma's family and friends would want him dead, the fucking paedo. Doesn't mean any of them killed him though, does it?' He finished off the dregs in his glass, tossing back his head so as not to miss a drop. 'I can't think of anyone who wouldn't want him dead,' he said, nearly choking on his laughter. 'Even had an old boyfriend of hers down here when he heard the paedo was getting out.'

'Oh, who was that?' asked Gayle.

Tommy just snorted and Rachel volunteered Matt's name. 'He's my friend's son. Lovely lad. He was sweet on our Emma, or Eva as she was then... just a kid's crush really, or so I thought. I was very surprised when he turned up here. He said he'd seen on the internet that Cooper was going to be released. He was really concerned about Emma. Said he couldn't sleep for worrying about how devastated she would be feeling. He wanted to talk to her, but she'd gone by then. I know he wrote to Emma just after we moved here, but she didn't reply. I suppose I thought he'd just forgotten about her. It's been a long time. But how wrong can you be? He asked me to ask Emma to contact him when we next spoke to her... I don't know whether or not she did...' Rachel paused before adding, 'You'd be wasting your time interviewing him. There's no way he could kill anybody.'

'Well, we'll certainly need to rule him out,' Gayle told her. 'And we may need to speak to you both again, but for now I think we're done so we'll leave you in peace.' With a glance at Tommy, who had returned to his laptop, she made her way to the door. 'Thank you both for your time, and don't forget to ask Emma to ring me if she happens to get in touch.' Turning back, Gayle handed Rachel her card. 'My number's on there.'

'Yeah, go and do some real policing,' muttered Tommy. 'Instead of bothering innocent folk like us.'

'Bye, Tommy. You've been very helpful,' said Gayle, not without irony.

CHAPTER THIRTY-ONE

'I've had no breakfast,' said Gayle, prompted by the sound of her stomach rumbling. 'Tell you what, let's push the boat out. We're early, so let's stop off at the Nineteenth and grab a coffee. And a bacon sandwich. My treat.'

Georgia glanced over from behind the wheel. 'Ooh, that sounds good, I'm starving. The Nineteenth's at Close House, isn't it? The golf place? I've never been there.' Georgia tossed back her head, red curls glinting in the bright sunlight.

'You're always starving,' observed Gayle. 'Just take the turning for Heddon-on-the-Wall. It's coming up soon. It's not far from there. I'll keep you right. The Satnav would probably try to take you over a field, so ignore it and listen to me.' Gayle had been misdirected by her own Satnav once before and a local resident had come to her aid, explaining that he was forever re-directing people whose equipment was trying to get them to cross the field beside his house.

Georgia did as she was asked and soon they were driving slowly down the long, winding drive towards Close House, navigating the harsh speed bumps with care. It was a blustery day, the trees waving and bowing to them as they passed.

'You see over there?' They were nearing a bend in the road, and Gayle pointed to a pale three-storey mansion house in the near-distance. 'That used to be a fab hotel and restaurant. I once had lunch there with a guy who was trying to impress me. But now it's a private home for the owner and his family.'

Georgia took a quick look over towards the big house nestling in the trees at the end of its long, lawn-flanked drive and wistfully muttered 'Imagine living there...'

'Sharp right here,' said Gayle, indicating the car park. Following her directions, Georgia neatly parked in the steeply sloping car park in front of the Nineteenth. 'Make sure you leave it in gear,' warned Gayle, unfastening her seatbelt. 'Don't fancy having to fish it out of the lake.'

The place was busy, but the waitress managed to find them a small table next to full-length windows overlooking the lake and the award-winning Lee Westwood golf course. As they munched on their sandwiches, Gayle idly watched a group of golfers in the distance, while Georgia looked around the spacious restaurant with its long, gleaming bar and fantastic views. After ordering the sandwiches and coffee, Gayle idly perused the menu, thinking *forty quid for 20ounce Northumberland Sirloin to share, cheap at half the price.* The *truffle scented French fries with parmesan* sounded good. Getting her mind back on the job, she heard Georgia asking if Emma's brother had been surprised to get her call requesting an interview.

'Sam Jackson? Hard to tell. Seemed to take it in his stride,' said Gayle, taking a sip of coffee. 'Of course, he would already know that Cooper's body has been found. His parents will have told him straight away, so he'll probably have been expecting to hear from us. We'll soon find out.' The sandwiches were very satisfying, the bacon crispy, just the way Gayle liked it. With her napkin, she wiped crumbs from the corners of her mouth and told Georgia, 'Finish your coffee, I'll go and pay.' She got up and made her way to the bar.

Georgia, impressed by the venue, chuntered on as they exited the Nineteenth. After crossing the short bridge that led from the entrance, they made their way up the steep incline to the car. 'I judge places by how nice the Ladies are. They're lovely in there. Solid wooden doors, nice flowers, individual towels, luxury hand cream,' she said, sniffing the back of one hand in appreciation. 'Mmm...'

'Bacon sandwiches aren't too bad either,' said Gayle, thinking that Georgia was a funny mixture of naive schoolgirl and serious police officer. Gayle pretended to be surprised that the car was still where they had left it, and not in the lake, despite Georgia's dubious parking skills. Back on the A69, they continued west towards Corbridge, before taking the first exit at the next roundabout, on to the A68, heading south towards the Derwent Reservoir and the border with County Durham. Their destination was the small village of Edmundbyers.

Gayle loved the Northumberland countryside, just as much as she loved its spectacular coastline, and took the opportunity to take in the landscape as Georgia drove. Even in the depths of winter, with most of the trees bare, the scenery was spectacular, with sweeping views over rolling hills. She knew that Northumberland had recently been named by the Campaign for Rural England the country's most tranquil spot and she could understand why. After passing into County Durham, the Satnav guided them along narrow country lanes and after passing the sign for St Edmund's Church, Gayle had a glimpse of a beautiful old stone church standing beyond an ancient graveyard. A mile or so further on, they turned off the road, following a signpost for "Kiln House", which turned out to be a lovely, detached Georgian country house. After navigating the circular driveway via a long, winding approach road, Georgia brought the car to a standstill, the sound of the tyres making a satisfactory crunch on the gravel.

'Like something from a movie,' said Georgia, gazing up in awe at the ivy-covered facade of the stone-built mansion, its tall casement windows aglow in the winter sunshine. 'Must have a bit of money to live here... Look,' she exclaimed, pointing to two large birds strutting around at the side of the house, 'are they peacocks?'

'Yeah,' said Gayle, equally impressed. She knew from Rachel that Emma's brother was with the Ministry of Defence, and wondered just how high up the ladder he must be to afford a place like this. She looked around at the immaculately landscaped gardens set in beautiful open countryside and as they approached the wide, ornately carved front door, it was opened by a man of about thirty. Tall, black hair curling around his shoulders, slightly rugged face, hooded eyes, not exactly handsome, but interesting thought Gayle. Was that make up on his eyes?

'Sam Jackson?' asked Gayle, flashing her warrant card. 'DCI Gayle Jones, and this is DI Georgia Green.' She indicated Georgia next to her, who nodded.

'Simpson,' he corrected. 'I kept my original name. Do come in. I've been expecting you. Did you have any trouble finding the place? SatNavs don't always accurately pinpoint us.' He continued to make small talk as he led them across a wide hall, through double doors into a large drawing room. Gayle tried not to look impressed as she looked around at the polished, dark wood floors with a smattering of Chinese rugs in hues of navy, gold and cream. Lofty, ornate ceilings, intricately carved and gilded friezes, two huge sparkling chandeliers. 'Please, take a seat,' he said, indicating a large, plush, gold-coloured settee. 'Would you like coffee?'

'No thank you, we've just had breakfast,' said Gayle, sitting on one end of the settee. Georgia perched herself on the other. The spacious room was bright and pleasant, with high casement windows on three walls, letting in lots of sunlight, which bounced off the pale-yellow walls. A large abstract oil painting, which to Gayle's untutored eye looked vaguely familiar, took up much of the fourth wall. She would like to have taken her time to study it properly.

'Thank you for seeing us, Mr. Simpson. We're making preliminary enquiries into a suspicious death...' she began.

‘Yes, so I understand,’ interrupted Sam, sinking into a dark blue velvet armchair opposite them, legs splayed. ‘My mother told me about your visit. Ian Cooper, I gather he’s been found dead? By the way, do call me Sam.’

‘We’re ruling people out of our enquiry at this stage. Talking to friends and family of Emma, building up a picture. Can I ask, Sam, what was your reaction when you heard that Cooper was to be released from prison?’ asked Gayle.

‘Dismay, shock, anger. I was fearful for Emma’s mental health, to tell you the truth. I didn’t think she’d be able to cope, knowing he was back on the streets.’ He sat up straighter, crossing one leg over the other, displaying a bare ankle above a white tasselled loafer.

‘Can you tell us where you were from the twenty-fourth to the twenty-seventh of December, Mr Simpson?’

He raised one eyebrow. ‘Over Christmas?’ he asked. ‘Is that when he was murdered?’ There was no response from Gayle, and he continued, ‘I was here, with the family. We always celebrate Christmas here.’

‘Who exactly was here?’ asked Gayle.

‘My wife, Olivia, my mother, father and grandfather, Olivia’s parents,’ he said. ‘And Emma, with a friend, Gerda, and Gerda’s Cousin Eric. Also, my cousin Craig, for part of the time.’

‘Quite a houseful. We’ll need contact information for everyone, please. DI Green will take their details before we leave. Just to rule people out of the equation so to speak. Tell me, Sam, were you here for the whole of the time?’

‘We like a big crowd. The more the merrier. We all did various things at different times, but yes, I was here the whole time. I think my movements can probably be corroborated. Why? Am I in the frame for murder?’ He looked amused; his mouth twisted in irony.

‘At this stage, we’re simply eliminating people from our enquiry, Mr Simpson. We’re talking to anyone who might potentially have a motive for killing Ian Cooper, As the brother of his victim, you fit into that category, wouldn't you agree?' asked Gayle. 'How would you describe your feelings at the time he assaulted Emma? We have been informed that you were "incandescent with rage". Is that true?'

'Whoa. What are you implying here?' he laughed. 'I do believe you think I could have done it. This is quite thrilling. Do I need to call my solicitor?'

'No, you don't need a solicitor,' Gayle responded in a calm voice. 'At least not at this stage. But this is a murder enquiry Sam, and it's no laughing matter. Awkward questions have to be asked. Can you tell us how you reacted when you learned of the assault on Emma?'

Folding his arms, he said, 'You heard correctly. I was incandescent with rage.' His face darkened for a moment. 'What brother wouldn't be? Knowing what that filthy pervert did to my kid sister? I believe I even threatened to kill him at the time.'

'And did you?' asked Gayle. 'Kill him?'

'I did not,' he responded, 'but I salute whoever did.'

'And do you have any idea who could have killed him?' asked Gayle.

'Phew... any number of people, I should think. I don't have any theories as to who actually did it, but I can think of quite a few who would like him dead. Starting with myself. Anyone who cared for Emma would want to see that monster done away with, and they would all be outraged at his early release.'

'Ok, Sam. We'll leave it there for now. We may need to speak with you again, as our enquiry progresses,' said Gayle, getting to her feet. 'Thank you for your time... By the way, do you have an address for Emma? We'll need to speak with her, too.'

'I'm afraid I don't,' he said, levering himself out of the depths of the chair. 'Poor kid's so paranoid about Cooper finding her, she's not given anyone her address, or even her phone number. She contacts me from time to time, on a throw away phone. All I know is that she's somewhere in Berlin, with Gerda... and before you ask, I've no idea what Gerda's surname is or how she can be contacted. I'm only grateful that she's there for Emma. God knows, she needs someone to keep her sane.'

'We'll be able to trace her, I'm sure. If she hasn't already heard about Cooper, no doubt she'll be very relieved to hear the news.' Gayle turned to leave. 'Oh, by the way,' she said, turning back, 'is your wife in? We'd like a word with her too.'

'I'm afraid not. She's out on a hack this morning. I hope she's home soon. The weather's beginning to change. Strong winds and rain forecast. But she's on a steady mount, so I'm sure she'll be ok. Can I get her to give you a call later, once she's back?' he offered, leading the way to the front door.

'No need. One of my officers will be in touch with her shortly. Thanks again for your time.'

As they left, Gayle noticed that while they'd been talking, the weather had indeed begun to change. Now, dark clouds obscured the sun, threatening an imminent rainstorm. 'Looks like the lady of the manor is going to get very wet on her hack,' smirked Georgia, as they got into the car.

Sure enough, before long there was a sudden torrential downpour, and with the wipers working overtime, Gayle had to raise her voice to make herself heard. 'What did you make of him?' she bellowed. There was no reply from Georgia, who was hunched forward, concentrating on the road ahead. Gayle decided to let her be for the moment, knowing that driving would become a lot easier once they reached the main road. She began mentally going through what Sam Simpson had told them. There was no doubt he had a strong motive, but did he have a strong alibi? Until they'd spoken to everyone else who'd stayed at his place over Christmas, they wouldn't be able to assess that. South Shields was approximately an hour's drive from his house, so it was feasible that he could have driven there, murdered Cooper, loaded his body into the boot of the car, and driven up to Rothbury. All doable, but it would necessitate him being away from his home overnight on the twenty-seventh of December, the night of the blizzard in Rothbury. It was essential that they establish who, if any, were missing that night.

Georgia's voice cut into her thoughts, and she became aware they had now reached the main road. The rain was easing, the wipers not quite so frantic. 'He's a cocky bugger, isn't he?' she commented, glancing at Gayle. 'Typical Oxford graduate, I should think.'

'And how many Oxford graduates have you come across in your life, madam?' teased Gayle.

'Well, you know what I mean. Such bloody confidence. Bet he never doubts himself.'

'Hmm, I think that's partly a man-thing. Women tend to have far more self-doubt than men. I once read a magazine article about it. Even some of the most successful women in the country suffer from Imposter Syndrome. There was one, an editor of an up-market women's magazine, I forget which one, who admitted that she secretly can't believe what she's achieved. She appears so confident, yet says she always has a fear she'll be found out as a fraud. Never heard a man saying anything like that. In my experience, if anything, men tend to over-estimate their abilities.'

'Yeah... But what a house,' exclaimed Georgia. 'How many bedrooms do you think it has? Must be at least ten, don't you think?'

'At least,' murmured Gayle. 'Now, let's concentrate on what we need to do. Which of the crowd that were there over Christmas do you think could have a motive for the murder?'

'Well, there's the avenging brother, Lord Snooty himself, for starters,' said Georgia. 'Then the father, Tommy Jackson. I suppose Rachel too, though I doubt she could have done it on her own. Could be both together. Then we have Emma herself, although she had clearly laid plans to flee, to get away from him, and she couldn't have done it on her own anyway, although she could have had help from Gerda and Eric. Then there's the cousin, Craig... basically everyone who was there at Christmas had a motive, apart from Sam Simpson's parents.'

'Don't forget it was a man who tried to dispose of the body, so even if it was a woman who did it, she would have to have an accomplice,' said Gayle. 'We need to interview everyone who stayed at the house and get full details of their movements and recollections. By cross-referencing their stories some anomalies might come to light.'

CHAPTER THIRTY-TWO

Amazing thought Gayle, gazing up at the white structure that was the Brandenburg Gate. 'Wow,' she said to Georgia, as they walked through the high arch and made their way down the wide Unter den Linden, 'can't you just feel the sense of history in this place? Imagine what it was like to be here in the nineteen thirties?'

It was Gayle's first visit to Berlin, and she was trying hard not to appear overawed. She hadn't seen much of the world at all, really, a situation she vowed to correct in the future. World War 11 held a fascination for her, and she'd read quite extensively on the subject. To be here in the heart of Berlin was just awesome.

'Picture it, Georgia. There would be huge swastikas flying from every lamppost. Hanging from every window. The whole place a sea of red, black, and white. When Hitler became Chancellor, in nineteen thirty-three I think, there was a torch lit parade through this very gate. Imagine SA and SS forces goose-stepping down this very street.'

'How do you know about all that?' queried Georgia. 'You know about lots of different stuff. I remember when those bodies were found in Kielder Forest, you knew all the bloody trees that grew there. The only one I recognised was a Christmas tree.' Georgia was referring to a case they'd worked on several years earlier, when two putrefying bodies had been found in a car hidden deep in the forest.

'I read, Georgia. You'd be surprised what you can learn from books, or from the internet. This place fascinates me,' Gayle explained. 'As did Kielder Forest. If I'm interested in something, I research it. You should try it sometime. You'd be surprised what you can find out.'

Georgia shrugged nonchalantly, the sense of history going whoosh over the top of her auburn curls.

'It must have been terrifying to be a Jew in Germany or Poland at the time of the Second World War. Even you must have heard of the gas chambers and what happened to millions of Jews in the concentration camps?'

'Well, yeah. But I've never really thought much about it,' said Georgia, looking up at the sky. 'Nice day,' don't you think?'

'You see that hotel there?' asked Gayle, ignoring Georgia's disinterest. She was pointing to an austere-looking building, set back off the Unter den Linden. 'The Adlon. It was the best hotel in Berlin, full of high society. The famous and wealthy used to flock there, many of them wealthy Jews. Until Hitler came to power. Jews were banned by decree from using the hotel. Can you imagine being turned away from a hotel where once you'd been fawned over and treated with deference? Suddenly you aren't even considered good enough to cross the threshold. Can you imagine the humiliation?'

'Oh, is that the sort of thing that happened, then?' asked Georgia, her interest piqued at last by the thought of someone losing their social standing.

'That was minor. The Jews were systematically stripped of all their rights. Their businesses were taken from them. All Jews were made to wear a yellow star on their arm, with JEW written on it.'

'Why was that then?' asked Georgia and Gayle marvelled inwardly at her complete lack of knowledge of such an important part of history.

'It was to humiliate them. And to mark them out clearly as Jews, so they could be more easily rounded up for deportation. And you know what happened to them after they were carted off to the camps. Genocide. Heartbreaking and sickening.' Gayle was silent for a few moments, feeling an overwhelming sense of sadness, before picking up her pace. 'Right. Enough of that. Let's find this bloody apartment.'

They were in Berlin to interview Emma. She'd taken some tracking down, but with the help of Interpol and the authorities in Berlin, they'd finally got an address. Gayle hoped they'd find her in. They'd soon find out.

***

As dawn broke, Gerda made her way down the narrow alley leading to her tiny apartment. Although not far from the Unter den Linden, it was worlds away from the tourist areas; rather run-down and dilapidated. "Apartment" was a fancy term for the tiny, cramped room which served as living room, bedroom and kitchen. A curtained off alcove barely concealed a shower cubicle, with a toilet and the tiniest washbasin. Still, she thought, it was a roof over their heads, and it was just until they found something more permanent. Although they kept the place scrupulously clean, they couldn't quite get rid of the smell of damp, nor eradicate the faint sewage odour that seeped up from the grate on the shower room floor.

Picking her way carefully along the cobbled alley, she reached the high, double fronted doors to the apartment block. Once painted red, they were now largely grey, bleached wood, with the odd flakes of the original pigment bravely clinging on here and there like small flowers in the desert.

The doors were never locked, and she pushed hard, shouldering aside one heavy door, before entering the dim hall within. Taking the bare stone steps two at a time, she ran up the three flights, past graffiti covered concrete walls, until she reached neunzehn. She inserted her key into the tarnished brass lock and pushed open the door, calling out as she did so.

'Just me, Emma.' There was no response and Gerda realised Emma must still be sleeping. The place was in darkness, so not wanting to wake her, Gerda quietly closed the door before kicking off her shoes and quickly undressing. As her eyes adjusted to the gloom, she could make out the form of Emma, a hump under the coverlet. She gently slipped in beside her. Emma stirred, sleepily turning over and putting an arm around Gerda's waist.

'Hi. Have fun?' she asked in a voice thick with sleep.

'It was ok, but I prefer it when you are with me. I should have come home when you did. How are you feeling now Liebling?'

'Much better,' Emma murmured. 'My headache's gone, thank goodness.'

'Do you feel well enough for this?' Gerda asked, taking Emma's face into her hands, and lowering her head until their lips met.

'Oh, I think so,' whispered Emma, entwining her fingers in Gerda's long hair, eagerly returning her kiss. Later, they both fell into a deep sleep, only waking mid-morning when there was a loud rap on the door.

'Ja?' called Gerda, hastily disentangling her long limbs from the sheet, and jumping to her feet, pushing her thick chestnut hair from her face.

'Police' came the reply, 'Polizei'

After grabbing her robe from where it rested on a chair, and struggling to get her arm into an inside-out sleeve, she looked at Emma. 'English police?' she whispered, 'Einen moment bitte,' she called out.

Emma scrambled out of bed, reaching for her clothes lying on the floor. She quickly slipped into her jeans before pulling a blue sweater over her head. She looked at Gerda and shrugged. Gerda, pale blue dressing gown now in place, raked her fingers through her hair once more before straightening her back and opening the door.

'DCI Jones,' said a slim blonde woman, holding out her warrant card. 'And this is DI Green.'

'Ja?' said Gerda. She had expected to see uniformed officers and was surprised to see two women, both dressed in dark trousers, the older one with a navy parka, the younger a green woollen jacket.

'Sorry to trouble you. We're looking for Emma Jackson. Is she here?' asked Gayle.

'Err... Ja. Yes, come in please,' said Gerda, stepping back and opening the door wider to allow the two women to enter.

The dim room was suddenly flooded with light as Emma, by now fully dressed, pulled back the faded blue curtain covering the window. The nearby rooftops and chimneys were revealed, set against a bright blue sky.

'Emma Jackson? We've been looking everywhere for you,' said Gayle, looking around the room, taking in the tiny, cluttered space and the tumbled sheets on the newly vacated bed.

'How did you find me?' asked Emma, her eyes widening in alarm. She went to stand by Gerda and held on to her arm, as though she expected to be dragged from the room at any minute. 'Did my parents send you? They can't make me go back. I'm old enough to make my own mind up where I want to live.'

'No, no, Emma. It's nothing to do with your parents. You're not in any trouble. We just need to ask you a few questions.' Gayle explained.

'Oh... Well... if my parents didn't send you, why are you here?' Emma loosened her grip on Gerda's arm. 'It's just my dad gave me so much grief at Christmas when I wouldn't give him a forwarding address, I wouldn't put it past him to have me dragged back home.'

'No, don't worry, nothing like that. Actually, we met seven years ago, Emma. Don't you remember? I was in charge of the investigation.' Gayle studied Emma's face as she spoke, noticing her eyes widen again as comprehension dawned.

'Oh my God. Yes... I remember...' Emma looked puzzled and a bit dazed.

'Emma, I don't want to upset you, but I have to ask you some questions in connection with a current enquiry,' explained Gayle. 'Can you tell me when you came to Berlin?'

'What enquiry?' Emma asked, without answering Gayle's question.

'We're investigating the murder of Ian Cooper,' Gayle said quietly.

Emma's mouth gaped. 'What?' she eventually whispered. 'He's dead...? Murdered?' She shook her head in disbelief, glancing up at Gerda, who had come to stand beside her, a protective arm around her shoulders.

'Can you tell me the date you came out to Berlin, Emma?' repeated Gayle.

'Why are you asking? Wait a minute... you don't think I did it, do you?' Emma blurted, looking at Gayle, her eyes like saucers. 'You can't be serious.'

'We're simply trying to rule people out of the investigation at this stage, Emma. We're talking to everyone we know who was connected in any way to the victim. Just routine questions.' Gayle let that sink in. 'Now, how long have you been in Berlin?'

'We came out in December... the twenty-eighth I think?' She looked at Gerda for confirmation. 'Yes, the twenty-eighth. We thought about coming out before Christmas, but the flights were too expensive. Anyway, we went to my brother's over the Christmas period.' The colour was returning to Emma's face.

'What made you decide to come here?' asked Gayle.

'I wanted to be with Gerda,' Emma shrugged.

'We know you left home initially when you heard that Ian Cooper was being released on parole.'

'Do you blame me?' Emma looked up sharply. 'That pervert. Free?' She pushed back her long light brown hair and spoke in a low voice, 'I was scared he'd come to get me... I had to get away... somewhere he couldn't find me.'

'He was under a supervision order...' began Georgia.

Emma whirled round, scorn in her voice. 'Supervision order? Do you really think a Supervision Order would have stopped him? Did you even see the message he sent me from prison? Do you have any idea what he was capable of? He would have come after me. I know he would. I had to get away from home. The last straw was when I thought I saw him watching me in London. I freaked out. I didn't feel safe there anymore.'

'And now he's dead,' said Gayle. 'Do you know anything about what happened to him, Emma?'

Emma stared at her. 'How could I possibly know? I was here, in Berlin.'

'So, you say you went to stay with your brother for Christmas? Tell me about what you did, where you went whilst you were there. We are trying to build a picture of everyone's movements. Were you at your brother's the whole time?'

Emma resumed her seat before answering quietly. 'My brother suggested we stay with him and some of the family over Christmas. So, we did. Gerda's cousin, Eric, stayed too.' She looked up at Gayle, 'Is he really, really dead? I can't believe it.'

'Yes, he's dead Emma. Now, you need to tell me about your movements over the time you stayed with Sam. When did the three of you go to his house?' asked Gayle.

'We got the train up, on the twenty-second. Sam paid the fares for the three of us. The manager of the pub wasn't too happy at us leaving at the busiest time, but... I wanted to see my brother before we left. We've always been close.'

'So, you were there from the twenty-second to the twenty-eighth? Did you stay at the house the whole time?'

'Well, most of the time. Gerda and Eric were getting a bit bored by Boxing Day, so we told my brother we had to visit Gerda's aunt. But, really we sneaked off to an all-night club in Newcastle.'

'You told him porkies?' asked Georgia.

'Well, a white lie. I didn't want to hurt his feelings by letting him know we needed a bit more excitement. We went back to his place the next morning.'

'Where is your cousin, Eric, now?' asked Gayle, turning to address Gerda.

'He's living at his mother's,' replied Gerda. 'Do you need to see him? He lives not so far from here. Just a short walk.'

'Yes, we'll see him while we're here,' confirmed Gayle, nodding to Georgia to take down the address. 'We are taking details of the movements of everyone who was at Sam's over the Christmas holiday. Just for elimination purposes,' Gayle explained. 'As I've said, these are preliminary enquiries.'

'Why...' began Emma. 'I mean, when exactly was Cooper killed?'

'We believe sometime between the twenty-fourth and twenty-seventh of December,' Gayle informed her.

After Georgia had made detailed notes of their movements and their recollections of the movements of the others at Sam's, the clubs they'd visited, and obtained contact details of Gerda's cousin, Eric, Gayle told them, 'We might need to speak to you again. What are your plans for the next few weeks?'

Emma looked at Gerda. 'She will be here with me,' said Gerda, taking Emma's hand. 'Won't you my darling?' Gayle noted the tender look that passed between them.

'Yes. Yes, of course I'll be here,' answered Emma, blushing faintly. 'We're not planning to go anywhere.'

'Good. Well, thank you both for your time, you've been very helpful.'

As they retraced their steps, Gayle spoke. 'So, the three of them were out all night at the crucial time? We need to triple-check their alibis. Let's see what this Eric has to say for himself. If they've anything to hide, no doubt they'll be on their phones right now, getting their stories straight.'

Eric turned out to be a twenty-four-year-old, tall, blonde, Teutonic looking young man. He confirmed the details given by Emma and Gerda and seemed eager to please and willingly agreed to voluntarily provide a sample for DNA purposes. After Georgia had obtained the swab, Gayle let him know they may need to see him again and got his confirmation that he'd be available to answer further questions should it be deemed necessary.

'We've just got time to fit in that sight-seeing tour my sister told me about. It doesn't take more than two hours. What do you think, boss?' There was a hopeful note in Georgia's voice and Gayle was intrigued that she was even interested in seeing the city. They were making their way back to the Unter den Linden, walking carefully over the cobbles in the back streets, avoiding overflowing bins and bags of garbage in the narrow, graffiti-strewn alleys.

'Ok, then,' said Gayle. Truth be told, there was nothing she'd like to do more than see the sights of Berlin. 'There's just time if the guide can get here soon. Go on, give him a ring.'

Georgia grinned and took her mobile from the pocket of her trousers. 'My sister recommended this tour. She was here a few weeks ago, with a friend on a city break. She told me this guy is amazing. He's South African, and he does this amazing whistle-stop trip. She said you see all the major sights of Berlin from the comfort of his car. My sister says he's lived in Berlin for a long time and knows everything about the place and the history and everything.' Georgia paused for breath. 'And she says he's so funny, and witty and very politically incorrect. And he's gorgeous,' she added for good measure.

'Ah, that's the attraction, DI Green. Might have guessed.' Gayle teased. The guide arrived within ten minutes, drawing to the kerb in his silver Mercedes, and soon their whistle-stop tour was underway. He told them his name was Mike, and he turned out to be just as irreverent as Georgia's sister had described and soon had them laughing at his risqué comments and political views. Basically, he believed all politicians, of whatever persuasion, were unscrupulous lying bastards and not to be trusted. Very soon he was pointing out an ordinary-looking car park, beneath which, he told them, Hitler's bunker had been found. The very one where he and Eva Braun had committed suicide. He told them the place had deliberately been left unmarked, so as not to become a shrine to Hitler.

They passed the sombre Jewish Cemetery memorial, made up of symbolic stark concrete blocks, then the remaining, rather unimpressive, bit of the Berlin Wall that was still standing. Mike had them laughing when he pointed out the touts selling 'genuine' bits of the Wall to gullible tourists.

'The bloody wall would have had to be as long as the Great Wall of China, to give a piece to every bloody tourist,' he laughed. 'This is Checkpoint Charlie,' he explained slowing alongside a Checkpoint booth with American soldiers standing guard. A myriad of tourists, mainly Japanese and American as far as Gayle could tell, posed for selfies with them. 'It's just symbolic now, mainly for the tourists.'

Gayle was surprised to learn that although Berlin had been extensively bombed, many of the grand buildings had been rebuilt exactly as they had been before the war. Drawing their attention to the plethora of bullet holes in the facades of many buildings around the city, Mike explained they'd been deliberately preserved as a reminder of what the people had endured during World War 11.

All too soon, they were dropped off at the bustling Schonefeld Airport just in time to catch their two-hour flight to Newcastle. Once on board, and seated, they at last had time to discuss the interview with Emma.

'I don't think Emma had anything to do with it,' said Georgia. 'Her relief when you told her you were investigating Cooper's death was real. There was a transformation in her, not just her face; her whole body slumped in relief.'

'I think you're probably right, but they were gone from Sam's house for a good eighteen hours after lying to him about where they were going. We need to cross reference what the three of them have said, with the accounts of others. See if we can place them at the nightclubs in question. They all have CCTV. See if there are any anomalies.' Just then, the crew with the drinks trolley reached them and they each ordered a large gin and tonic. 'Just as well we got a lift to the airport, or you'd have to have an orange juice and watch me drink my gin,' laughed Gayle.

Georgia laughed. 'That Mike was a bit of alright, don't you think? I could have listened to his lovely South African accent all day.'

CHAPTER THIRTY-THREE

Sitting at a wooden trestle table, Gayle watched the distant figures bobbing around in the surf, hoping to catch a wave. The tide was on the turn, but still well out, revealing a huge expanse of golden sand. At that distance, the swell didn't look very high to her untutored eye, although she could see that each wave was topped by a crest of white as it rose and rushed towards the shore. It was hard to make out any detail, the surfers all looked like black blobs, but after a while she noticed a figure emerge from the sea and begin to walk up the beach in their direction.

'That could be him now,' said the waitress, placing two coffees in front of them, the steam from each curling upwards into the cold air. Shading her eyes with one hand, the girl screwed up her face as she peered down towards the sea. She watched the surfer for some time, biting her lip.

'Is it him then?' Gayle asked, wondering how the girl could discern who the figure was at such a distance.

'Just a minute...' the girl said still focused on the beach. 'I think... yeah, that's him,' she confirmed, nodding her head. 'I can tell by his swagger. Cocky. Full of himself.'

'Thank you,' said Gayle. 'Very helpful.'

Having been unsuccessful at catching him at home, Gayle had learned from one of his neighbours that Brian Turner could probably be found on the beach at Tynemouth, where he regularly surfed.

'You wait here, Georgia, we don't want to lose the table,' said Gayle to the DS. Even on a very cold morning such as this, most of the outside tables were taken, many by dog-walkers or families out for a morning stroll. 'I'm going to have a word.'

Getting to her feet, she left the terrace fronting Crusoe's Cafe, stepping down on to the pale, soft sand. To the north, she could see St Mary's Island, the white painted lighthouse gleaming in the bright winter sun; to the south, the ruins of Tynemouth Priory stood proudly on the headland. She never tired of this view of the Northeast coast. If only the weather was warmer, this would be the most idyllic holiday spot. On the other hand, she thought, best keep it to ourselves; let the hordes stay south of Watford Gap, unaware they are missing such splendour.

As she got closer to the sea, Gayle could see that the waves were actually quite big, affording the surfers some great rides. The figure in black strode across the firm sand in her direction, and as the distance closed between them, Gayle could see his tall, athletic build and self-confident stride. His features became clearer as he neared, and Gayle estimated his age at around forty. She watched him run his fingers through tousled wet hair with one hand, his surfboard tucked under the other arm. The sun highlighted the droplets of water running down his wetsuit, some dripping from his raised elbow. The waitress was right; he did have a cocky air about him.

'Brian Turner?' asked Gayle, approaching him. Close up, he looked older than she had at first thought. Maybe mid-fifties? His weather-beaten face had deep crinkles around the eyes, and she guessed he laughed a lot.

'Yeah... who wants to know?' he asked, coming to a halt, and looking curiously at her as he wiped his wet face with one large hand, a gold signet ring catching the sun.

'DCI Jones, Northumbria Police,' she said, holding out her warrant card. 'I was told I'd find you here. You're a hard man to get hold of.'

'Am I?' he asked, raising his eyebrows. 'I didn't know anyone was looking for me... what's this about then?' His eyes appraised her. 'Am I under arrest?' He was being playful, and Gayle couldn't help but smile.

'We'd just like a word with you,' she said. 'Down at Crusoe's?' She turned, and he began to walk with her in the direction of the cafe. Gayle was glad of her thick parka in the brisk easterly wind. 'Was the surfing any good?' she asked. 'The waves look quite high.'

'Aye, not bad at all. Got some good breaks. It'll be better later when the tide turns. Mid-tide gives the best conditions around here,' he explained. 'Where have you been looking for me?'

'We've been trying to contact you at home, but you haven't been there,' explained Gayle. 'One of your neighbours told us the best place to find you would be here. We just need to ask you a few questions if that's ok?' She gestured to the cafe as they approached it. 'Fancy a coffee?'

'Well, yeah, but I'll need to get changed first,' he said, waving vaguely ahead. 'What do you want to ask me about?'

'It's in connection with an ongoing enquiry. I'll explain when you've changed.'

'How did you know it was me anyway?' he looked amused.

'The waitress,' said Gayle. 'She recognised your walk.'

'Ah, Christina? I see. One of my devoted fans.' He grinned, before turning to head towards the cars parked on the slope leading from the main road down to the beach. Gayle couldn't help but notice the well-developed muscles rippling as he walked. *Hmm...* she thought, *lovely bum.* The wet suit left nothing to the imagination. He called over his shoulder, 'Won't be long. Black, one sugar, please.'

Despite the brightness of the morning, the icy chill in the January air made Gayle grateful for the polystyrene cup of hot coffee waiting for her. She settled back into her chair, taking tentative sips of the warming liquid, as she and Georgia waited for Turner to return.

'God, there's nothing I would like less,' she said to Georgia, 'than to be out there in the freezing cold sea at this time of year.' She nodded towards the many tiny black figures dotted around in the surf.

Georgia, who had been admiring her own reflection in the cafe windows, liking the way the sun turned her red hair to fire, twisted her head around to look. 'Makes you shiver just to look at them. I wouldn't fancy it either.' Turning back, she cradled her cup, warming her hands. 'What's he like then?' She nodded in the direction Brian Turner had taken.

'Bit of a cynic, I'd say,' said Gayle. 'He's just gone to change, won't be long.'

Turner returned just as his coffee arrived. 'Well, here I am,' he said, pulling out a chair. 'What can I do for you?' He had a look of amusement on his face, the creases around his clear grey eyes deepening as he smiled. He'd changed into a thick grey fleece, dark grey joggers and white trainers.

Gayle introduced Georgia before broaching the subject she wished to talk to Turner about.

'I understand you head up a Vigilante group, in Newcastle?' she began, 'Fair Justice?'

'Yeah...' said Turner, elbows on the table, cupping his hands around his coffee cup. 'This smells good,' he commented, looking steadily at her, waiting for her to continue.

'I need to find out if the group has had any involvement with someone called Ian Cooper?' said Gayle.

'Ian Cooper...' he repeated slowly. 'The convicted paedophile? Yeah, as a matter of fact we've been keeping an eye on his on-line activity since he came out of prison. Why are you asking about him?'

'His body has been found,' Gayle was blunt. 'And we're treating his death as suspicious.'

'He's dead...?' Turner looked surprised. 'And you think he's been murdered?'

'Did you know him personally?' asked Georgia.

'No, I haven't met him myself,' he said, turning to Georgia. 'But I know he was being monitored by the Group. As I said, there's been some on-line activity that we've been keeping an eye on.'

'What on-line activity would that be?' prompted Gayle.

He turned back to her. 'Look, you know that we expose adults who solicit and groom minors on the internet? Always within the law, of course. We put the bait out there and if they take it, we keep an eye on them. Eventually, if it's appropriate, we arrange a meet up. They think they're meeting an under-age person and find us waiting for them.'

'And is that what Ian Cooper was up to?' asked Gayle.

'Yeah, he was having sexual conversations with what he believed to be a twelve-year-old girl. Indecent communications. We set the trap.'

'And did you lure him into the trap?' asked Gayle, watching his reactions.

He shook his head. 'As a matter of fact, no. I was told he didn't turn up at the rendezvous... God, this probably explains why...' He took a deep breath, shaking his head and wiping his face with one hand. 'Exactly when was he killed?'

'Sometime over the Christmas period, Mr Turner. But, regarding Cooper's activity, you should have come to us. He was breaking his bail conditions and would have gone straight back inside.' Gayle's voice betrayed her annoyance.

He looked directly at Gayle, seeming to consider his response, before replying. 'With all due respect, DCI Jones, the police always suggest we should have gone to them. Recently the Detective Superintendent of the Serious Crime Directorate even warned that vigilante groups could make paedophiles more evasive. Said we should leave the job to the police. But you know, we're not going anywhere.'

'But in this instance, you would have known we'd pick him up straight away?' she persisted.

'We wanted to make sure he was caught in the act of meeting an under-age girl, so he'd go away for as long as possible. Not just get his knuckles rapped for breaking bail.'

'We would always encourage anyone with concerns to report these to us, rather than take matters into their own hands,' said Gayle. 'Especially when it's a known offender.'

'Oh, I'm sure you would,' said Turner with a hint of sarcasm. 'But let me tell you that's not going to happen. The police can sit in their ivory towers all they want and tell us not to do it. Call us amateurs. But while there are predators out there in their hundreds, preying on kids, we will exist.'

'Who was involved in setting this trap?' asked Gayle, choosing not to respond to his tirade.

'A guy called Craig Burton was leading the team on this one... he's one of the senior members.'

'Craig Burton?' repeated Gayle. 'We'll need to speak to him. Where can I find him?'

'Well, he lives in Howden. But he's away on holiday just now. Tenerife. With a couple of mates.'

'And he's due back when?' asked Gayle.

'He's been away over week now... let's think... he'll be back on Friday I think... yes that's right, Friday.'

'Ok. We'll catch up with him then – if you could give Georgia his contact details?'

'No problem. You know,' he said, leaning across the table to emphasise his words, 'we only confront paedos when we know they're meeting up with someone under-age. We keep an eye on their on-line activity, but unless we observe any criminal activity, we don't approach them.' He sat back in his chair. 'With this case, Craig told me he wanted to expose Cooper quickly, and get him put away before he could do any more harm, especially with him being on bail.'

'Right. Well, we'll speak with him as soon as he gets back,' said Gayle. 'Hear his side of the story.'

'We work strictly within the law,' Turner repeated, his voice steady and serious, at pains to explain how Fair Justice worked. 'I'm sure you'll find that Craig's handled this in a professional manner. You know, our activities have so far led to fifty convictions and helped snare over a hundred sex crime suspects. Ninety-nine percent of the public have nothing but love for what we do. And we're grateful for their support. We recently won a high court ruling to say we can continue with our activities. The judge said there was no legal requirement for the activities of the group to be subjected to controls.'

'Do you recall the date the trap was set for?' asked Gayle, not responding to his statement, although personally she had sympathy with most of what he'd said, despite it not being the official line.

'It'd be late December, I think. I can check the exact date and get back to you if you like?'

'That would be helpful,' said Gayle, handing him her card. 'Just give us a call.'

'We do good work,' Turner persisted, 'The powers that be say "leave it to us" but we left it to them with Jimmy Saville, with Rotherham, with Rolf Harris. The so-called experts had their chance. It's time for them to admit that we've shown them something that works. Now, they want to get on the bandwagon. A while ago, a government minister announced twenty million pounds funding to extend an initiative where undercover detectives operate in internet chat rooms and forums used by suspected offenders. A tactic perfected by us, Tyneside-Based Fair Justice.'

Gayle rose to her feet. 'Well, thank you for your time, Mr Turner. You've been very helpful. That's all for now, but we might need to speak with you again.'

'I'll be around. I'm not going anywhere.' He looked at her and with a cheeky grin added, 'Why not bring your wetsuit next time?'

Gayle grinned, 'Not my scene, I'm afraid.' She began to walk away, before turning back, calling 'Don't forget to let me have that date.'

Turner made a mock salute, 'Yessir'.

As they walked back up the slope towards their unmarked car, Georgia began waxing lyrical about the 'gorgeous' Brian Turner. Gayle would have been surprised if Georgia had failed to notice such an attractive man. But however much she might agree with her, there were more important things to discuss.

'Craig Burton?' Gayle pondered. 'Isn't that the name of the cousin who was at Sam Simpson's at Christmas? Emma's cousin? We need to check if it's the same person. If it is, that would be very interesting.'

'You're right. It *is* the same name. I'll get on to it and check him out,' said Georgia.

'Brian Turner didn't mention any connection... if there is one, I wonder if he's aware of it. We need to pursue this. Let me know what you find out,' said Gayle. On the way back to the station, the conversation returned to the role of vigilante groups. 'Just between us, Georgia, they do a really good job of catching paedophiles. Turner was right, they've got quite an impressive track record. But, as you know, the official line is we can't condone people taking the law into their own hands.'

'Pity, really,' said Georgia. 'Wouldn't it be better if the police worked with them rather than disapproved of them?'

'You have a point, but I don't think that's going to happen any time soon. Anyway, let's see what Craig Burton has to say on Friday. The sooner we can speak with him, the better, so I think we'll catch him at the airport. In the meantime, do some background checks Turner as well as Burton. See if there's anything further we should know about either of them.'

CHAPTER THIRTY-FOUR

Craig Burton looked out of the window as the plane banked sharply to the left, heading inland over the coast, on its descent towards Newcastle International Airport. He never tired of this sight, a birds-eye view of Saint Mary's Island, with its majestic lighthouse and the red-shingled roofs of the nearby cottage buildings.

As he watched, a shaft of sunlight broke through a gap in the rainclouds, bathing the tall column in dazzling white light, contrasting it in sharp relief against the almost black sky. He could see that the tide was well out, revealing the rocky outcrop on which the island sat, and from his vantage point, he could just make out a colony of seals basking on the rocks below the sea wall. He sighed deeply, glad to be home. He loved the North East of England and couldn't imagine living anywhere else.

'Welcome to Newcastle where the temperature is a balmy four degrees, on this delightful winter's afternoon. Weather... a brisk westerly wind, with intermittent rain showers.' The captain's laconic drawl came over the public address of the Jet2 Boeing 757, his announcement eliciting a collective groan throughout the cabin. Time for the returning holiday makers to get back to reality.

The rain began as he made his way towards the terminal, whipped up by strong gusts of wind. *Nice welcome* he thought, hurrying across the tarmac, head down. He'd had a great time in Las Americas with his two mates, and despite being glad to be home, he wasn't happy about having to get back to work. Not when it meant leaving them to enjoy themselves for another week. Lucky buggers.

Notified by airport security that he was on his way through, Gayle kept an eye on the opaque automatic doors at Arrivals. 'He's wearing a grey hoodie, carrying a blue holdall,' she told Georgia.

They stood watching the doors opening and closing, disgorging holidaymakers of all shapes and sizes, many still wearing their skimpy summer clothes, some in shorts despite the bitter chill. After a few minutes, the doors opened to reveal their target. Early thirties, short dark hair, shaved at the sides, faded blue jeans, ripped at the knees, and the ubiquitous grey hoodie. The blue holdall did not look as though it could carry enough gear for one week's holiday let alone two observed Gayle. Some people could travel much lighter than others. *Maybe I'm too high maintenance* she thought, making a mental note to try harder with her packing in future. Not that she had any holidays planned for the foreseeable.

Gayle strode towards him. 'Craig Burton?' she asked, holding out her warrant card. 'DCI Jones. And this is my colleague DI Green.'

He paused, momentarily taken aback at the sight of the warrant card, looking from one to the other. 'Yeah, that's me.'

'Mr Burton, sorry to ambush you at the airport, but it's important that we speak to you without further delay. We'd like to ask you some questions in relation to an on-going enquiry,' said Gayle.

Gayle watched as understanding dawned on his face. 'Oh... right... this must be about Ian Cooper. Brian rang to tell me he'd been found dead. Told me you wanted to speak to me.'

'Did he?' Gayle wasn't surprised to learn that Brian Turner had warned him. 'We'd like you to come to the station now to answer a few questions, if you don't mind? It's on your way home, so it seems the logical place to talk. Is that ok with you?' She gestured towards the exit, expecting him to come with her.

'Hang on,' he said sharply, clearly irritated, and not making any move to go with her. 'I didn't expect to be hauled down to the station from the bloody airport. I mean, do I have a choice? I've just got back from a long flight. Can't it wait til tomorrow?'

'The flight's not that long, Mr Burton,' Gayle said wryly. 'But, yes, you have a choice. We can come to your home if you like?' she offered. 'But, no, it can't wait 'til tomorrow. We need to speak to you today. We've already had to wait five days for you to get back into the country.' She kept her steady gaze on him.

'I could give you a lift home, afterwards,' offered Georgia. 'It's the least we can do, under the circumstances.'

He looked from one to the other again, thinking through his options, before conceding 'Alright... I'll come to the station. Come to think of it, me mother wouldn't be too pleased to have the police at the house.' He heaved his holdall on to one shoulder and began to follow them across the Arrivals Hall. 'It'll save me a taxi fare, if nowt else, I suppose,' he added.

'You live with your mother, then?' asked Georgia, making conversation as they headed for the nearby short-term car park, where they'd left the maroon Ford Mondeo.

'Aye. For the time being. Since me and the ex broke up. Nice to get spoilt for a change,' he grinned. 'Me ma's a lovely cook... and she washes and irons me gear.'

'Didn't your ex do that for you then?' asked Georgia, holding the car door open for him.

'Not bloody likely,' he laughed, sliding into the back seat, and reaching for his seatbelt. Gayle gave her DI a warning look across the top of the car. Georgia's flirting would get her into real trouble one of these days.

Twenty minutes later, they were ensconced in Newcastle Central police headquarters, in Wallsend, seated at a metal desk in one of the small interview rooms, Burton on one side, the two detectives on the other.

'This all feels very official,' Burton observed, looking around at the pale green walls and dusty grey filing cabinets. 'Should I be worried? Am I a suspect or something?'

'No, Mr Burton, you are not a suspect at present. At this stage we are simply trying to rule people out of our enquiry. We need to speak to you because we know you were leading the Fair Justice investigation into the activities of Ian Cooper, and we'd like to ask you some questions about that,' Gayle explained.

'Fair enough,' he responded. 'Ask away.'

'Tell us how long you've been with Fair Justice?' asked Gayle. 'And why you joined them in the first place?'

'Just over five years, I'd say,' replied Burton. 'As to why I joined them, well... what do you think my motive was? It's a good thing to do. To save vulnerable young kids from perverts. Me and Brian grew up together and when he told me about Fair Justice and asked if I'd like to join, I thought "why not?" Computers are my thing, so I was sure I could help. Anyway, it's not as if the police are any good at catching them, is it?' He ran one tanned hand through his hair and sat back in his seat. 'We save a lot of kids from harm.'

'Tell us about Ian Cooper,' said Gayle. 'Why were you investigating him?'

'I think you know the way we work?' he said, leaning forward, folding his hands in front of him on the desk. 'We get into kids chat lines and look out for perverts getting in touch. We don't use any coercion. We let things take their course until they walk into the traps. If they suggest a meeting, we set it up and then meet them, with a camera. Usually, we call the police at the time of the meeting, and they pick them up. Anyway, I put the bait out there and, lo and behold, true to form, the bastard took it. Just out of bloody nick. That bastard's learned nowt. Thought a twelve-year-old girl was talking to him.'

'So, talk me through the process. Why were you in charge of this particular case?'

'No reason, really. It was my initial email he responded to, that's all.' He shrugged and sat back into his chair. 'And I was experienced enough to handle it.'

'How do you know the identity of the person you are messaging?' asked Georgia. 'Surely he doesn't give his real name?'

'That's a good question. Usually, we don't. We only have the name they choose to use online. And we don't know who they are until they turn up at the rendezvous and are arrested. But, in this particular case, posing as the girl I asked him for a photo and unbelievably, he sent one of himself. Taken quite a few years ago, of course, but I recognised the bastard.'

'Do you recall the date and time you set the trap for?' asked Gayle.

'Aye. Course I remember. It's not something you do every day. It's a tense, nerve-wracking time and I was hyper all day. Couldn't settle to anything, waiting for the time we agreed to meet. It was six o'clock on the twenty-seventh of December. I was looking forward to giving the bastard his Christmas present. Absolutely gutted when he didn't show up.'

'Hmm... and when was the last time you saw him?' asked Gayle, shuffling through some papers, before looking up at him.

'Saw him?' he raised his eyebrows. 'I never saw him. I've just told you he didn't turn up at the meet.'

'What about before that, Craig?' asked Gayle, watching his reaction carefully.

'Before that?' he asked, raising his chin. 'I've told you that's not the way we work. We don't meet up with the paedos until they take the bait.'

'Really? What about at his trial? Didn't you see him then?'Gayle looked down, straightening the papers on her desk. 'Surely you attended the trial of the man who attacked your cousin?' Once her papers were in a neat pile, she looked up at Burton. 'When did you plan to tell us that you are related to Emma Jackson Mr Burton?'

She watched as he blanched, blinking in surprise, before lowering his eyes. 'You even saw her at her brother's house over Christmas. At around the time the murder took place.'

After a few seconds he mumbled, 'Yeah, she's my cousin. 'But...'

Gayle cut him off. 'She's your cousin. And did you let Fair Justice know that your cousin was the victim of a paedophile?' she asked.

'Well, I wouldn't, would I?' he asked, a note of sarcasm creeping in. He paused, and then continued, 'They probably wouldn't have let me join if they'd known. We must be fair and objective, and maybe they'd have thought I couldn't be objective. That I'd be too emotionally involved with cases.'

'Well, they'd certainly know you couldn't possibly be objective with this one,' Gayle snapped. 'So, have I got this right? You were leading the team trying to entrap Ian Cooper. And you knew his identity. The man who, seven years earlier, had attacked and raped your cousin?' Gayle stared him out. 'And you kept to yourself the fact that you were related to the victim?'

He nodded, biting his lip. 'I knew they would take me off the case if they'd known. I wanted to be the one to catch the bastard. I didn't want to leave it to anyone else. I wanted to look the bastard in the eyes and let him know we had him. That he was going away for a very long time... He was mine.'

'He was yours?' she echoed. 'You must have hated him, after what he did to Emma? I know I would, if he'd done to a relative of mine what he did to your young cousin...'

'Course I hated the bastard,' he raised his voice, his face turning red. 'But I didn't kill him, much as I'd like to have done. I wanted him put behind bars again, for the rest of his fucking life.'

'So, Cooper took the bait, thinking he was talking with a young girl. Arranged to meet up with "her" but then simply didn't turn up at the rendezvous?'

'That's right. I went along to the meet with a couple of the team. It was in a supermarket car park. Morrison's at North Shields. We staked out the place, got into position and waited. The bastard didn't turn up. We were gutted. Me, more than the others, but they didn't know that of course.'

'So, what did you do then?' asked Gayle, sitting back in her chair, arms crossed.

'Went back to the office. Sent him a message, as the girl, asking why he hadn't come to meet me. Saying I was disappointed. But there was no reply.'

'Do you find out where these paedophiles live in the course of your enquiries?' asked Georgia.

'Not usually. And never as part of the official investigation. But sometimes, you know, rumours get around and you hear where the odd one lives. But we never go to their home or harass them. We work by a strict code. Do things properly, within the law.'

'Did you know where Ian Cooper was living?' asked Gayle.

'As a matter of fact, I did. A smart penthouse in South Shields. Too good for that bastard. But I swear I never went near it. I wanted to do everything by the book. That would have fucked the whole operation up and I didn't want to jeopardise catching him in the act.'

'And did you have any contact with Ian Cooper after his no-show?' asked Gayle.

'No. I went holiday a few days later. Before I went away, I tried a couple of times, posing as the girl, to contact him online. But there was never any response... Do you think he might already have been dead by then?'

'You see, what I'm having difficulty with is this, Mr Burton. You went to a lot of trouble to make sure you dealt with this case personally. You really wanted to get this paedophile who had beaten up and raped your cousin. He doesn't show up, and you just meekly accept that and go off on holiday? When you knew where he lived? I don't believe you. Come on, you must have been tempted to go round there and confront him?'

Burton jumped to his feet. 'I've bloody told you I didn't go near his flat. We don't do that. We have to act professionally; otherwise we can blow the whole case.'

'Sit down, Mr Burton. Tell me about your movements over the Christmas period. We know you stayed with Sam Simpson.'

'Yeah, I was just there for Christmas Day. Me mother was volunteering at the soup kitchens and Sam asked me to join him and the rest of the family at his place for Christmas dinner. I just stayed the one night, then went back home to me mothers. It was a nice surprise to see Emma all grown up. Hadn't seen her since before the attack... She was unnerved to know Cooper was back on the streets. I think that was her motivation for going to Berlin.'

'Well, I think that's all for now Mr Burton. Thank you for your time. We'll probably need to speak with you again at some stage, 'said Gayle, getting to her feet. 'Do you have any plans to go away again in the near future?'

'No. I'll be around. Not planning any more trips for a while,' he confirmed.

'Before Georgia takes you home, would you mind if we take a swab for DNA? Just for elimination purposes?'

'No worries,' Burton said, grinning. 'I've got nowt to hide.'

CHAPTER THIRTY-FIVE

'DCI Gayle Jones. Here to see the Governor. He's expecting me.' Gayle showed her warrant card at the desk. 'This is DI Green,' she gestured to Georgia, beside her.

They followed a portly guard as he waddled ahead of them, their footsteps echoing and bouncing off the drab grey/green walls of the corridor. It was Gayle's first time inside Frankland, and she couldn't help but be reminded of the evil within its walls. She knew that the high-security prison housed many notorious criminals. Ian Huntley, the murderer of those two sweet little girls, Jessica and Holly, was here. She wondered where Huntley's girlfriend, Maxine Ann Carr was living now, feeling sure she must have completed her sentence for providing Huntley with a false alibi. *A Teaching Assistant*, thought Gayle, *how could she?* Levi Bellfield, the killer of little Millie Dowler was also here, and prior to his death, Peter Sutcliffe, the Yorkshire Ripper. She remembered he'd murdered thirteen women and attacked many others...

Her thoughts were interrupted by a wide-eyed Georgia. 'This is where Michael Adebolajo is kept,' she whispered, referring to the killer of Fusilier Lee Rigby in 2013. Gayle could swear she saw Georgia shiver. Clearly, she was affected to some degree by being under the same roof as so much unadulterated evil. Gayle didn't like to admit, even to herself, that despite having become inured to most violent crime over the years, she too felt pretty much the same, *I wouldn't fancy working here*, she thought.

The Governor greeted them cordially, shaking their hands and offering refreshments, which they declined. He indicated two chairs opposite his large, rather imposing desk, before taking his own seat, facing them. Well built, short grey hair, acne scars. Not bad looking. Gayle estimated him to be in his late fifties.

'You told me on the phone you're investigating the death of one of our former inmates... Ian Cooper?' He peered steadily at Gayle over his rimless glasses, getting straight down to business. No small talk, clearly a busy man. 'What would you like to know?'

Without preamble, Gayle outlined the circumstances in which the body had been found and its subsequent identification from DNA, as Ian Cooper. 'Obviously we're looking at all avenues, one of which is to check whether his death could be linked to his time in prison, given that he was only released a few weeks ago...'

'I made a few enquiries following your phone call,' the Governor said, rubbing the side of his nose before opening a buff-coloured file on his desk. 'He wasn't popular. Hardly surprising. Child molesters are given a rough ride here. He was seriously assaulted a number of times over the years...' He leafed through the contents of the file. 'Let me see... yes, the first time in 2013, soon after his arrival. He was badly beaten in his cell. Sexually assaulted. Fractured skull. His attackers weren't identified on that occasion. Subsequent assaults took place from time to time, none quite as serious as the first.'

'I thought you segregated paedophiles, for their own safety. You know, to prevent this sort of thing happening?' commented Gayle.

'Not completely, and let's face it, where there's a will, there's a way. Inmates can be incredibly inventive once they've identified a target.' There was steeliness to his voice, giving Gayle the distinct impression that he didn't altogether disapprove.

'Hmm... Anything else that might be relevant? 'asked Gayle, sensing there was more information to come.

'He's a nasty piece of work. As I'm sure you already know, he's been dealing for most of his life, albeit he's adept at avoiding prosecution. Word is he was heavily involved with a county lines gang in Durham, not long before his arrest. The two activities can go hand in hand, plenty of opportunity to sexually abuse the young kids they recruit to courier drugs for them. The bastards use sexual assault to intimidate and humiliate the kids, keep them in line. Make them more amenable. And more and more, they're using young girls to make the deliveries. Less likely to be suspects apparently. Anyway, we're pretty sure he was organising stuff from here. We know from CHIS there was plenty of communication with gang members on the outside. Nothing we could prove, more's the pity. And believe you me, we tried. The grapevine in here can be very accurate, but short on providing evidence. Phones get smuggled in; snatches of conversations overheard... but nothing concrete. May be worth you checking it out though. Could be some gang-related thing. Maybe someone didn't like him being back in circulation?'

'Hmm, we're aware he's a dealer. A particularly slippery one. We'll check out the County Lines angle, thanks.'

'There may be nothing in it,' replied the Governor. 'Just thought I should mention the rumour. Now, is there anything else I can help you with?' he said, glancing at his watch. 'Only I have another meeting to attend.'

Gayle got to her feet with Georgia following suit. She held out her hand. 'No, you've been very helpful. Thank you for taking the time to see us.'

'Pleasure. If you think of anything else, just give me a call. Pearson will show you out. I'd wish you luck in finding the perp, but I couldn't really care less. One more animal off the streets is no tragedy in my book,' he said with a grimace.

CHAPTER THIRTY-SIX

'Let's sum up where we are,' began Gayle. A few of the team were in the MIR, Kris leaning against a windowsill, Georgia at her desk, a few DCs tapping away at their computers or on the phone.

Gayle, absently fiddling with the gold locket at her neck, a habit she vowed to break after a colleague told her it made her look nervous, was perched on the corner of a desk beside the Murder board. Now festooned with photographs, notations, and yellow post-it notes, she studied the display for a while, before turning to Kris. 'So, what have we got?' She pointed to one of the photos. 'First of all, there's the Fair Justice link, and Craig Burton she said, tapping his photo with her index finger. 'A cousin of Emma Jackson, the girl brutally raped by the vic. He's definitely in the frame. What else have you found out about him, Kris?'

'Well, as we know, he didn't leave the country until the twenty-ninth of December, so he was still around when the murder took place. No clear alibi for the days before he flew to Tenerife, other than for Christmas Day when he was at Sam Simpson's house with the rest of the family. Works as a self-employed decorator but was on holiday from work from the twenty-third of December. Lives in Howdon with his mother since splitting up with his partner. He could easily have driven through the Tunnel to South Shields, committed the murder, stolen the vic's car and driven the body to Rothbury. We've got the Tyne Tunnel people checking their records over the relevant four day period, to see if they can find his car going through.' Kris got to his feet, rubbing the back of his neck. 'We've dug into his background. No previous, apart from a couple of driving convictions when he was younger. His mother is Emma's mother's sister. She and Rachel are pretty close, and used to see a lot of each other, before the move to Walton Bridge. He grew up with Emma in his life and was fond of her. He was devastated when she was attacked. Definitely gives him a motive.'

Resuming his seat on the windowsill, he continued. 'Burton's mother claims that he didn't stay out late on any of the nights in question. However, she also told us that she is in the habit of going to bed around eleven, so she could easily have been asleep and unaware of the time her son came home.

'We've shown Burton's photograph to the residents who took in the driver of the car, but their reaction was pretty vague. None could say it was definitely him, but there again they couldn't say it wasn't. Same with the manager at the hotel. They all say, he was of similar build, but as he wasn't seen without his hat and had a scarf obscuring much of his face, they can't ID him.

'We found a taxi driver who picked up a man from the hotel in Rothbury at eight thirty on the twenty-eighth. He took him into Newcastle, dropped him off at Central Station. He remembers it well, because it was a good fare to get at that time of the morning. Told us he was a bit dubious, with the weather being so bad, but he needed the money, so he accepted the job. We showed Burton's photo to him, but he told us the guy was muffled up in a scarf and hat and appeared to be asleep the whole journey, so there was no conversation, and he never got a good look at his face.'

'Was he paid in cash too?' Georgia asked.

'Afraid so,' replied Kris. 'Hard cash, so there's no record of a credit card.' Getting up from the windowsill, he scratched the top of his number two cut.

'Hmm...' said Gayle, moving Burton's photo to the right of the board. 'We'll keep him as a person of interest for now. Now, what do we know about the other guests at Sam Jackson's place over Christmas?'

'Of everyone who was there, those with the strongest motives would be Sam Jackson himself. Always been protective of his little sister. He's a bit eccentric, odd. Doesn't want to take a DNA test, doesn't like his privacy being invaded. Then there's Emma's father, Tommy Simpson' he began, counting them off on his fingers as he spoke. 'The grandfather...'

'Grandfather?' interrupted Gayle. 'How old is he, for God's sake?'

'Early sixties. Joe Simpson. Was a bit of a firebrand in his younger days. Several convictions for disturbing the peace, obstructing the police – used to go on demos and liked a good fight apparently. Nothing recent, but he's a robust guy still, so he can't be ruled out. Emma's his only granddaughter. When she was attacked, according to his friends, it unhinged him for a while. He went on benders, got mortal, made all sorts of threats.'

'Can he account for his movements?' asked Gayle.

'As much as any of them can. We're still working on it. There's a vagueness about who was where, and when. People were coming and going all over the Christmas period. It's like a bloody Agatha Christie novel. All kinds of activities going on. Joe Simpson said he did a lot of walking, mostly with his wife. I've checked and apparently, they're both hikers. Members of walking groups back where they live, in Durham.'

'Come on Kris, we need to pin all of them down. In particular we need to know if anyone was away overnight. Use more people if you need to. We need exact details of their whereabouts, with as much corroboration as possible. We know the perp didn't leave Rothbury until the morning, and then presumably had to get back to Cooper's flat to pick up his own car, then get back to the house, so we need to establish beyond doubt if anyone was missing from the house for all of that night.' Gayle was pacing now, frantically sliding the locket at her throat back and forth. *Damn,* she thought, irritably, *I'm going to have to stop wearing this thing.* 'Without an exact date of death, we have a window of a few days. Therefore, we need to establish the movements of them all over the whole of the potential time frame.'

'I'm aware of that, boss. We're still working on it,' responded Kris, his tone conciliatory, indicating he considered the boss was in a bit of a strop this morning. 'Almost there.'

'We're amassing quite a list of persons of interest,' commented Georgia. 'So many people seem to have a motive for wanting him dead.'

'True,' said Gayle briskly. 'We also need to look at Emma's boyfriend, Matt. The one she left behind in Wallsend. He still has strong feelings for Emma, according to her mother. He's at Newcastle University now.' She turned to Georgia leaning against a nearby cupboard. 'Make contact with him. Arrange for us to have a chat. Tell him we're just conducting preliminary enquiries, etcetera.'

'There's the prison connection, too,' said Kris. 'The team you put on that is still digging. Looks like he was heavily into people trafficking.'

'Thanks, Kris,' said Gayle. 'Also, arrange to speak to all the other ex-cons staying in the bail hostel where Smith was sent before moving into his flat. We all know paedos are not well tolerated by the criminal fraternity. Villains code of conduct and all that. Could be that one or more of them found out what he'd done time for and decided to mete out their own form of punishment. Make sure they're all interviewed. Thorough background checks too. Ask for DNA, to rule them out.'

'And of course, it could be a stranger who just doesn't like paedos. Some vigilante, taking the law into his own hands,' said Kris.

'There's a lot of work to do. We need to whittle down the list and home in on a prime suspect.'

CHAPTER THIRTY-SEVEN

'Ma'am, you might want to see this,' said PC Tracey Andrews, approaching Gayle's desk. A fairly new addition to the squad, Tracey was still learning the ropes, and was very keen to please. She looked excited but was clearly trying to compose her elfin features in an endeavour to act in a professional manner.

That morning Gayle had instructed the team to once more go through every inch of the CCTV footage obtained from Devonshire House, covering the period between the twenty-third and the twenty-seventh of December. She wanted them to double-check that they had photos of every single visitor.

Confirmation that the victim was killed in the flat meant someone had to have gained entry. It was unlikely the rear entrance could have been used as it could only be opened from the inside, so by that logic, the killer had to have entered through the front entrance. And therefore had to be on the CCTV covering the front entrance. The problem was, with it being Christmas there were a lot more visitors to the block than usual, all of whom had to be checked out. They were trying to match each visitor to a particular flat, a task which involved every one of the forty or so residents studying all one hundred and twenty stills taken from the video.

'What have you found for me, Tracey?' she asked, looking up from her screen.

'Everything's been checked and double checked, and we've definitely now got photos of every visitor to the block,' she began. 'And we've also managed to speak to each of the residents and go through all the photographs with them. It wasn't straightforward, boss, because some of the residents were away. A few of them are elderly and don't seem to know what day it is, never mind remember who their visitors were a few weeks ago.'

She fished a tissue from her sleeve before blowing her nose vigorously. 'Excuse me. Got a cold.' She sniffed, pushing the tissue back inside the sleeve of her blouse. 'There were a few visitors not recognised by anyone, so we went back to each individual in the block and asked them to take a second look at those particular photographs. One was identified. He'd been missed by the tenant first time round, as he was a friend of a friend, and the photo was a bit fuzzy. We checked it out with the friend, who confirms the ID.' She paused, clearly excited to be imparting such important news. 'No-one knows who this is,' she said, picking up two photographs from the nearby desk and handing one to Gayle.

Gayle studied the photos carefully. The first showed a middle-aged woman, slightly built. Wearing a thigh-length, black quilted jacket, its fur-trimmed hood obscuring part of her face. Slightly turned towards the camera, part of her face could just be seen, though not clearly. In the second, the woman had turned her head and looked up at the camera, giving a clear shot of her face. Gayle's breath caught in the back of her throat. 'I know this woman,' she said. 'Let me see the video footage.'

'Well, well, well. I think we'll pay this lady a visit. Good work Tracey.'

CHAPTER THIRTY-EIGHT

'Hello Sandra,' began Gayle. 'Remember me, DCI Gayle Jones? It's been a long time. You helped us to identify Ian Cooper and send him to prison seven years ago.' Wearing a pair of black leggings, teamed with an emerald green tunic, Sandra looked smarter than Gayle remembered her, but the lines on her face had deepened considerably and her skin had a dull, greyish look.

'Oh, oh yes... of course I remember you. This is a surprise... how are you?' Sandra looked momentarily taken aback to see Gayle on her doorstep. 'What...?'

'I'm ok thanks,' interrupted Gayle. 'We just need to have a word with you if that's alright. This is my colleague, DI Georgia Green.' She indicated Georgia standing next to her.

'Oh... right,' said Sandra. 'You'd better come in then.' She stepped back, opening the door wider to admit them. It was a sunny yet blustery day, and a blast of cold air accompanied them through the door. They followed Sandra up the stairs, Georgia, pulling her fingers through her windswept curls in an unsuccessful attempt to tidy them.

Gayle looked around. Sandra's living room looked very different from how she remembered it seven years earlier. More up to date, she thought, with fresh white walls and pale laminate floor. A sage green long-pile rug, leafy green plants and two pale green settees completed the new look.

'The place is looking lovely, Sandra,' Gayle observed. 'The plants are a really nice touch.' She rubbed a leaf on the nearest plant between her finger and thumb, realising it was artificial, but very realistic. 'Now,' she looked directly at Sandra, 'we need to speak to you about Ian Cooper. We have a few questions for you if you don't mind.'

'Ok...' Sandra almost whispered, looking down and patting her pockets fruitlessly. 'What questions?'

'When was the last time you saw him?' asked Gayle.

'Saw him?' said Sandra, turning away to rummage in a drawer. 'I haven't seen him for years. I did hear that he was released from prison... quite a shock. Far too quick.' She carried on searching, finally pulling out a packet of cigarettes, followed by a battered plastic lighter.

'And you haven't seen him since he was released?' asked Gayle.

'No... no, of course not,' said Sandra, turning to face Gayle. 'Why would I want to see him? Why are you asking?' She shook a cigarette into her hand, put it to her lips and grappled with the lighter, flicking it several times before successfully igniting her cigarette and taking a deep drag. Gayle noticed her hands were trembling, as she struggled to open a window to blow out the smoke.

'Ian Cooper's body has been found.' Gayle paused for effect. 'We're treating his death as suspicious. As part of our enquiries, I wonder if you could you tell us where you were and what you were doing on the twenty-seventh of December?'

'His body? He's dead?' stammered Sandra. When Gayle continued to look at her she continued, 'Shit... the twenty seventh, let me think. That was the day after Boxing Day so I wouldn't be at work. I think we just had a quiet day. We'd had a busy Christmas and Boxing Day with Katie and her kids, so we just chilled that day.'

'And did you leave the house at all that day?' asked Georgia.

'No... I don't think so... No, I'm pretty sure we didn't. We just watched TV and chilled.' Sandra inhaled, blowing a thick plume of smoke out of the window.

'And you say you haven't seen Ian Cooper since his release?' Have you ever been to his flat in South Shields, Sandra?'

‘No. How would I know where he lives? And why would I want to see him?’ asked Sandra, drawing deeply on her cigarette, before stubbing it out in an overflowing ashtray on the windowsill.

‘Very well. Sandra, I’d like you to come to the station for an interview under caution,’ Gayle told her. She watched Sandra’s reaction, noting her lack of surprise. Her only barely discernible reaction was a sudden stillness as she processed what Gayle was saying.

‘Okay...’ Sandra said, slowly. ‘Do you mean now? Am I under arrest?’ She didn’t show any emotion, seeming almost resigned to the situation.

‘You’re not under arrest at this stage,’ Gayle replied. ‘But I’d like you to come in voluntarily tomorrow morning. We’re in possession of some information that we’d like to ask you about,’ she explained. ‘There’s no compulsion but obviously it won’t look good if you refuse to come in. Do you know the address of the police station?’

‘Yes, in Wallsend. But what new information?’ Sandra asked. ‘Why don’t you ask your questions now?’

‘We’ll cover everything at the station. It will be a formal interview, which will be recorded. You might want to have your solicitor present. We’d like you to come in for eleven o’clock.’

Sandra opened her mouth to say something, then closed it again, seeming to consider Gayle’s words, before asking ‘If I’m not under arrest, why do I need a solicitor?’ She was struggling to light another cigarette with shaking hands.

‘You don’t have to have one Sandra. We must let you know that you are entitled to legal representation, should you wish. If you don’t have your own solicitor, you’ll be entitled to legal aid. It’s up to you,’ Gayle informed her.

‘Just a minute, it must be quite serious if you want me to come to the station?’ The question was rhetorical, as she looked from one to the other. 'I don't have my own solicitor... so yes, you'd better arrange legal aid for me.'

'We'll do that,' Georgia assured her. 'No problem,' she added, following Gayle's lead, and getting to her feet. 'He or she will be at the station before eleven tomorrow.' She smiled at Sandra in an attempt to give some reassurance as she watched her finally manage to light her cigarette with shaking hands.

'We'll see ourselves out,' said Gayle, walking to the door. 'And we'll see you at eleven tomorrow.'

Back in the car, Georgia observed, 'Well we know she's lying, and she's not very good at it. She had guilt written all over her face.'

'It'll be interesting to find out what she has to say when we show her the tape,' said Gayle.

CHAPTER THIRTY-NINE

The next morning, the interview commenced at eleven eighteen.

'Sandra, you have come into the station this morning voluntarily, at our request. You are not under arrest and are free to leave at any time. Do you understand?' began Gayle.

On one side of the table was Sandra, looking Gayle thought as though she'd had a sleepless night, the dark shadows beneath her eyes highlighting the strain clearly evident in her face this morning. Sitting next to her was the duty solicitor, a prim-looking young woman dressed in a plain grey short-sleeved dress, the matching jacket draped over the back of her chair. Georgia was on Gayle's right.

Getting the interview under way, Gayle listed those present, for the benefit of the tape. 'DCI Gayle Jones, DI Georgia Green, Ms Sandra Howard and her legal representative, Ms Claire Etherington. Sandra, we've asked you to come in for interview this morning because some information has come to light that we want to ask you about. Before, we get to that, can you tell us what you were doing during the period from the twenty-fourth to the twenty-seventh of December?'

'The twenty-fourth to the twenty-seventh? That's four days,' said Sandra, counting them off on shaking fingers. 'How am I supposed to remember everything over four whole days?' She looked enquiringly at her solicitor, who nodded at her.

'Tell us what you do remember. It was over the Christmas period, so it shouldn't be too difficult to recall where you were and who with,' said Gayle. 'Take your time. Start with Christmas Day if you like; you must remember what you did then.'

Sandra began wringing her hands before realising what she was doing and quickly putting them out of sight, under the table. 'We stopped work on the twenty-second, for the Christmas break and over the next couple of days I did some last-minute shopping,' she began. 'How much detail do you need? Have I got to remember where I was every minute?'

Slowly, painfully, Sandra worked through each day, trying to remember the banal detail of her Christmas break. 'Christmas Day, we had Katie and her two children for the day. They came over in the morning and stayed overnight. It was lovely having the children there, seeing their little faces.' She smiled briefly, remembering. 'Boxing Day we all drove to the beach and went for a long walk. From Whitley Bay to Tynemouth and back again. It was cold, but the kids loved it.'

'Did they stay overnight on Boxing Day too?' asked Gayle.

'No, we dropped them off home when we came back from the beach. That would be about five-ish. Marek and me went home, had a few drinks, watched the telly and had an early night.'

'What about the next day? The twenty-seventh,' asked Gayle. 'Did you go out at all?'

'The twenty-seventh? You asked me about this yesterday. I can't remember the detail... let me think. We didn't do anything special... no, we didn't go out. I remember we played scrabble. Marek likes to play, he's not very good at it but he says it improves his English. God, it's hard trying to remember everything... we made a curry together from scratch, using up the last of the turkey...'

'So, you didn't go to South Shields at any time on the twenty-seventh?' Gayle asked, studying Sandra's reaction.

'South Shields? No, definitely not. Why would I go to South Shields?' Sandra was wringing her hands again.

'Georgia?' said Gayle, turning to her. Georgia pressed a few keys on her computer before turning the screen so they could all see it. The monitor came to life, and they sat in silence watching the comings and goings through the doorway to the block of flats where Ian Cooper lived. 'Slow it down... there... go back a bit Georgia.' The screen froze, showing a slim woman, wearing a black quilted jacket, with a fur-trimmed hood pulled over her head. As they watched, the woman turned her head and looked up at the camera. It was clearly Sandra, from whom there was an audible gasp before she clamped her hand over her mouth. 'You can see the date in the corner of the screen, Sandra. Twenty-seventh of December 2022,' said Gayle, pointing to the monitor. 'This is CCTV footage taken from a camera sited at the doorway to the apartments in South Shields, where Ian Cooper lived. Is that you, entering the building?'

Sandra opened her mouth to speak, but Claire Etherington placed a hand over hers to quieten her. 'I'd like a break now, to confer with my client,' she announced. Gayle agreed and they all got to their feet, to the sound of chairs scraping on the vinyl floor covering.

'Interview suspended eleven forty-five,' Gayle told the tape, rising to her feet, grateful for a chance to ring her mother. Guilt at not doing enough for her seemed a permanent part of her psyche these days. Her heart told her she really should halt her career for now to care for her mum on a full-time basis, but her head said otherwise. She knew things could go on for a quite a while yet, and she was realistic enough to know that financial implications aside, she wouldn't be able to cope with that. 'We'll re-convene at twelve fifteen,' she told them, before hurrying to her office to make her call. When the interview resumed, some thirty minutes later, Claire told them her client would like to make a statement. Gayle nodded, settled back in her seat, and looked enquiringly at Sandra.

'I did go to South Shields,' Sandra confessed. 'I wanted to see him. Ian Cooper. But I didn't kill him. I swear I didn't kill him,' she said, vigorously shaking her head.

'So, tell us what did happen, Sandra,' suggested Gayle, putting both elbows on the table, resting her chin on her hands.

'It's a long story,' said Sandra, looking directly at Gayle. 'You know about my history with Ian Cooper. How desperate I was to get away from him. I never wanted to see him again, ever.' She paused, lowered her eyes, and began wringing her hands. 'But I found out something, something so terrible I had to confront him with it. I wanted to see his face when I told him I knew what he'd done.' Her voice had reduced almost to a whisper.

'Go on,' said Gayle, eyebrows raised. ''What was it you found out?'

'There's a woman called Anne, who sits next to me at work. She's a terrible gossip. Anyway, she knows people in the police and social services and she's always nattering on about things she finds out. She told me stuff... about the girl. The one he attacked.'

'Eva?' asked Gayle. 'Or Emma as she's now called,'

Sandra nodded and continued. 'Anne and her husband sometimes have dinner with some neighbours of theirs who moved up from London. Antonia and Declan. She's a social worker and she's apparently very good friends with another social worker called Charlotte who lives in London. Anyway, this Antonia told them some things about Emma's history. Said she felt sorry for the kid as she's had a shit life. Told them Charlotte had had to take the kid away from her mother and father when she was just a baby... the father was violent and both parents were drug addicts... Brought back all my old feelings of guilt and self-loathing, to hear about a kid being removed like that.' She hung her head for a few moments before continuing.

'Then, just before Christmas, I was at work and Anne said something that completely freaked me out. She said the social worker had told them the girl had been put into the care of her grandparents at first. Then she said the grandparents had both been killed in a car crash on the motorway and the girl was alone again and eventually adopted.' She stopped talking, stared at the table.

'Why would that freak you out?' asked Georgia. But Gayle was already putting two and two together.

'That's exactly what happened to my Chloe,' Sandra whispered. 'The girl must be my Chloe. My daughter... And his.' Sandra kept her eyes on the desk, unable to meet their eyes.

Gayle leaned over the desk, looking intently at Sandra. 'You're saying you think the girl he attacked is Chloe, the daughter who was taken from you when she was three? You are saying you believe Ian Cooper attacked and raped his own daughter?' Her tone was gentle but firm. 'Is that what you went to tell him?'

'Yes,' nodded Sandra, her face a picture of misery. 'To confront him. To tell him what an evil bastard he is. I wanted to know if he knew, somehow, that she was his little girl when...' Her eyes filled up. A tear spilled over, running down her cheek and splashing on to the desk. 'She has to be my daughter,' she reiterated. 'It's too much of a coincidence. Chloe was given to my parents, and they were both killed when a van crossed the central reservation. That was less than a year after Chloe had been taken from me. It was a terrible time.'

'So, what happened when you went to see him, Sandra?' asked Gayle, getting her back on track.

Another deep breath and Sandra continued. 'When I knocked on his door, I was shaking; my knees were literally knocking together. I was terrified... I nearly ran back down the stairs. But then he came to the door. It was horrible, seeing him again. All the old fear came flooding back. I'd been conditioned to be frightened of him, and I was. He looked gobsmacked to see me at the door. Told me to come in.' She hesitated, wringing her hands, twisting the narrow silver ring she wore on her little finger round and round.

'Are you alright, Sandra?' asked Gayle, noticing the colour drain from Sandra's face. 'Just take your time. Have some more water.' She pushed the water glass nearer to Sandra.

Sandra took a sip, her hands shaking. 'I told him about the girl... That she's his daughter. He didn't believe me at first. Got belligerent and nasty. Just like he always used to. He asked what the fuck I was talking about,' she said, taking a tissue from the box Georgia pushed towards her. 'I kept calm,' she sniffed, 'and explained about the girl's grandparents being killed in a car crash, just like Chloe's. We were still together when my mother and father were killed, so he already knew the details. That Chloe had been in the car and brought out unhurt. That she'd been adopted. I told him it was all too much of a coincidence for the girl he raped not to be Chloe.'

'What was his reaction to that bombshell then?' asked Gayle.

'He... he started to laugh,' said Sandra. 'He actually started to laugh... Then he said he still didn't believe me; I was making it up. He paced around the room, trying to process the information. Back and forth, back and forth…' Gayle could see Sandra picturing the scene. 'Then he seemed to accept what I was saying and came to a halt in front of me. I was standing near the door, and he put his hand on the door frame and leaned into my face. *So, I fucked my own daughter, then?* he asked. He looked pleased, grinning to himself. *Fucking hell, wait til I tell the lads about this. They're gonna love it. That little virgin was my own kid. They'll want to hear every detail over and over again...'* She paused, shaking her head from side to side, breathing deeply in an effort to pull herself together.

'I was appalled. I... I couldn't believe what he was saying. He was actually proud of what he'd done. Couldn't wait to tell his sick paedo friends. It was going to give him some extra kudos. It didn't seem possible that even he could be so sick. So evil. I was disgusted, angry. I swore at him, called him a filthy pervert. I needed to get out of there, away from him. I turned to open the door, but he grabbed my wrist and dragged me away from it. I managed to pull myself free and ran into the kitchen, trying to find another way out. He followed me... and...' she stopped and put her head into her hands, taking deep breaths.

Gayle exchanged glances with Georgia; this was turning out to be quite a harrowing interview. She gave Sandra some time to compose herself, before offering her more water. Claire asked if she needed another break. Sandra shook her head and wiped her eyes again, before continuing.

'He taunted me. Said the real reason I'd gone to see him was because I missed him. Wanted him. Said I was gagging for it... He grabbed my shoulders and pushed me across the kitchen... He had me backed against the bench, started breathing hard... feeling me up. I was trying to push him away, but he was too strong... I felt around on the bench behind me for something to defend myself with and I felt a knife... I picked it up and tried to stab him...' Dropping her head in her hands once more, Sandra began rocking back and forth in her seat, little keening noises coming from her.

Claire put a hand on Sandra's shoulder and asked if she was alright to continue. When Sandra didn't respond, she got to her feet. 'Clearly my client is too distressed to continue at present,' she said. 'I think we need to stop there...'

'No,' interrupted Sandra, pushing her hand away. 'No, let me finish... I need to tell them.' She looked at Gayle as she pushed Claire's arm away and sat up straighter in her chair, taking a deep breath. 'It's alright. I'm ok now.' She put her hands together on the table, clasping them so tightly that the knuckles stood out, starkly white.

'If you're sure, Sandra?' asked Gayle, hiding her relief. The last thing she wanted at this juncture was a break in the interview. She waited for Sandra to speak, but when she seemed to be struggling to get the words out, opening and closing her mouth a couple of times, Gayle asked her, 'What happened then, Sandra? Did you stab him?'

'No... no... I couldn't. I would have if I could. But... I wasn't strong enough. He laughed at me, took the knife off me, and threw it on the floor, out of reach. He taunted me, saying stuff; *this is what you came here for...* Called me a dirty whore. Said if I wanted it rough, that's what I was going to get. He turned me around... forced me forward over the bench, ripped my tights down. I fought as hard as I could... cried out... but... he raped me.' She dropped her head into her hands again. 'I couldn't stop him...' she whispered through her fingers. 'I could hardly breathe... The bench was digging into my ribcage. He was too strong... too strong.' She shook her head and began to sob again. This time Claire was successful in calling a halt to the interview.

'Interview suspended thirteen fifteen,' said Gayle, before switching off the tape.

'Bloody hell,' said Georgia, once they'd left the room. 'That's a turn up for the books. You know, if she had managed to stab him, it would have been self-defence under those circumstances.'

'That's true,' said Gayle. 'No doubt we'll find out a bit more when we reconvene. And I want Marek brought in straight away. I don't want them to have a chance to confer before we hear his side of this. This is getting very interesting. It puts Sandra in the flat and explains in advance any fingerprints of hers that may be on the knife, or elsewhere. And we need to get a warrant to search their flat. Look for any bloodstained clothes or other evidence.'

'I'm on it, boss,' said Georgia. 'I wonder if Ian Cooper really was Emma's father?' she pondered. 'Sandra certainly seems to be convinced that he was. If that's not motive enough to kill someone, I don't know what is. A father raping his own daughter and then laughing about it. Doesn't get much more devastating than that.'

'Interview recommencing fourteen hundred hours,' intoned Gayle, reiterating for the record the attendees. Sandra seemed composed and looked as though she'd made an effort to tidy herself up a bit, had even applied a trace of lipstick. 'Sandra, I'd like to start by thanking you for you telling us about your ordeal at the hands of Ian Cooper. That took a lot of courage. It can't have been easy for you to talk about it. Going forward, if you need any help in dealing with the trauma, we can put you in touch with a rape counsellor. There's a lot of support available these days for people who are victims of sexual assaults.' Sandra nodded in acknowledgement, and Gayle asked, 'Do you feel up to continuing? Are you able to tell us what happened next, after the assault?'

'Yes...' Sandra hesitated. 'I... I felt humiliated. Disgusted with myself for getting into a position where he could do that to me. Realised how stupid I'd been. I should never have gone there alone. What had I hoped to achieve? I straightened my clothes as best I could. He was blocking the doorway to the living room, one hand on each side of the frame, smirking, saying foul things. I noticed another door and tried that. It turned out to be the back door, leading to the fire exit. He didn't make any move to stop me. I ran along a corridor, down the stairs and out through the fire door at the bottom. Then I ran round to the front, got into my car, and drove off. I stopped in a lay-by a few streets away and tried to pull myself together. I couldn't go home in that state. Couldn't tell Marek what I'd done – what Cooper had done to me. So I went to Katie's, where I'd told Marek I was going in the first place. She wanted to ring the police, but I wouldn't let her. I didn't want anyone to know. In the end, she said she'd keep my secret. Cleaned me up, gave me some spare tights so I could look normal when I got home.'

'What happened once you got home, Sandra?' asked Georgia.

'I... I said I had a migraine. It was hard to act normal, so I thought that was the best excuse. I do get them from time to time, so Marek wasn't suspicious. He put me to bed, full of concern, checked on me from time to time. By the next day I was able to function more or less as usual.'

'But, Sandra,' said Gayle, 'why didn't you tell Marek? Surely that would have been better. You would know that Cooper would have been picked up immediately and returned to prison if you'd told the police. Why didn't you?' It wasn't making sense to Gayle that Sandra would keep all that to herself.

'If I'd told Marek, he would have killed him. No doubt at all. He's a kind, decent man, but he hates injustice. And he loves me. He would have found him, and he would have killed him. I didn't want that to happen, I didn't want him going to prison.' Sandra closed her eyes for a few seconds, before speaking again. 'When you came last night, I guessed you must have something, maybe a witness who saw me in South Shields. I knew I'd have to tell you. So, I sat Marek down and told him everything. I've never seen him so upset, so angry, so raging mad. I did the right thing not telling him at the time. He would have torn Ian Cooper limb from limb.'

'I see,' said Gayle. 'Ok, we'll leave it there for now. Obviously, we'll be checking all this out with Marek. He's in an interview room just down the corridor. Will his account be the same as yours?' asked Gayle, watching for Sandra's reaction.

Unperturbed, Sandra said quietly, 'Of course it will. Because it's the truth.'

CHAPTER FORTY

'Mr Kowalska, we've asked you to come in today to answer some questions in relation to our enquiries into a suspicious death.'

'Why you want to speak to me?' he demanded in heavily accented English as he strode into the room. 'What it fucking matter who killed the dirty bastard? You bloody English... too bloody soft. This country going to shite... Getting like third fucking world... I leave Poland for this...?'

Gayle surveyed him coolly, noting he was neatly dressed in a black leather jacket, black jeans, and beige suede loafers. She was mildly surprised at his volatility. The picture Sandra had painted of her partner was one of a kind, caring, man, albeit one she considered capable of murder under the right circumstances. She couldn't quite picture her with this volatile man, with his unruly bohemian hair and interesting vocabulary.

'Thank you for coming in Mr Kowalska,' Gayle interrupted. 'Please take a seat.' Georgia pulled out a chair for him, indicated with her hand that he should take it. 'We are investigating a murder, and are interviewing a number of people,' continued Gayle. 'At this stage, we are simply trying to rule people out of our enquiry. We'd like to ask you some questions,' she said, taking a seat opposite him.

'You got my Sandra here too. Why? Why you bloody people interrogate defenceless woman? You think she strong enough to kill that wanker bastard?' He let out a short, derisive laugh, shaking his head in disbelief.

'We need to establish your movements on the afternoon and night of twenty seventh of December Mr Kowalska, the day after Boxing Day. Can you tell us what you were doing during that time?' Gayle spoke crisply, with authority. This one was going to take some keeping in line.

'You fucking people. Why you waste time on that wanker? In my country...'

Gayle put her hand out, palm forward 'Stop, Mr Kowalska. I am asking the questions here, not you. Just answer please. What were you doing on the twenty-seventh of December?' She steepled her hands and waited.

'How can I fucking remember?' he started. 'Day after Boxing Day?' He rubbed his chin, his stubble making a rasping sound. 'Ah, yes, I was at home all day. We have hectic Christmas, and we just need to chill,' he sat back, job done.

'Was Sandra with you all day?' asked Gayle.

'I think so, yes...' he rubbed his chin again. 'Oh, hang on, I remember now. No, she go to see her friend for short time. Why...?'

'Which friend was that?' asked Gayle, folding her arms and leaning back in her chair.

'She go to see Katie,' he muttered, nodding his head. 'Said one of her kids is ill.'

'And how long was she away, Mr Kowalska? And what happened when she came back?'

He muttered about her being gone for about two or three hours. 'She not feeling well when she come back. Headache... migraine she say. So, she went to bed.'

'And then?' asked Gayle.

'Then?' asked Marek. 'I just watch television, have little doze. Check on Sandra. What else do you want to know? If I use toilet?'

Gayle said nothing. Let the silence stretch, watched him getting more uncomfortable, looking around the room. Anywhere but at Gayle. Eventually she decided to put him out of his misery.

'Why don't you tell us what really happened, Marek?' Gayle watched the changing expressions on his face. He sat very still, biting his lip and staring at the desk.

'She told you?' he muttered eventually, raising his eyes to meet Gayle's. I didn't know for sure if she was going to tell you... she only tell me about it last night...'

'She didn't have much choice,' said Georgia, indicating the computer beside her on the desk. We have CCTV footage of Sandra entering the building where Ian Cooper lived, at eleven twenty on the morning of the twenty-seventh of December.' On the screen was the shot of Sandra looking up at the camera.

Marek's eyes widened, before he set his lips in a hard line, and nodded in acceptance. 'Everything I tell you is true,' he said. 'Until last night I know nothing different.' Speaking in a subdued voice, he explained. 'It is true she tell me she go to see Katie. Katie having some problems, I don't know, something to do with one of her kids. Anyway, when Sandra comes back, she quiet, very pale. Said she didn't feel too good. Had migraine, felt sick. She went to bed.' He paused, rubbing his hands over his face. His face darkened. 'But last night, you tell her you want to talk to her. After you go, she tell me she needs to tell me something... that's when I find out what he did to her.' He dropped his head into his hands. 'I can't believe what she is telling me...'

'What exactly did she tell you last night?' asked Gayle.

'She went to tell him that girl is his daughter. That he attacks and rapes his own daughter. She told me he laughed. Boasted he would tell his wanker mates he fuck his own daughter. Thinks it's a real turn-on... Can you imagine? What kind of fucking monster...?' Visibly upset, he took a sip of water, his hand shaking.

'What did she say happened next?' prompted Gayle.

'Sandra said he told her the real reason she was there was to see him... She tried to leave but he dragged her away from the door. She ran in kitchen, to get away from him. She saw knife on the bench, pick it up to defend herself, but he laughed again. She only small. No match for that bastard. He took it from her. He pushed her over the bench and... He raped her.' Wiping his eyes with his knuckles, he repeated, 'The bastard raped her.'

Gayle gave him a minute to compose himself, before continuing the questioning.

'How do you know she was no match for him? Have you ever met him?'

'I see pictures of him from when he rape that girl. I Google him and see he is big bastard.'

'I see. What time did Sandra return home, Mr Kowalska? Can you remember roughly how long she was away?'

He looked at her with dull eyes. 'I already tell you. Maybe around two hours? She told me she sat in car park to calm down before she come home.' He took another sip, still shaking. 'She went to Katie's to get cleaned up and borrow some clothes.'

'Why did she not tell you straight away what had happened?' asked Georgia.

'She thinks I would kill him,' he said simply. 'And she is fucking right. If she tell me what that bastard wanker did to her, I kill him with my bare hands.' He looked down at his hands, turning them over, examining them. 'I could still kill him, but someone beat me to it and got the cunt,' he added. His face flushed with mounting anger; he shouted in frustration 'Why she not fucking tell me? It would be pleasure to remove that piece of shit from this earth.' He sank back into his chair, breathing heavily.

'So, going back to when Sandra went off to bed with her migraine,' continued Gayle, 'what did you do then?'

'Do? I do nothing. Watch a bit of telly, doze on and off. Make myself something to eat. Check on Sandra couple of times, take her a cup of tea up. I have early night. I sleep in spare room to give Sandra some peace.'

'And can anyone vouch for you?' asked Gayle.

'Vouch? Oh, you mean is anyone else with me? No, just me. And Sandra upstairs.'

'Can you remember what you watched on television?' asked Georgia.

'Bloody hell, let me think... No, I don't know, some variety shit, I think, but I can't remember. Can you remember what you watched on the twenty-seventh of December?'

'Did you leave your flat that day, at any time, for any reason, after Sandra returned from South Shields?' asked Gayle.

'No, I stay there all day and night,' Marek confirmed.

'Mr Kowalska, we've obtained a warrant to search your house. The team are ready to go in as soon as you return home.' Gayle watched the shocked reaction on Kowalska's face. 'And we need to check your mobile phone records.'

'I tell truth. You find nothing at house. Or on phone. Fucking waste of time...'

'Ok. Interview terminated at sixteen-forty. Thank you for coming in, Mr Kowalska. We may need to speak to you again, but for now you are free to go... Oh, just one more thing, would you be agreeable to letting us take a swab for DNA purposes, and your fingerprints before you leave? For elimination purposes, you understand.'

'I tell truth,' he repeated. 'I do swab and fingerprints. And here is my fucking phone.' He fished his mobile from his back pocket and threw it on to the desk.

'The forensic team will be at your house when you arrive there, Mr Kowalska. If you co-operate with them, the search shouldn't take too long.'

Once he'd left, Gayle and Georgia joined the others in the Control Room, some of whom had watched the interview through the two-way mirror. 'Well, he seemed genuine,' said Gayle. 'But he has no alibi. He and Sandra could have cooked up their story together. If Sandra did in fact tell him about the rape, he would have had a very strong motive. He could have carried out the murder and driven to Rothbury to dispose of the body that afternoon. We need to check any CCTV around his flat and en route to the murder scene. It's possible Sandra was with him. If he did it, someone would have needed to bring his car home. It's not likely he would leave his own vehicle there while he drove the body up to Rothbury in Cooper's car. We certainly can't rule him out just yet.'

'DNA sample and fingerprints have been taken, so we'll see if there's a match to anything in the vic's flat.' Gayle said. 'Could even be that Sandra did kill him and Marek helped cover it up by mutilating the body afterwards? Go through the CCTV footage again. Double-check there's no sign of Marek going into the building, 'Gayle continued. 'Of course, there's always the possibility he could have gone in the back way since Sandra was aware of that entrance. I want background checks on Marek, find out his history, any previous in Poland, etcetera. Let's see what we can find out about him.'

Gayle sighed. 'Kris, how did you get on with the childhood sweetheart, Matthew White?' she asked.

'I caught up with him at university and had an informal chat with him. Nice kid, helpful. He confirmed that he was devastated for Eva, as he calls her, when he heard that Cooper was getting out – saw it on the internet apparently- and said he felt compelled to see her, to make sure she was alright. He confirmed he'd gone down to Walton Bridge try to see her. That was on sixteenth December and as we already know, she wasn't there. His parents corroborate his movements. Stayed in Wallsend with them over the whole of the Christmas and New Year period. They confirm that although he went out Christmas Eve, he was home before midnight and over the next three days he didn't go out, other than to walk the dog. And, a major point, he doesn't have a car and hasn't yet learned to drive.'

'Hmm... put him on the back burner for now,' said Gayle. 'Can't rule him out absolutely. These kids can often drive long before they get a licence. And he was upset enough at Cooper's release to make the journey to Walton Bridge to try to see Emma.'

CHAPTER FORTY-ONE

'Sam?' Rachel sounded agitated. 'Sam, your father's gone missing again. He... he went out early this morning, I'm not sure what time, but he wasn't in bed when I woke up at six... I don't know what's going on with him. His phone is just going to voicemail. When he is here, he's remote. Won't speak to me... refuses to tell me what's wrong. Honestly Sam, I'm at the end of my tether... I don't know what to ...'

'Look, mum,' interrupted Sam. 'Sorry, can't talk just now. I'm in a meeting. Can I call you back in a couple of hours? Try not to worry, he'll turn up eventually. He always does.' Sam spoke rapidly; obviously she'd chosen a bad time to call.

'Ok.' Disappointed and crestfallen, Rachel ended the call and sat motionless on the end of the bed, staring out of the window, watching rivulets of water chasing each other down the pane. Something was very wrong with Tommy, but he wouldn't open up to her. Just got angry when she tried to get to the bottom of it. Could it be... she hardly dared let the thought form in her head. Could he have...? She thought back to Christmas. That's when he really started to get weird, although thinking about it, he hadn't been the same since the Victim Support woman's visit with the news about Cooper's impending release. She made herself think the unthinkable. Could he have murdered Cooper? He disappeared that night at Sam's, and he'd lied to the police when they asked about his movements. That was on the twenty-seventh, so it fit in with the timescale given by the detective. By omission, they'd all lied. No-one had volunteered the fact that Tommy had disappeared for a whole night. Did Sam have his suspicions too, she wondered. Oh, she needed to talk this through with Sam. He would know what to do...

She sat there for a long time, almost in a trance. A sharp knock at the front door brought her to the present and she jumped up and hurried down the stairs, wiping her wet face with one hand. She hadn't even realised she'd been crying. The rapping came again, louder this time.

'Coming,' she cried. 'Give me a chance.' She could see through the frosted glass two large dark shapes and a flash of fluorescent green. Her heart missed a beat as she opened the door to reveal two grim-faced police officers, one wearing a green tabard.

'Mrs Rachel Jackson?' asked one, holding out her warrant card. 'I'm Sergeant Isabelle Grant and this is PC Jayden Daniels. May we come in?'

She nodded, unable to speak, a feeling of dread stealing over her. She led the way into the sitting room, followed by the two officers.

'Is there anyone with you, Mrs Jackson?' asked the young PC, looking around. He looked fresh out of college, just a boy really. When she confirmed she was alone in the house, he nodded and asked her to please sit down.

'My husband should be here...' she began, taking a seat on the settee, 'but he went out early this morning and I can't get in touch with him...'

'That's why we're here Mrs Jackson,' the sergeant said, sitting down beside her. 'I'm so sorry, there's no easy way to say this. A body has been found in the woods down by the river and we believe it to be that of your husband, Thomas.' She took Rachel's hand. 'We found his wallet in his pocket, containing his debit card and a photograph.' The PC held out a polythene evidence bag, the debit card clearly visible, and her mind registered the name Thomas R Jackson. Next to it was a photo of the two of them on their wedding day. 'Is this your husband's?' she asked.

'Yes,' she whispered. 'But, how...? There must be some mistake. How can he be dead? What's happened?' Rachel couldn't take in the enormity of what she was being told.

'I'm afraid he was found by a jogger at eleven o'clock this morning,' the sergeant said gently. 'Hanging from a tree.'

Rachel's vision went dark. She couldn't speak, felt faint. She felt the sergeant take a firm hold of her arm and heard her instructing the boy to make her a cup of tea, with plenty of sugar.

'Is there anyone we can contact Rachel? A relative, close friend, a neighbour?' she asked. 'You can't be alone at a time like this.'

'My son... Sam... But he's busy. He's in a meeting... He has a very high-powered job...' she trailed off.

'Give me his number and I'll call him,' she instructed. The call went to voicemail, so Isabelle text him asking him to contact her urgently. Within thirty seconds he rang back, and she went through to the hall to speak, where she briefly outlined the situation.

There was a stunned silence at the other end of the line. 'I'm in Canary Wharf,' Sam eventually told her. 'It'll take me about an hour to get there. Don't leave mum on her own, will you?'

'PC Jayden Daniels will stay with your mum. He's been assigned as your Family Liaison Officer. He'll be here to help your mother and all the family in any way he can. He'll keep you informed of any developments.'

'Thanks, leaving now.' Isabelle could hear the barely controlled emotion in his voice. Sometimes she hated this job.

Returning to the sitting room, the sergeant resumed her seat beside Rachel and took her hand again. 'Rachel, we also found two letters with the wallet. One is addressed to you; the other was for Detective Inspector Gayle Jones of the Northumbria Police.'

Rachel looked up at her sharply, her face wretched.

'We've had to keep the originals for forensics and the coroner, but I have copies for you here.' Reaching into her case, she withdrew two pieces of paper. 'Are you up to reading them just yet?' Rachel nodded, and the sergeant handed one of the letters to her. 'This is the one for you,' she said gently.

Hands trembling, Rachel took it, biting her lip as she read the document.

> My Dearest Rachel
>
> By the time you read this you will know that I have gone. I
>
> I haven't always been kind to you and for that I am really sorry.
>
> What I am about to do will upset you, but you know I've always said if I got to the stage where life was unbearable, I would end it.
>
> I'm sure in time you will realise this is for the best and I hope you go On to meet someone else who treats you far better than I ever have.
>
> Back in October I was diagnosed with terminal, aggressive lung cancer.
>
> The kind that stays hidden til it's too late. I didn't want to burden you With that knowledge or have you nurse me and watch my deterioration.

I don't want the suffering or degradation. This way brings a swift end, and I'll be at peace. I'm enclosing a copy of a letter I've written to DCI Jones.

Please understand this was the best and only thing I could do for Emma.

I want you to know that although I haven't always shown it, I have always loved you, Emma and Sam and always will even beyond the grave.

Tommy

Tears coursing down her cheeks, Rachel wordlessly put out her hand for the second letter.

DCI Gayle Jones

If you are reading this, then you will already know that I am dead.

Although I haven't always been pleasant to you, I want you to know that I did appreciate you finding Eva for us, seven years ago, after she went missing. And you did a great job in bringing her attacker to justice. But for the bastard to be let out after only seven years inside for what he did is a joke. The criminal justice system in this country is broken and the only way to get justice for my daughter was to take matters into my own hands.

This is my full confession to the murder of Ian Cooper. I acted alone and told no-one what I was going to do, nor what I had done afterwards. I have no remorse and would do the same thing again. I could no longer bear to see the fear in my daughter's eyes at the thought of that evil bastard seeking her out and coming for her again. Through a private detective I found out where Cooper was living. I went to his penthouse in South Shields, and I stabbed him through the heart. I wrapped him in a sheet, put him in the back of his own car and drove to Rothbury to dump his body. There was a blizzard, and the rest you know. Oh, Inearly forgot to mention, I also hacked the bastard's balls off. He won't be raping anyone else any time soon.

Tom Jackson

'I realise all this is a lot for you to take in, Mrs Jackson. I'm sure your son will help you to cope with everything. He should be here very soon. I have to tell you that DCI Jones, the officer heading up the enquiry into the murder of Ian Cooper will be coming to see you to discuss the note,' the sergeant explained. 'She asked me to tell you she'll be here in the morning.'

***

'Must you do this now?' asked Sam the following day, grief and frustration etched into his face. 'Can't you give us a few days to grieve?' He scowled at Gayle as he led her through to the kitchen.

‘Mr Jackson, I’m really sorry to hear about your father, but this can’t wait. I need to talk to both you and your mother.’ Her tone was sympathetic, but firm. ‘This is still a murder enquiry.’

Gayle thought Rachel looked dreadful, but she was calm as Gayle expressed her condolences. She listened quietly as Gayle asked why neither of them had mentioned Tommy’s overnight absence from Sam’s house when they were giving details of their movements over the Christmas period. Rachel and Sam looked at each other as Gayle told them they could be charged with perverting the course of justice.

‘Neither of us thought for a minute that my father had murdered Cooper,’ explained Sam. ‘He’d been acting weirdly, going missing for protracted periods of time. We thought he was having some kind of mid-life crisis. My mother even thought he might be having an affair. But... murder? No. And when dad omitted to mention being away overnight to your officer, we just sort of followed suit... I suppose.’

‘That’s right,’ nodded Rachel.

‘Georgia will take new statements,’ she told them. ‘We need the full details - the time he left and returned, and so on. The truth this time, with no omissions. And we’ll need Tommy’s mobile and laptop for analysis.’

‘He only used his laptop to gamble and play games as far as I know,’ volunteered Sam. ‘I’ll get it for you, and the phone. Can I ask why you need them? You’ve got his confession, what more proof do you need?’

‘Corroborating evidence is always important in cases like this,’ explained Gayle. ‘Belt and Braces. The more evidence we have to support your father’s claim, the sooner we can close the file on the case.’

CHAPTER FORTY-TWO

When I got the call from Sam to tell me my dad had been found dead, my knees gave way and I slumped against the bed. Not my dad, surely? Please not my dad. All I could think of was how horrible I had been to him the last time I saw him. That was at Christmas, at Sam's. He was so grumpy and not being very nice to my mother, putting a cloud over all the Christmas celebrations. I cringed with shame at my last words to him before I left for Berlin, after I saw my mother in tears at his behaviour.

"You're being an absolute pain in the arse, Dad. Don't know why you bothered coming. You should have stayed at home with your own misery for company." I'd screamed at him. And now he was dead... and I couldn't feel worse. An hour later, when she returned from shopping, Gerda found me in the same position, head in hands, sobbing. It took me three attempts before I could voice the words I didn't want to say, 'My dad's dead.'

Gerda took control in typical Germanic fashion, and soon flights to the UK were booked and suitcases packed. She refrained from asking any further questions while she was busy, but then, in a sympathetic voice she asked, 'What happened, Leibling? How did he die?'

'I... I don't know. Sam wouldn't tell me any more on the phone. Said he would meet me at the airport and give me all the details then.'

In the Arrivals Hall, Sam embraced me like he'd never let me go, and we were both tearful. 'What happened?' I asked.

'Not now, Emma. Let's all get to the car.' But once in the car, he still wouldn't be drawn and when I persisted, in asking, he snapped at me. 'Please, Emma, wait until we get to mums. We all need to be together when we talk about this.' He turned his head to glance briefly at me in the back seat. 'Ok?' Turning his attention back to

the M25, which as ever was like a gigantic car park, he braked, slowing as we approached a line of stationary traffic.

'Patience, Emma,' said Gerda, squeezing my hand tightly. 'Listen to your brother. He must have his reasons.'

***

'He hung himself?' I screamed at my mother. 'My dad? I don't believe it. How could he do that? Why would he do that?' Sam held on to my arm as it finally sunk in that it was true. I turned to him and whispered 'Why, Sam?'

'He left a note. He was ill, Emma. Inoperable cancer, aggressive. He knew he would die soon anyway. He didn't want a prolonged ending. Didn't want us to see him go like that. He did it to spare mum, and us.'

I'd once seen a photo of a man who had been hanged from a lamppost by the Nazis and this image came into my mind, only it was my dad's contorted face I could see, his head at an unnatural angle, his body swinging, turning in the breeze.

'Oh my God,' I groaned. 'Spare us? How is this sparing us?' My heart was breaking. 'How could dad do this to us?'

'There's something else you need to know, Emma,' said Sam after a while. 'Sit down.' I did as I was told. 'Dad left a note for the police before he died, confessing to the murder of Ian Cooper.'

I was stunned. 'What? No... No... he couldn't kill anyone. Dad's not a murderer, Sam... he can't be...' But even as I was saying the words, I knew I had doubts. Given the right provocation, perhaps dad was capable... and after what that beast had done to me... 'I can't process this just now,' I said. 'I need to lie down. I'm going upstairs.' Gerda followed me up and mum appeared a few minutes later with a tray of hot chocolate.

Her voice was steady and sad. 'It's a lot to take in, Emma. I think we're all in deep shock. You have a sleep now and we can all talk it through when you're rested.' She set the tray down on the dressing table.

Gerda lay with me, not saying anything, just being there. Miraculously, I must have fallen into a deep sleep and when I woke three hours later, I felt much calmer, and at last gave some thought as to how my poor mother must be feeling. Hurrying downstairs, I ran to mum and flung my arms around her, whispering how sorry I was for the pain she must be feeling. We cried together then, and over the next few days talked endlessly, trying to make sense of all that had happened.

Knowing that my father killed Ian Cooper to save me from a lifetime of worry filled me with so many conflicting emotions. My head was all over the place. I felt immense relief that Cooper was no longer alive, horror that my dad had actually killed him, pride that my dad loved me enough to do such a thing for me, more horror at what he'd done to Cooper's body, though I could understand the sentiments that must have driven him to carry out the mutilation.

CHAPTER FORTY-THREE

'Well Gayle, that wraps up that one nicely, wouldn't you say?' Chief Superintendent Gordon McAllister sat back in his winged chair, a look of satisfaction on his face.

'Yes, sir. On the surface, it does close the case...'

Leaning forward, he put his elbows on his desk, steepling his hands. He peered at her over his rimless glasses. 'Do I detect a "but" DCI Jones?'

Why do all Supers steeple their hands? wondered Gayle, *do they teach them that in superintendent training school?* 'Well, I'm not one hundred percent convinced that Jackson did it, sir,' she ventured. 'When someone is going to die anyway, there have been cases, as I'm sure you know, where they've confessed to a murder... to save someone else.'

'And you think that's what's happened here? What are you basing that on? Who do you think he's trying to save?'

'There are a few untidy ends, sir. We have at least two suspects linked to Tommy Jackson who don't have firm alibis. The Fair Justice guy, Craig Burton is one. He's a nephew of Tommy Jackson, his wife's sister's son. The other is Emma Jackson's childhood sweetheart, Matt White. Although he does have an alibi from his parents, I would like more time to test it and check him out further. White's parents are close friends of Tommy and Rachel, so it's feasible that Tommy would want to protect their son.'

'Were either of those two prime suspects?' the super asked.

'They were persons of interest, sir, as was Tommy Jackson. Our prime suspects were Sandra Howard and Marek Kowalska. However,

Tommy Jackson didn't know these people, so of course he would have no reason to protect them.'

'And do you have any hard evidence against either of these two persons of interest Gayle?' he asked, watching her keenly. 'Or indeed against your prime suspects?'

'No, sir. Not yet. Sandra Howard has admitted to being in his apartment and handling the knife. And...'

'Yes, yes, I've read the report,' the superintendent interrupted. 'But hard evidence?'

'No, not yet, but given more time…' she began.

'The Super got up, walked round to the front of the desk, and rested his ample backside on the edge. 'Listen Gayle,' he said, hands on thighs, leaning towards her. 'This is what I think. A piece of scum has been murdered, and we have a full confession from a suspect with a very strong motive for ridding the world of his daughter's rapist. From your report, I can see that his assertion that he obtained Cooper's address from a private investigator stacks up, and he was missing from his son's house all night at the relevant time. He also knew details of the crime that weren't in the public domain. Why waste further scarce police resources in challenging that confession? Let's close the file. It's a win/win situation. We have a successful case, good for our stats, and you can now go off on the six months compassionate leave you've applied for to spend quality time with your failing mother.'

Gayle opened her mouth to protest, then paused. In the grand scheme of things, how much did it matter if Tommy had given a false confession? The work involved in continuing all the current lines of enquiry was significant and at the end of the day may only prove that it was a genuine confession. There was no doubt in her mind that the world was a safer place for children without Ian Cooper in it. Then she thought of her poor mother coming to the end of her life and of how much she needed Gayle to be with her. There was no contest really, the Super was absolutely right.

'Agreed Detective Chief Inspector Jones?' the Super enquired, raising his eyebrows.

'Agreed sir.'

CHAPTER FORTY-FOUR

I am coming to terms with losing my dad, and mum is coping better since we moved back up to the Northeast, where she has relatives and old friends nearby. Mum found a nice little house, not far from the sea front in Whitley Bay. We didn't think moving back to Wallsend was a good idea.

When dad committed suicide, I was in turmoil. Getting my head around losing him was tough enough. Heartbreaking. But thinking of him putting a noose around his own neck and kicking away the stool he'd taken specifically for that purpose was gut wrenching, and still is if I let myself think about it. There's some consolation in the coroner's report, which confirmed his cancer was so advanced that he would have been lucky (or unlucky) enough to survive a few more weeks.

A month or so after dad's death, mum said she had something to show me. Packing up the house for her impending move back to the north, she'd come across a large bundle of letters tucked into an old shoe box at the bottom of Dad's wardrobe. All addressed to me, in a loopy, cursive script and all unopened. Intrigued, I eagerly opened the first one from the top of the pile, to find it was from Matt. They were all from Matt. Wow. Dad must have hidden each one, unopened, as it arrived over the years.

I always thought Matt had given up on me too easily, and felt hurt and abandoned, even though I couldn't bring myself to see him. Why didn't dad give me the letters? Why did he do that to me? I can only think he must have thought I'd be upset at being contacted and reminded of the life I used to have. Typical control-freak dad. I felt a momentary burning anger at his absolute certainty that he knew what was in my best interests. Always sure he knew what was good for me instead of letting me make my own decisions, even after I was grown up. Over the next couple of days, I read through each one of the letters, and shed tears for Matt. He had never stopped caring about me, the early childish letters giving way to heart-rending love letters as he grew older.

Discussing it with mum, she said she hadn't known about the letters, but confessed that many years ago my dad warned Matt about trying to see me, saying the reminder of my previous life would be too upsetting for me. He had asked Matt not to send any further letters, but Matt must have continued to send them, not realising that they weren't getting to me. Then she told me about Matt going down to Walton on Thames, looking for me after hearing that Cooper was to be released. I was living in London by then and fairly incommunicado, but dad had insisted she didn't mention it to me during our infrequent conversations. Although, she insisted they both meant well and just wanted to protect me, I nevertheless felt furious with them both.

A few months later, I finally met up with Matt, after moving up to Whitley Bay with mum. It was bizarre. I felt an immediate connection. Almost instantly I knew that we were meant to be together, just as he told me later, he'd always known. I know that sounds corny, like something from a Mills and Boon novel, but to my complete surprise, that's exactly how I felt. Me, who couldn't bear any man to touch me, felt completely at home and safe when Matt first wrapped his arms around me.

It was difficult telling Gerda, who was waiting patiently in Berlin for my return, and I know I broke her heart. I flew over to tell her in person and I'm grateful that we've somehow managed to remain good friends.

'Liebling, I knew something had changed,' she told me tearfully. 'When you delayed your return, saying your mother needed you around for longer, I was worried. Then when you told me that you had met up with Matt, I could hear the joy in your voice. Though you tried not to let it show, I just knew.'

Four years have gone by since then. With Matt's encouragement I picked up my education where I left off, and six months ago graduated from The University of Northumbria with a 2:1 in forensic science. A year ago, we set up home in a small flat in Whitley Bay, not far from mum. I love it here, a short walk from the sea, and for the first time since the attack, I can say that I'm happy. And now I'm pregnant. Not great timing, career-wise but we're both looking forward so much to the arrival of our daughter.

'Babe, there's some post for you,' said Matt, coming into the living room, sifting through the mail. 'Most of it looks like junk... except this one.' He held out a buff-coloured envelope.

I took the letter, the hand-written address intriguing me. I quickly opened it, scanned through the untidy scrawl. 'Wow... I can't believe this. It's from a woman claiming to be my birth mother. She wants to meet me if I'm ok with that.' Open mouthed, I looked at Matt, and handed him the letter.

'I didn't think birth parents were allowed to contact a child directly,' he said, skimming through the letter. 'Aren't there regulations about having to go through an intermediary? I mean, how does she even have your name and address?'

'I don't know... but I'm curious... I wonder how mum would feel about me meeting her. Do you think she'd mind?' I got to my feet, looking for my mobile. 'I think I'll just run it past Sam first. He's always full of good advice.'

A week later, I found myself sitting nervously in a pub car park, plucking up the courage to go into the Briar Dene on the sea front at Whitley Bay. I was alone, despite offers from Matt and Sam to come with me. Walking in, I scanned the bar, seeking out the red jacket she said she'd be wearing. Was that her? A thin, grey-haired lady, sitting at a table, a glass of coke in front of her, nervously biting the side of her finger. She looked up. No, she was too old to be my mother with her careworn face and sallow skin.

'Emma?' she said, and smiled, getting to her feet. 'Thank you for agreeing to see me.'

It was weird. I didn't feel any emotion on seeing her, though she was clearly moved to see me. She stared at me, seemingly drinking in my appearance, unable to tear her gaze away. I noticed tears in her eyes.

'I've got so much I want to say to you, Emma, and when I've finished, you'll probably hate me. But I think you have a right to know everything. And I want you to know that whatever you decide to do next, I won't hold it against you, and I'll never stop loving you.'

She was so intense and although I was curious to hear what she had to tell me, I felt uncomfortable in the busy bar. 'Why don't we go for a walk?' I suggested. 'We can leave the cars here and walk down to St Mary's Island. Maybe get a coffee from the van down there.'

'Emma, I don't know what you've been told about me, about your background?' she asked as we walked.

'Not much to be honest, I know I was with my real grandparents for a while, and they were killed in a car crash.' For the next twenty minutes or so, Sandra talked without interruption, sparing herself nothing. She painted a picture of such degradation and despair that I could fully understand how I came to be taken away from her. Her life had been wretched and the guilt at losing me had never left her. I believed her when she said she had never stopped loving me and when she begged me to forgive her, I gave her all the reassurance I could.

'I've had good parents, Sandra. My dad's dead now and he was always a grumpy sod, but he took care of me and loved me in his own way.' I told her about my mum and Sam and what a lovely brother he was. We'd reached the headland by then and decided to get a couple of ice cream cones instead of coffee. We sat on a nearby bench to eat them. It overlooked the sea, which on a bright sunny day was as blue as the Mediterranean.

'Emma, this is very hard, but there's so much more I need to tell you.' She looked so troubled; I wondered what on earth more she could have to say. I stayed silent, waiting, licking my ice cream. 'I know what happened to you,' she said.

'Oh...' I said, taken aback. 'You mean...?'

She told me about working in the factory and her gossipy mate there. How they'd all read about the attack at the time. She explained how, through this mate's contact with social workers, she'd been able to work out from the details given that it had to be her long-lost daughter who had been attacked.

'Heavens, I don't know what to say... that must have been quite a shock for you...'

'There's more, Emma. When the attack on you took place, I identified the perpetrator from photographs the police showed me... that's how they arrested him so quickly...' She hesitated, 'It was your father, your biological father, Emma.'

'Whoa, whoa... Ian Cooper was my father? No.' I was stunned. 'No, I can't take this in. I can't deal with this. Why are you telling me all this now?' I got to my feet, began walking fast, back the way we'd come. Hurrying to keep up with me, she put

her hand on my arm. 'It's taken me four years to pluck up the courage to tell you, Emma. But I didn't want you to go through the rest of your life without knowing that your dad, the dad you know, is innocent.'

'What?' I came to an abrupt halt and whirled to face her, dropping the remains of my ice cream cone. 'What did you just say?'

'Emma, your father didn't kill Cooper... Please, come and sit down again. Let me explain.' Holding my arm, she guided me towards the nearest vacant bench. In a daze, I complied. 'I realise all this is a big shock for you, but I think you have the right to know the truth,' she said in a quiet voice.

'When I realised that it was you that Cooper attacked, I went to confront him about what he'd done to you, his own daughter. He attacked and raped me. I managed to pick up a knife and I stabbed him in self-defence. I should have called the police there and then, but I was in a panic. I left and went home and told Marek, my partner. He disposed of his body. We should have told the truth to the police at the time, but Marek already has a criminal record. A one-off crime committed in Poland when he was young, and we were worried he would be sent to prison, and I just couldn't have coped without him. I was in a terrible state... I'm so sorry we didn't set the record straight about your dad.'

'Look,' I said, trying to absorb all the implications of the bombshells she'd just dropped on me. 'I can't think straight. Why are you telling me about this now? Why now, after four years?'

'I've been trying to pluck up courage all these years. Then when I heard, on the grapevine at work again, that you're expecting a baby, I couldn't leave it any longer. I don't want your child to grow up believing its grandfather to be a cold-blooded murderer.'

'That's some bloody gossip shop you work in,' I said, angry. 'How on earth does this woman know so much about my life? This is all too much... I'm sorry but I can't take it in right now. I need to go. I need to talk to my family about all of this.' I got to my feet again.

The woman was gabbling, out of breath trying to keep pace with me as I hurried back to the pub car park. 'I'll go to the police and tell them everything if that's what you want...'

'Wait a minute...' I said, slowing my pace as the thought occurred to me. 'Why did dad say it was him when it wasn't?'

'I don't know. We puzzled about that... Marek and me, but we couldn't work it out.'

'Did Marek mutilate his body then?' I asked, suddenly remembering how horrified I'd been to think of my dad doing that.

'Yes... I think he was out of his mind with rage and grief at what Cooper had done to me. He disposed of his body... he told me he'd done it then.'

'Oh my God... So much to think about...'

'Emma...' she began.

'No. No more, please. 'I held up my hand to silence her. 'I'm going home.' I could feel my bottom lip quivering and I didn't want to break down in front of her. 'I'll contact you later.' We reached the car park, and I quickly dived into my car, started it up and screamed away without even doing up my seatbelt, my mind absolutely whirling.

CHAPTER FORTY-FIVE

Matt was appalled at the state I was in when I got home. My face blotchy from crying, I was shaking like a leaf, and almost incoherent. At first he couldn't understand why or how seeing my 'mother' had caused so much distress. Eventually, I calmed down enough to quietly relate everything to him. He was as astonished as I was. We spent the next couple of hours going through all the implications, before deciding to ring Sam. As luck would have it, Sam was at home in Edmondbyers. After listening to a brief summary of what had transpired, he suggested we held an urgent family conference the following day.

The next morning found us sitting around the blue painted table in Mum's garden, a jug of Sangria on the table, and a glass of lemonade for me. It struck me as bizarre to be discussing death, murder, deceit and rape in the warm sunshine.

I went through everything that Sandra had told me, and a stunned silence followed as Sam and Mum absorbed and processed the information. Matt smiled encouragingly and squeezed my hand under the table.

Sam was the first to speak. 'So, can I just sum up where we are? Your birth mother,' he made inverted comma signs with his fingers, 'worked out that you must be her daughter from information she was given at work, second-hand. Aside from everything else, we need a DNA test to confirm or otherwise her theory.' Sam sounded like he was chairing a meeting, which I suppose in a way he was.

'As she had already identified your attacker as her former partner, she therefore concluded your birth father had molested his own daughter. On that premise, she went to see him, to confront him and let him know exactly what he'd done. And for her trouble, was attacked and raped herself. She picked up a knife to defend herself, stabbed and killed him. I wonder why she didn't just ring the police then? It would have been self-defence.' Sam wiped a hand across his face.

'She said she panicked,' I informed him.

'Putting that to one side for the moment, the big question is why did dad say he'd done it? Why put his family through the additional pain of thinking him a murderer?' Sam looked at the faces around the table.

'That's what I'd like to know,' I said. 'It hurt so much to think that dad was a murderer. Why would he say that if it wasn't true? It doesn't make any sense.'

Mum hadn't uttered a word up to then. With a faraway look on her face, she had been sitting there in silence, deep in thought.. Now she glanced at Sam before focusing on me and speaking in her soft voice. 'I think I know why.' We all looked at her in surprise, waiting expectantly to hear her explanation. 'I believe your dad thought he was protecting you, Emma. You see, I'm sure he thought that you had killed Cooper. You and Gerda and Eric...'

'What...? But why on earth would he think that?' I asked, puzzled.

'Well, if you remember, on Boxing Day the three of you borrowed one of Sam's cars and said you were going off to see Eric's aunt in Jesmond. And then you were gone all night? Only you didn't go to see an aunt, did you? Your dad told me he overheard Eric speaking with Gerda, telling her he thought we'd all fallen for your story. He was laughing, saying he didn't even have any aunts, other than Gerda's mother in Berlin. I think your father must have put two and two together and made five. He knew the police had gone to Berlin to question the three of you.'

'Oh my God. Are you saying that's why he killed himself? Because of me?' I was horrified.

'No Emma, of course that's not why he killed himself.' Mum's voice was fierce. 'He was ill. He killed himself because he was terminally ill. He's always said he believed in euthanasia and if he ever got to the stage where he was in pain, and there was no hope, he would want to die. He couldn't bear the thought of other people having to watch him waste away. So, no, he did not kill himself to protect you. He took the blame for the murder to protect you, because he thought he was saving you from prosecution. He had nothing to lose as he knew he wouldn't be around anyway.'

Sam's voice broke into my thoughts. 'Well, that makes a lot of sense, mum. If he thought Emma might be charged with murder, that's exactly what he would do. I agree too about him not wanting to go on living under certain circumstances. I remember Dad telling me on several occasions that if he ever got to the stage where he couldn't wipe his own backside, he'd rather kill himself than suffer the humiliation and degradation.'

'Sam, I'm sorry I lied to you about that night...' I began. 'The others wanted to sample Newcastle nightlife and we didn't want to offend you... didn't want you to think we were bored at your place...'

'I see. Right.' He gave me a disapproving look and I could see how disappointed he was that I'd lied to him. 'Well, forget it, that's not important now. What we have to decide now, the sixty-million-dollar question: Do we contact the police, or do we leave things as they stand? What does everyone think? You first, Emma, you've had the longest to think about it.'

I took a breath. 'Well... I've thought of nothing else since I saw Sandra,' I began. 'And Matt and I have talked it over at length. Whether DNA proves she's my birth mother or not, and I think she is, by the way.' I turned to mum. 'In my eyes, I will only ever have one mother, and that's you. You know that.' Mum had been pragmatic when I told her about Sandra making contact, now she smiled and reassured me again that she had no problem with me seeing my birth mother.

I continued. 'Sandra's reasons for believing she's my mother stack up and anyway there's a likeness. Something about her eyes. They look just like mine. Anyway, this is what I think. She's had a shit life. Abused for years since she was fifteen, turned into a drug addict, had her daughter wrenched away, parents killed in a road accident. Her kid gets adopted and she never sees her again. Eventually she runs away, gets help from a Women's refuge, gets clean, and is just settling down to some kind of normality when she identifies her ex as a rapist and paedophile. And then the shock of finding out he's raped their own daughter. And then he rapes her. I wouldn't blame her for killing him.

'As for whether we should go to the police... I don't think we should. Because if we do, Marek will certainly go to prison, even if they accept that he only mutilated and disposed of the body. He'd be an accessory after the fact or something like that. I don't know what that would do to Sandra. I get the impression she's right on the edge.' I took a deep breath. 'I've been thinking that it was possibly Marek who killed

him. He sounds volatile and you can imagine his rage if she went home and told him she'd been attacked and raped. I think she could be saying that it was her who killed him so it can be put down to self-defence in the event we do report her.' I sat back.

'Well, listen everyone,' mum said. 'This is what I think. All this has come as a shock, especially to Emma. She meets her birth mother out of the blue and at the same time finds out her biological father could be the man who attacked her. There's a lot to come to terms with there. Then to be told that the man she knows as her father is not a murderer after all, well it's all a bit much to take in all at once. I think she needs our support now more than ever.

'As for going to the police... Now that I'm back living up here, amongst my family and friends again, I can see that your dad's thought of as a bit of a hero, rather than a murderer. After what that man did to Emma, nobody I know blames him for getting rid of him. Some of the men say it's what they would have done in the same circumstances. Why cause more misery for the person who actually did it? Whichever of them did it, their motives were understandable. And let's be honest, they've done us all a favour. I say let sleeping dogs lie. I think it's what your father would want under the circumstances... What are your thoughts, Sam?'

'I agree with both of you,' Sam said in a sombre tone. 'For the reasons you've both given, it would seem pointless to drag all of this up again. Also, if dad's looked upon as a bit of a hero, I think that's far better than risking people finding out that Emma was raped by her own biological father. This is a really important point. If there was a trial, this could well be used as a mitigating factor. Imagine what a field day the press would have with that if it ever came out? I don't think you could withstand that, Emma.' He sat back, grim-faced.

'You're right, Sam,' I said, shaking my head. 'I'd be an object of curiosity and gossip all over again. I really couldn't bear that.'

'What's your view, Matt?' asked Sam. 'You should have your say too.'

'Well, to be honest I don't really give a toss who killed him, as long as he's dead. And, I agree with you Rachel, Tommy is regarded as a hero around here, so there's nothing to be gained as far as I can see by the truth coming out. People would wonder why he took the blame when he was innocent and that could start all kinds of speculation. And, most importantly, I don't think any of us want Emma dragged

into any future court proceedings and all that that could do to her mental health all over again. I say leave well alone, for Emma's sake.'

'Well said, Matt,' said Sam. Looking around the table, he summed up. 'So, we're all agreed. We don't go to the police. I suggest you contact Sandra as soon as possible Emma. Let her know, before she decides to report all this to the police.

***

Isn't life strange? My call to Sandra was just in time. She and Marek had decided the best thing to do was to go to the police and confess. I dread to think what a can of worms that would have opened up for me and my family, but thankfully we need never know now.

I was filled with horror at the thought of my own biological father raping me, but I had to know the truth. Sam used his influence to get access to Cooper's DNA profile. The strange bit? The irony? DNA tests have confirmed that although Sandra is in fact my birth mother, Ian Cooper was not my biological father. That came as a shock to Sandra, as well as a relief. Although she always believed Cooper to be the father of her child, she now concludes because of Cooper's perversions and her drug-addled state at the time, she must have been mistaken.

I don't know which is worse, thinking I was the child of a paedophile and rapist or the offspring of a man who paid to rape my mother while her partner looked on. I have decided to put it out of my mind. The only father I ever want is the one I've known all my life, who loved me enough to brand himself a murderer in order to protect me.

I feel the warm mound of my belly and think of the child within me. Already I love her so much, I know that without a doubt I would do anything to protect her. Anything. It's time for the healing to begin.

THE END

About the Author

Georgia E Brown was born and raised in Whitley Bay, in the North East of England. 'When I Find You' is her second crime thriller. Following a long business career Georgia decided to devote herself to writing. Her first novel 'The Stalker's Song' was published in 2019 and received many five star reviews on Amazon and some great reviews in the local media. Georgia's novels are gritty, down-to-earth crime thrillers, depicting the darker side of life, where ordinary people, through no fault of their own, are thrust into unimaginably traumatic situations.

www.georgiaebrown.com

GEORGIA E BROWN

AUTHOR

I hope you enjoyed reading *When I Find You.*

It would be greatly appreciated if you could kindly leave a review on Amazon.

Printed in Great Britain
by Amazon

31243145R00162